G000095124

UNDER THE IMPRESSION

Dennett Press

UNDER THE IMPRESSION

KYLE DARCY

DENNETT PRESS

CANTON, MASSACHUSETTS

2020

Dennett Press
95 Washington Street
Suite 104-212
Canton, MA 02021
USA

Printed in the United States of America

Dust Jacket:
Design & Lettering by Dave Bailey (davebailey.xyz)
Illustration by Forest Stearns (draweverywhere.com)

For Mary

TABLE OF CONTENTS

Introduction

European scientists realized the importance of the coca plant in the nineteenth century when they began to study cocaine. Advances in chemistry included development of a group of drugs known as alkaloids which led to new pharmacological compounds such as quinine, morphine and cocaine. German chemist, Albert Nieman, was first to extract cocaine from coca leaves in 1859, however, the process proved difficult to replicate outside laboratory conditions and it was decades before it eventually became commercially available. Eminent scientists and doctors, including Sigmund Freud, studied the drug and lauded its apparent wondrous healing properties. In the 1890s when Karl Koller, a German ophthalmic surgeon, discovered its numbing effect on the protruding eyes of frogs, he realized he had discovered the first local anesthetic. Until then, patients had two options for invasive surgery; they could either remain conscious throughout the operation, or undergo the procedure under the effect of a general anesthetic. An aqueous solution of cocaine applied to the eye revolutionized Koller's branch of medicine as well as many others. Meanwhile, Freud uncovered another breakthrough. It appeared any ailment could be treated by applying cocaine to the nasal passages. The immediate improvement in each patient's spirit supported Freud's theory that each organ in the human body had a correlating region in the nasal passage. By coating the area with powdered cocaine, patients experienced an instant miraculous recovery. As cocaine became more prevalent, the consequences and side-effects of its use became more evident. Many medical practitioners, including Freud himself, came to realize the perils associated with the drug.

These European pioneers, however, lagged behind their South American counterparts by centuries. In the ancient Inca civilization, skillful medicine men perfected the practice of trepanning which involved drilling a hole in the skull to relieve pressure. By spitting on the wound while chewing coca leaves and lime powder, the numbing effect of the saliva was enough to subdue a patient while sharpened stones ground a hole into the skull. This primitive anesthetic was also used when wounded Inca warriors needed surgery.

The coca plant, indigenous to South America, has been part of the region's culture for thousands of years. Initially, the Incas believed it was a gift from the gods. At the height of the Inca empire, in the fourteenth through sixteenth centuries, the coca plant was the fuel, which drove their economy. Without it, one of the largest empires ever known could not have flourished to the degree that it did. A network of roads stretching thousands of miles allowed its army to mobilize and travel freely. This network was also an important component in the communication infrastructure. Relay runners were able to carry messages to outposts along these routes which enabled the Emperor to communicate efficiently with every region. None of these athletes would be able to pass an Olympic drug test today.

Centuries later, the Catholic Church realized poor, wretched South American natives were being oppressed as much by the coca plant as by the Spanish rulers who had conquered them. The Church repeatedly made overtures to the King of Spain condemning use of the coca plant to sustain slaves working in silver and mercury mines. These protests from the Vatican continued until Spain agreed to give the Catholic bishops 10% of all silver taken out of South America.

Cocaine use flourished in America and Europe during the first half of the twentieth century. It was a common ingredient in a variety of elixirs, which became household names and were consumed without knowledge of the drug's addictive power. Eventually, its social consequences could no longer be concealed by its addicts nor pharmaceutical companies engaged in underhanded marketing practices. Advances in anesthetics replaced cocaine with less dangerous alternatives. Today, the import of processed coca leaves into developed countries, such as the United States, is strictly regulated. A large legitimate customer for this commodity is a Maywood, New Jersey corporation, which historically has processed coca leaves for a range of clients including the *Coca-Cola Company*.

Chapter 1

GERMANY - 1945

THE ESCAPE

6:35PM - Sunday April 8th 1945
Furstenfeldbruck Air Base, GERMANY

K laus Bremner did not consider himself to be an ace pilot, but he was a fortunate one. No one could deny that. On several occasions the fuselage of his *BV 222 Wiking* transport aircraft had been ripped apart by automatic gunfire from *Spitfires* and *Grumman Wildcats*. Fortunately for him, the pilots of his *Messerschmitt Bf 110* escorts were more than a match for their British, Canadian and American counterparts.

His luck, however, was not limited to the skies. He had the good fortune to have been born into the Bremner Pharmaceutical empire. After graduating from Hamburg University in 1938, he immediately went to work in the family's main manufacturing plant in Cologne. His duties were to oversee quality control and assist research chemists isolate alkaloids for the company's cocaine based medicines and methamphetamines. Access to these substances enhanced his rise through Luftwaffe ranks and endeared him to his superiors who appreciated the value of having their own private pharmacist permanently on call. The young pilot's skill at handling the massive *BV 222*, and his close relationship with the upper command, made him an obvious choice for the evening's crucial, top-secret mission.

Germany's surrender was weeks, if not days away. Ordinarily, no one would have authorized such a perilous operation, but there were no other options and time was running out. It would require every skill possessed by Bremner and his co-pilots for the plan to succeed. The situation became abundantly clear to him as he listened to the final briefing. The *Blohm & Voss BV 238*, which he had flown the previous week for the first time, had been meticulously modified based on feedback he had given to its engineers. Although two *BV 238* seaplanes had been built, company records made reference to only one. The second model's existence was a closely kept secret. Its exclusive purpose was to provide a swift escape for a group chosen from the highest echelons of the Third Reich, along with their ill-gotten assets. In September 1944 the first *BV 238*, with its one hundred and eighty-nine foot wing span, had been easy prey for two *P-51 Mustangs* from the US 361st Fighter Group. The monstrous machine had been docked on Lake Schaalsee, practicing repeated water take-off and landing exercises, in preparation for the Bolivia mission. Its destruction sealed the fate of the second *BV 238* which underwent limited pre-flight testing and was concealed in its hanger to await the critical mission. Bremner could see it on the runway encircled by mechanics finishing their pre-flight checks. He would have two co-pilots and two navigators, and a small escort of Messerschmitts which would turn back once they had crossed over Algeria. The twenty passengers and cargo were bound for La Paz, Bolivia where they planned to establish a secret Third Reich compound. During the briefing he learned how the seaplane would rendezvous for refueling in the South Atlantic with a specially modified U-Boat. Every detail of the flight plan had been scrutinized to safeguard the cargo of: twenty million US dollars; forty-five million in gold bullion; a priceless fine art collection; and chests of flawless diamonds.

There was, however, an additional piece of information only he knew. Out on the runway one of the mechanics checking the plane was, in fact, his wife Gabriele. Bremner's access to narcotics enabled him to have excellent intelligence sources. Once he learned the true purpose of the flight, he managed to sneak her onto the base. The couple had only one hour's notice. They understood the mission would be dangerous but Gabriele knew something even Klaus did not. She was pregnant and did not want to raise their child alone, and certainly not in a Germany occupied by forces of the Allied Command. By the time Klaus Bremner and his crew prepared to taxi, Gabriele was carefully concealed in the cargo hold.

Chapter 2

BOLIVIA - 1945

NEW BEGINNINGS

1:05AM - Monday April 9th 1945
Lago Titicaca, BOLIVIA

The *Daimler-Benz DB 603G* inverted V-12 engines gently set the *BV 238* seaplane down at the edge of the Bolivian side of Lake Titicaca, just south of the border with Peru. It taxied to the predetermined remote rendezvous location to avoid detection by either Peruvian or Bolivian authorities. Three boats signaled, as arranged, and approached to welcome the weary travelers. An eight-man Kriegsmarine unit had been dispatched several months earlier. The elite naval contingent executed their orders efficiently and effectively, reflecting the practice and preparation that had gone into their intense training.

It would take several hours to ferry the plane's passengers and cargo to shore. The massive and secluded lake-front property had been secretly purchased the previous year. Finally, just before dawn, the huge *BV 238* was deliberately destroyed by the Kriegsmarines. The muffled synchronized explosion of strategic detonations scuttled the seaplane, causing it to sink to the bottom of the lake. Within minutes, all trace of the aircraft, and the sole mission for which it had been developed, was forever erased.

9:15PM - Sunday October 5th 1947
Lago Titicaca, BOLIVIA

K laus and Gabriele were the proud parents of twins, Steffen and Klaudia, who were almost two years old. Security at the compound was tight and entrusted to the Kriegsmarines who had ferried the group to shore, two years earlier, in the waning days of World War II. Celebrating Oktoberfest was a way to remember their heritage, while promising to avenge the annihilation of *The Fatherland*.

The private lake-shore compound proved to be the perfect base for their new South American home. The proximity to the border with Peru meant they could escape Bolivian authorities if their Nazi identity were to be uncovered or their mission compromised. Bremner and his colleagues had begun to establish business interests in the nearby city of Nuestra Señora de La Paz and were already providing a substantial economic reward to the local community. Despite the history of previous European invasions, the indigenous community showed little interest in the background of their visitors who made sure to bribe the appropriate regional officials for their silence and loyalty. Construction projects on the compound provided employment, and donations to Roman Catholic churches and schools, in neighboring towns, endeared the German immigrants to the natives. Nevertheless, interaction with the local population was limited. Consequently, no one in the community was aware the location was, in fact, home to a post-World War II Third Reich cell.

The escape plan had been developed prior to the conclusion of hostilities and without Hitler's knowledge. High ranking Nazi officials envisaged six such cells throughout the world. Bremner and his group had been assigned the code-name, "Wolf 238". Their objective was to methodically infiltrate cities in South America using identities supported by counterfeit passports and documentation. The original twenty passengers included twelve who were chosen for their experience in commerce. The masterminds behind the exercise had identified the importance of establishing self sustaining units. Accordingly, each contained several married couples with the stipulation the wives had to be members of the NS-Frauenschaft, the Nazi party's women's organization.

Committed to regaining the glory of their beloved German *Fatherland*, each group was sworn to secrecy and instructed not to communicate until April 20th 1989. Forbidding communication between cells minimized the risk of capture during post-war efforts to eliminate all Nazi culture. On April 20th 1989, the one hundredth anniversary of Adolf Hitler's birth, an advertisement would be placed in Berlin newspapers seeking homes for six Rottweiler puppies. Predetermined answers to specific questions would confirm a caller's credentials, and further instructions would be imparted.

Bremner established contacts at La Paz University and started a modest pharmaceutical business. Advances in medicine meant cocaine was falling out of favor as a local anesthetic. The drug's aggressive addictive characteristics, however, were exactly why it was so appealing to him. He was well aware of the destructive impact it had on society. He also believed America's meddling in European affairs had been a major contributing factor to the demise of Nazi Germany. Accordingly, he dedicated himself to the destruction of the United States using his weapon of choice: cocaine.

7:00PM - Saturday April 9th 1955
Lago Titicaca, BOLIVIA

It was the tenth anniversary of the *BV 238* landing on Lake Titicaca. Every year its passengers and crew assembled to celebrate the mission's success and hold their annual congress. In keeping with their original instructions, they had established businesses in Colombia, Ecuador, Peru, Chile, and Bolivia.

In one decade the group had managed to develop *The Phoenix*, a two hundred and fifty room luxury hotel and spa on the site of their original camp. The business provided a credible cover for their base operations. In addition to running his pharmaceutical company, Klaus Bremner operated an air taxi business, *Aymaran Air*, between El Alto Airport and the lake-side resort. The route was one leg of a larger corporate jet leasing business he had established to help limit Wolf 238's dependence on regular airlines. Trips requiring transportation of illicit cargo were always scheduled using his jet fleet. Accordingly, official manifest records on these flights were never accurate. His airline also provided a clandestine method for shipping cocaine paste to Venezuela, en route to the United States via Puerto Rico. Although he was capable of transporting it further north, Bremner wanted to minimize the risk of his legitimate enterprises being associated with the illegal narcotics operation.

2:15PM - Thursday October 20th 1955
Lago Titicaca, BOLIVIA

Ten year old Steffen and Klaudia Bremner knew little of the world other than life in the post-World War II Nazi compound at Lake Titicaca. Whenever they had a chance to travel, they were always accompanied by Klaus and Gabriele on one of their private planes. Their parents had restricted interaction with children from the local community and schooling was provided by private tutors. Their confinement was supplemented with a school curriculum rich in the principles and culture of the Third Reich. Every aspect of their upbringing had been closely monitored including the toys and books they were given as gifts. While children in the free world innocently enjoyed Hollywood cartoons, Klaus and Gabriele's disgust for Walt Disney's 1943 propaganda cartoon, *"Donald Duck in Nutzi Land,"* forced them to censor everything. To do otherwise risked the children mimicking the cartoon character singing, *"Der Furher's Face."*

There was only one way to describe young Klaudia Bremner. She was evil. She had planned the crime with precision and attention to detail. Her young victim finally stopped struggling when her last breath bubbled to the surface of the swimming pool. Klaudia waited two minutes before clutching the lifeless corpse and screaming hysterically for help.

Sadly, one of the first adults on the scene was the dead girl's father. He was employed as a landscaper in the compound and had no idea his daughter, Elena, had befriended a monster. Instead of feeling suspicious, he felt compassion for little Klaudia because she had witnessed his daughter's drowning. Her performance as a grieving distraught child fooled everyone. No one believed the death was anything other than a terrible tragedy.

Klaudia had callously drowned her little friend because Elena had confided in her that she had a crush on Steffen. Unfortunately, the young girl made the mistake of telling the one person who was determined to shield her twin from such amorous interests. Although she was only ten years old, Klaudia had absorbed her parent's teaching that relationships between the family and local Bolivians could not be tolerated.

Later, Klaudia sat in the lobby of the hotel and sobbed, appropriately and on cue. As she strained to focus through the tears, she gently leaned against Steffen's shoulder and resolved never to let anyone, or anything, ever come between them.

3:45PM – Sunday February 12th 1961
Washington Depot, Connecticut, USA

The Bremner twins had been enrolled at the prestigious boarding school in Connecticut since 1957. They shared some classes but slept in different dorm rooms and rarely got to see one another. On Saturdays there were sports schedules which only left time on Sundays for them to be together.

If the Connecticut State Police detective had known about the pattern of her previous weekends he might have wondered why Klaudia had chosen not to spend that Sunday with Steffen. She had opted, instead, to go hiking with her class-mate, Deborah Hearst. He had no reason to suspect Klaudia. All the evidence supported her version of events. Deborah had tripped and stumbled when the two friends were close to the edge of a ridge in Mt. Tom State Park. Follow-up interviews with the school's staff and other students confirmed the teenage girls were very close friends. "Inseparable," was how the assistant principal had described them. Unfortunately, a critical piece of evidence, the Valentine's card for Steffen that Deborah had given to Klaudia, was never presented.

Past pupils of the elite school were represented not only in the Office of the Attorney General, but also on the Board of Governors. Accordingly, the investigation progressed swiftly to the conclusion that the death was recorded as 'an accident' by the coroner. Other influential contacts ensured media coverage respected the school's wishes for its community to grieve in private. Consequently, Klaudia was shielded from aggressive police questioning and inquisitive journalists. No one, other than her parents, knew it was her second tragedy involving a close friend. If the Bremners were suspicious that events were not exactly as their daughter had described, they certainly gave no indication of concern.

Klaudia stared at the fire as it consumed the envelope and delicate hand-made card Deborah had entrusted her to deliver. Ironically, the last piece to surrender to the flames was the pretty pink heart Steffen's young admirer had drawn for him.

4:05PM – Sunday June 11th 1961

El Alto Airport, Nuestra Señora de La Paz, BOLIVIA

teffen and Klaudia Bremner cleared customs along with other pas-
sengers who had been on the final leg of their flight from New York.
Thirty minutes later, Klaudia was at the controls of a *Grumman G-73
Mallard* with her father in the co-pilot's seat.

"This is what I missed most," the fifteen year old announced as
she adjusted the throttle.

"Well, keep your voice down while I talk to the tower and get
us cleared for takeoff," her father interrupted.

The young girl finished the pre-flight instrument check and followed the tower's instructions. Steffen was asleep before they reached
a cruising altitude of eight thousand feet. He had also been taught to
fly but did not share his sister's passion. Not only did Klaudia want to
be in control of the plane each time she travelled with her father, but
she also wanted to know how the aircraft had been assembled. During
school vacation she enjoyed helping with maintenance of the fleet. This
affinity for aeronautical engineering was as much Gabriele's influence
as it was her father's. She loved to hear her mother's war stories about
working in the *Messerschmitt AG* aircraft factory in Augsburg. When
there was no maintenance project for Klaudia, she eagerly assisted with
administrative duties for the family's air taxi and freight business.

Gabriele oversaw maintenance operations at *Aymaran Air*. She
made sure all logs were correctly maintained and each aircraft's maintenance schedule adhered to in strict accordance with the manufacturer's
guidelines. The fact that her knowledge stemmed from building fuselage
components for the Nazi war machine was only shared with the twins

when they were old enough to understand. Since Germany had been defeated in World War II, it was crucial such information be kept secret. Nazi hunters, such as Simon Wiesenthal, were a constant and real threat.

Without realizing, Klaudia had touched down right above the hidden wreckage of the *BV 238* plane. She taxied cautiously over to the jetty at *The Phoenix* Hotel and Conference Center as her father grinned and marveled at his daughter's skills. The water landing was text-book and so smooth that her brother did not rouse from his sleep.

*****

It was ten o'clock the following morning when Klaudia awoke. A note on the kitchen table explained her parents had flown to Lima, Peru, to collect a party of corporate executives who planned to spend time 'strategizing' at *The Phoenix* resort. It also stated they would not return until the afternoon and finished with instructions for the twins to relax and recover from their jet lag.

Klaudia could not have wished for a better beginning to the summer vacation. She went back upstairs, but instead of going to her own room, she slipped under the sheets beside her brother. Steffen smiled without opening his eyes as his sister's naked body gently caressed his.

"Mother left a note. They've gone to Lima and won't be back for at least four hours."

The young man's body responded to the welcome news. For some time they writhed and wrestled, groaning and moaning as they indulged in their depraved and unnatural intimacy that knew neither guilt nor shame. They had been brought up to believe their Aryan blood was superior to that of native children whose parents worked in the hotel and conference center. As years passed, however, the Bremner parents had no idea the children's skewed, sordid behavior had overstepped the boundaries of even their immoral brainwashing. From Klaudia's perspective, there was no other option. Only three of the twelve children subsequently born to passengers of the *BV 238* flight were boys, and the oldest was five years younger than Steffen.

"You're out of control," he giggled as his sister produced one of the condoms she had purchased before they left the United States. Even if the local pharmacy had stocked prophylactics, it was an item neither she nor Steffen could purchase there. The sex crazed teenagers had endured five months of celibacy thanks to the logistics and circumstances of their boarding school. During the spring term, however, Klaudia had methodically stockpiled three months supply of condoms for their summer vacation.

The sound of a car door closing put an abrupt end to their illicit embrace. Immediately, she jumped out of bed and frantically began to gather her clothing.

"Clean up the rest of this," she commanded and scampered back to her room.

9:05AM – Friday September 1st 1961
Lago Titicaca, BOLIVIA

K laudia turned the nose of the *Grumman G-73 Mallard* into the wind blowing across the lake and gently pulled back on the throttle. The twins' summer vacation was over. Returning to their former school was not an option because its classes did not go beyond 8th grade. Mindful of the tragedy involving their daughter's classmate, Klaus and Gabriele decided to look for a boarding school outside Connecticut. They chose to enroll the twins in a prestigious academy in a suburb of Boston, Massachusetts. Klaus was sad to see his children leave. The vacation, more than any other, had demonstrated how grown up they were becoming. Both had helped with the air taxi and freight business during the summer and he was extremely proud of them. Obviously, he did not know everything the promiscuous teenagers had been doing. His ignorance of their incestuous activity was not a reflection on him. After all, Klaudia had maintained her composure during the questioning and interrogation that followed each of the two murders she had perpetrated. More importantly, one of those crimes was committed when she was only ten years old. If she had been able to deflect suspicion when she was the focus of an investigation, she would surely be able to conceal an incestuous relationship no one knew existed.

6:15PM – Saturday July 30th 1966
Wembley Stadium, London, ENGLAND

The Bremners could not get out of the soccer stadium fast enough. Steffen and Klaudia knew there was nothing they could say that would console their parents. West Germany had developed its soccer team in an effort to restore national pride following World War II. The 1966 World Cup final against England was viewed by everyone in Germany as an opportunity to do battle, once again, while the whole world watched. The England team, captained by Bobby Moore, was well aware of what was at stake and had the advantage of playing before a very partisan crowd. Tied 2-2 after ninety minutes, England's Geoff Hurst scored two unanswered goals during extra time. The English players emerged victorious and were presented with the coveted Jules Rimet Trophy by Queen Elizabeth II. For the first time, England was the World Cup Champion. An opportunity had been lost by West Germany. The next tournament would be in four years but no one could predict if the two countries would play each other at any stage, let alone in the final. Klaus Bremner just wanted to vomit. Seeing and hearing the obnoxious jubilant English fans sickened him. He remembered bombing mission briefings, in the early days of the war, when the stadium's iconic towers were used as reference points by the Luftwaffe.

Fortunately, there was a strong police presence when Klaus collapsed clutching his chest in agony. Within minutes he was being taken from an ambulance and wheeled into St. Mark's Hospital.

*****

It would be weeks before doctors deemed him healthy enough to fly back to Bolivia. Their advice for the forty-nine year old pharmacist and entrepreneur was that his mild heart attack should be regarded as a warning.

Once the family returned to their adopted homeland, he decided his medical emergency was a sign he should share more details of the Bremner businesses with his children. They already knew about the air freight company and the air taxi, *Aymaran Air*, as well as their part owner-ship of *The Phoenix* Hotel and Conference Center. They also knew their father owned and managed the *BV Pharmaceutical Corporation,* but had no idea about the vast amounts of cocaine this company processed and shipped illegally to the United States.

It took almost three hours for their parents to explain the full extent of the family's operations and interests, as well as their plans and desires for the future.

"I can't believe you sent us to a prep school in the United States if you disliked the country so much," Steffen observed.

"You need to know your enemy," Klaus explained. "I needed to immerse you in their culture. That's why I insisted you both go to uni-versity there. The more quality contacts you have in the United States, the easier it will be to flood its cities with our cocaine."

"Steffen and I are so proud of everything you have done for us, Father," Klaudia acknowledged. "We're looking forward to getting a chance to make you feel proud of us."

"Concentrate on getting through university first and everything else will fall into place," their mother advised.

11:45AM – Sunday May 24th 1970
Tufts University, Medford, Massachusetts, USA

Klaus and Gabriele Bremner could hardly contain their pride as their daughter walked across the stage to accept her Doctorate Degree in Pharmacy. The previous day they had been at Harvard Business School where their son graduated with a Masters Degree in Business Administration. The next generation was confidently emerging to help execute the master plan.

Later that evening the family dined in a small Italian restaurant off Hanover Street in Boston's North End.

"I think it's fortuitous we're in Boston to celebrate your graduations," the patriarch observed. "In six years time, America will be celebrating the two hundredth anniversary of its independence, and to think it all started in this city. So it's appropriate we raise our glasses and make a 'Declaration of Dependence.' Let's toast to making this country dependent on cocaine and whatever other fun narcotics we can supply."

"Prost!" Four glasses clinked as the family memorialized their commitment to American Drug Dependence.

"I've organized a well deserved vacation for you two," the senior Bremner announced as he removed an envelope from the inside pocket of his jacket. "After what happened in London neither Mother nor I will be going, but I've booked you two a trip to Mexico for the World Cup Tournament."

Klaudia got out of her seat and gave her father a huge hug. Over the months, she and her brother had rarely seen each other because of their studies, but she knew, once they got to Mexico, that would all change.

"If Germany ends up playing England, you'd better not even

watch the TV," she warned. "In fact, perhaps you shouldn't watch any of the games."

"There's no need to worry, I've never felt better," Klaus smiled to reassure his family. "Enjoy your vacation and when you get home, you can start getting more involved with the work at *BV Pharmaceutical* and *Aymaran Air*."

6:15PM – Sunday June 14th 1970
Estadio Leon – Mexico City, MEXICO

The Bremner twins understood the illegal aspects of the family's business made it difficult for their parents to recruit reliable and trustworthy employees. Cocaine production was not an issue and they were able to keep up with demand. There was, however, significant risk for the family's air freight business with its involvement in transportation of an illicit substance into the United States.

Thousands of German soccer supporters cheered and danced in celebration of the 3-2 win over England. Steffen, however, was thinking about something else as he and Klaudia watched the dejected English players as they were led off the field by their captain, Bobby Moore. The casual remark he had just heard made him think about his family's cocaine distribution problem.

"Thank you, Colombia!" a jubilant German fan yelled at the top of his voice. He was referring to the fact that, immediately prior to the tournament, Moore had been arrested and detained in Bogotá, for several days, as part of an investigation into the alleged theft of a gold bracelet. Not only did the incident unnerve their captain, but it also dampened the spirits and morale of the entire England squad. The incident occurred when England played Colombia in Bogotá in a friendly pre-tournament game. The team learned, along with their supporters and an entire nation following every detail in sensational tabloid reports, in South America there is no such thing as a friendly soccer match. The only evidence against the English soccer star was a statement from a female store employee. Moore cooperated fully with the police in an effort to resolve the matter expeditiously, however, the fact that England had just beaten

Colombia 4 – 0 did not endear him to local authorities. After objections had been lodged, at the highest diplomatic levels, the England captain was released in time for his team's first game of the World Cup tournament in Mexico. By then, the damage had been done. The defending champions neither played to their full potential, nor to the expectations of their fans. When Moore returned to Colombia to stand trial, subsequent legal proceedings uncovered flaws in the witness' account of how he had allegedly stolen the jewelry. As a result, the criminal case against him was dropped. It would take years to confirm Bobby Moore had been the victim of a scam, often perpetrated on unsuspecting tourists.

For Steffen the overheard remark was an epiphany as he realized how the Colombians could help his family. Klaudia, however, was totally immersed in the moment. She was completely oblivious to the fact that her brother's Harvard trained mind had become engrossed in solving their cocaine distribution problems. When their father landed the *BV 238* on Lake Titicaca in 1945, he could not have selected a better region in the world for cultivating coca. Erythroxylum Coca, also known as Bolivian Coca, is one of the best species for high cocaine yields. Klaus Bremner was well aware of that fact, hence the establishment of *BV Pharmaceutical*.

Thanks to a chance comment by a German soccer fan, Steffen had suddenly realized the Colombians, geographically and culturally, were better equipped to ship cocaine into the United States. Bolivia was somewhat remote and lacked an established and extensive trade network that could conceal illicit drug shipments. The following morning after breakfast, he shared his conclusions with Klaudia.

"I think we should concentrate on making cocaine and sub-contract its transportation to the Colombians. Our air freight operation can easily deliver it to them but that should be the end of our risk and involvement."

"Do you want to sell the Colombians our cocaine, or do you want to hire them to ship it to our own distributors in America?" Klaudia asked.

"Well," he paused, "they're both options but probably the best plan would be to sell them our product and let them take care of the rest. Our quality is better than anything they can produce and I've no doubt we can fill all the orders they'd place."

"There are several issues we'd need to address before I'd agree to that," his sister responded pensively, "but it certainly has the potential to increase our revenue. Right now, our distribution network can't match our production capabilities. So, I agree. If we can broker a good deal with the Colombians, we'll increase our profit. The biggest problem for me is that they would control our access to the market. Somehow we need to keep control of the process."

"You're right, it's not going to be easy, but we're not tapping the full potential of our production capabilities. We shouldn't make a hasty decision, but we need to give this serious consideration."

11:55AM – Saturday November 13th 1971
Lago Titicaca, BOLIVIA

S teffen and Klaudia each took one of their mother's arms as they followed their father's coffin out of the church, into the strong midday sunlight. Although the heart attack had been sudden, it was not unexpected. Nevertheless, despite the warning in London in 1966, the Bremners were not ready to say goodbye to their patriarch.

After the burial, mourners gathered at *The Phoenix* Hotel and Conference Center where they shared anecdotes and reminisced. One particular contingent acknowledged their special gratitude. Passengers from *BV 238* privately conveyed their condolences. They emphasized how they owed their lives to Klaus for skillfully flying them out of Nazi Germany in 1945. Each of the surviving members of 'Wolf 238' promised that same allegiance to his children and their mother.

The most poignant part of the day was when the parents of Elena Chavez came to comfort Klaudia. Her reaction gave them no reason to suspect they were consoling the very person who had murdered their daughter. Instead, she thanked them for their support and brazenly preached that her father and Elena were in heaven, together.

*****

One week after their father's funeral, the twins returned to the matter of finding a business partner to help expand their cocaine distribution network. They were committed to punishing the United States for entering World War II and had compiled a list of potential Colombian partners. Their father's untimely death reinforced their resolve to profit financially from flooding North America with one of the most addictive drugs known to man.

The selection process was meticulous and had taken almost eighteen months. Steffen and Klaudia were extremely particular since they could not rely on a conventional recruitment agency for assistance. Eventually, they managed to narrow their choice to Eduardo Santos.

Chapter 3

COLOMBIA - 1973

FAMILY TIES

3:00PM-Tuesday April 17th 1973
Zipaquirá, COLOMBIA

L ocated approximately fifty miles north of Bogotá, Colombia, the Santos family domain was a four thousand acre ranch on the outskirts of Zipaquirá. It was adjacent to the Tomine Reservoir where Eduardo's older brother, Fernando, raised 1,500 head of cattle. Eduardo also lived on the family estate where he helped his mother manage their iron and silver mines. She had assumed control in 1957 after her husband's death in an explosives accident.

Without his family's knowledge, Eduardo had branched out into cocaine production. His decision to diversify was driven by an admiration for the political doctrine of Simon Bolivar who helped free the continent from its imperial Spanish rulers, in the early nineteenth century. For generations, cocaine had been used to sustain the indigenous workforce who mined silver and mercury while their Spanish rulers raped the continent of its natural resources. From Eduardo's perspective, these tyrants had been replaced by multinational corporations that continued to interfere with Colombia's utilization of its natural resources. The main focus of the young man's ire, however, was America. He considered the import of coca leaves by the United States for the production of *Coca-Cola*, to be the height of hypocrisy. His father's death from the premature detonation of an explosive in a silver mine, reinforced these feelings. He despised the fact that, for centuries, Colombians had given their lives extracting the country's precious minerals for the benefit of foreign powers.

Eduardo knew his mother, Helena Santos, would not approve of his cocaine dealings. A devout Roman Catholic, she had reacted to her husband's death as a challenge from God. Her son utilized his knowledge of export operations by developing an international trucking and shipping subsidiary which provided services to third party entities. The ambitious Santos expanded his business to make it harder for United States Customs to uncover his illicit cocaine shipments. Colombia's legal exports ran a vast range of commodities including copper, nickel, emeralds, gold, silver, coffee, bananas and cut flowers. The perishable nature of some of these products put pressure on customs officials to process them promptly, a fact Santos regularly exploited. In Colombia, he formed clandestine alliances with local FARC revolutionary guerrillas, which ensured his coca plantations, and cocaine production facilities, were protected. As an added bonus, his family's mining operations were also permitted to operate without interference from the revolutionary army. Helena had always paid her workforce above the standard industry rate which endeared the Santos family, not only to the local community, but also to the Marxist revolutionary terrorist group. It certainly helped Eduardo when he negotiated with the guerrilla commanders. He and his FARC collaborators shared a common goal to keep their operations and pacts completely confidential. Agreements with business leaders ran contrary to their revolutionary doctrine, but the revenue from cocaine was an economic lifeline for them. Coca had been part of South American culture for thousands of years. FARC leaders understood they could not sustain their armed struggle unless they sold the drug where the market paid top dollar. That place was the United States and Eduardo Santos had an established shipping and distribution network to meet their need.

While all these attributes made him a good business partner for the FARC guerrillas, it was another criterion which attracted the Bremner twins. Eduardo Santos was single and that was a critical component of Klaudia's plan.

"There's only one way to ensure we'll be treated fairly and that's for me to marry him," Klaudia suggested as she caressed her brother's face. Steffen's initial reaction to his sister's plan was one of shock, but it only lasted for seconds. No one knew her better than he did so, upon reflection, her scheme did not really surprise him at all.

"It's not going to change how we feel about each other," she continued, as she straddled her brother's naked body, "but we need to know for certain we can trust this man with our livelihood. By infiltrating the Santos family and gaining his complete trust, we'll always know for certain what's going on."

"I don't know if ..." She placed her forefinger on his lips to prevent him from finishing the sentence.

"It's just business Steffen, that's all. Nothing's going to change between us. If anything, it will bring us closer."

"I'm glad Father isn't around to witness this. I don't think he would've wanted you to dilute our bloodline," Steffen acknowledged.

"The end justifies the means," she assured him. "We're going to be in control of the whole operation. Everything!"

2:05PM – Saturday April 27th 1973
Madera, California, USA

E duardo Santos worked hard, but he also liked to play hard. At least once a week, he managed to escape his hectic work schedule to ride his motocross bike across the family's vast estate. He had come to California to compete in several races on both his 125cc and 250cc bikes. In one of the events, he and another rider managed to open up a two second lead from the rest of the pack, and that gap increased as the race progressed. A missed gear change on the final bend caused him to slip into second place, as dirt from the spinning rear wheel of the new leader completely enshrouded his visor. When the dust cleared, he watched the rider pump a fist in the air as the black and white checkered flag signaled the finish. Irritated and frustrated, Eduardo pulled up beside the victor to offer his congratulations. He was completely stunned when long blonde hair tumbled out of the winner's helmet.

"Nice move at the last bend."

"That was close," Klaudia Bremner acknowledged.

It was the culmination of a year's preparation. Volumes of surveillance logs and photographs cataloged every detail in the life of the unsuspecting Eduardo Santos. Once she discovered his love of motocross, she purchased several bikes and spent months practicing and exercising in the gym to develop upper body strength. Having been practically raised in an aircraft hangar, she had a natural aptitude for engines and gearboxes which helped her transition into the sport. She had a keen ear for an engine's pitch on its power curve, so she knew when to select the optimum gear for hills and obstacles. For Klaudia, riding a motorcycle was similar to flying a plane. She became one with the machine. Not only did she master the skill, but she also enjoyed it immensely.

"Are you entered for the 250cc race?"

"No, this is it for me today," she replied as she ran her fingers through her long hair.

"Well, that's a shame," Eduardo lamented. "I'd like to get a chance to redeem myself."

"Perhaps another time," Klaudia suggested, trying not to sound interested.

For the Bremners, it was not going to be "perhaps." She and Steffen had booked adjoining rooms in the same hotel where Santos was staying. Their intentions were to see a lot more of him.

******

The following morning they arrived for breakfast in the hotel's restaurant at the same time as their prey. The Colombian was just about to enter the dining room when Klaudia stealthily approached from behind, and nimbly cut in front of him.

"I think we're next," she announced to the stunned hostess. "Wow! This is the second time I've beaten you at the finish line," she joked as Eduardo realized who had cut in front of him. "We'll take a table for three," she instructed. "I don't think we were properly introduced yesterday. I'm Klaudia Bremner and this is my brother, Steffen."

Breakfast for Santos went by too quickly. The more he learned about her, the more infatuated he became. She may have beaten him in the motocross race but he felt confident the next time they faced off, he would emerge the victor. He learned Klaudia was a pharmacist, an obvious asset if she were ever to be entrusted with knowledge of his cocaine business. She was also a pilot and her family owned an air-freight business with a fleet of aircraft; another obvious asset. There was also the fact she lived in Bolivia, the best place on earth to grow coca plants. Unknowingly, Eduardo Santos was reacting exactly as the twins had planned he would.

7:05PM – Sunday April 28th, 1974
Lago Titicaca, BOLIVIA

It was the day before the wedding and the culmination of Steffen and Klaudia's scheme to forge a relationship with Eduardo Santos. They had done their homework and could not have wished for a smoother and speedier outcome. It had only taken six months, from their first meeting, until he proposed to her. She let him know they shared a belief in the merits of Simon Bolivar's political doctrine: self determination for the native peoples of South America; and opposition to those imperial nations that raped the continent's natural resources. He had not confided in her about his cocaine operation, although they talked at length about fighting foreign interference in the commercial operations of South America. He cited the success of his family's mining business as a testament to Bolivar's doctrine. Both agreed the Bolivian economy was impeded by the vilification of cocaine by the rest of the world. In the sixteenth and seventeenth centuries, the imperialist occupiers had used the coca plant to sustain Inca slaves who were condemned to work in mercury mines. In the twentieth century, when it looked like Bolivia would benefit from the production of cocaine, the whole world had suddenly developed a conscience.

The Santos family, and a few close friends, were guests at the Bremner home for the wedding rehearsal dinner. That location was chosen because preparations for the reception were still ongoing at *The Phoenix* resort. The following day, Eduardo and Klaudia would be married and everyone, except Steffen, was thrilled for the couple. He, of course, could not share his feelings publicly and only he could appreciate the irony of the situation. Since his father had passed, the duty of giving

her away would be his responsibility. His sister was adamant her marriage would not change their relationship and insisted it was no more
than an international, economic alliance. Nevertheless, his MBA studies
at Harvard had not prepared him for their business stratagem which was
more the domain of European nobility. The siblings, however, appreciated
the alliance would help conceal the true nature of their relationship.

Eduardo had been preoccupied for some weeks when he resolved
to confide in his bride-to-be. Concern about her reaction caused him to
procrastinate, but it was the evening before their wedding and he had
no option but to take his fiancée onto the patio where they could talk
privately.

"I need to share something with you, mi amor," he began when
the couple was out of earshot of the guests who were more focused on
cocktails and hors d'oeuvres. She pretended to look concerned, even
though she suspected she already knew what he wanted to tell her. "I
want you to know my family's mining interest isn't my only source of
income. I have another export business which I can't report on my income
tax return."

"Before you say anything," Klaudia interrupted. "Not every
aspect of our business is completely legal either." She understood he
was at a disadvantage in the conversation because she knew much more
about his illicit operations than he knew about hers. While he was hesi-
tant and unsure, she knew exactly what to say in order to put his mind at
ease. "Cocaine is Bolivia's most profitable export and the US is trying to
destroy us?" she mocked indignantly. "*BV Pharmaceutical* augments its
legitimate drug manufacturing business by processing cocaine. Our air
freight business helps with its distribution to the United States. Unfortunately, that's where there's a bottle-neck in our operation. We have the
capacity to produce more cocaine than we're able to ship." Eduardo's

brain suddenly realized what she had known, long before they had ever met.

"It sounds like this marriage is a match made in Heaven," he announced, then passionately kissed her. "Or in Hell," she thought smugly to herself.

5:15AM – Monday April 29th, 1974
Lago Titicaca, BOLIVIA

K laudia smiled as Steffen slid quietly under the sheets and softly caressed her.

"I can't believe it's your wedding day and I'm giving you away," he whispered.

"No one's giving anyone away, my love. This is just a business merger. Nothing's going to change for you and me. The more cocaine Eduardo's operation shifts for us, the more opportunities we'll have to be together."

He rested his head on his sister's naked breasts and she gently stroked his hair. Slowly, the tranquil beginning transitioned into a passionate embrace. It was Klaudia's way of showing him actions speak louder than words.

"Today changes nothing," she insisted. "The outcome of World War II changed nothing. We were born to be together. It's our destiny to continue our parent's mission."

*****

Steffen escorted his sister down the aisle of their parish church. It was packed with family, friends and guests from both Bolivia and Colombia. As he sat beside his mother, he wiped away a tear that had suddenly, and unexpectedly, welled up.

"I'm so happy for her too, my dear. Doesn't my little girl look beautiful," Gabriele whispered. "I so wish Klaus were here with us today." Steffen put his arm around his mother and nodded.

"Father would be very proud of her," he agreed.

"Your sister thought of everything. Today is the wedding anniversary of our Führer, Adolf Hitler, to Eva Braun. It's a wonderful day."

11:35AM - Thursday June 2nd 1977
Boston, Massachusetts, USA

Everything about his new life in America was perfect, except for one thing: the traffic. Eduardo Santos and his bride, Klaudia, had immigrated two years earlier, just prior to the birth of their son, Xavier. It had been her idea to relocate to Boston. She emphasized the benefits of establishing legitimate commercial enterprises to conceal their cocaine imports and distribution network. Boston was the ideal place to live since she already had a network of friends from her college days. His regular trips to Colombia not only ensured everything continued to work smoothly there, but they also kept his mother in good spirits, especially when her grandson came along.

Eduardo pounded the steering wheel in frustration. Punctuality was a character trait he demanded of himself, as well as anyone who worked for him. He thought he had left his attorney's office with adequate time to make the 12:00 noon lunch appointment with Fr. Michael Foley. He had not allowed, however, for detours caused by the hazard of five hundred pound panels of insulated glass shattering down onto Clarendon Street. Boston Police cruisers and barricades surrounded the newly con-structed Hancock Tower. The building was making headlines around the world, but not for reasons anyone had anticipated when construction of the sixty story skyscraper broke ground in 1968. The architectural firm and structural engineers were frantically working to resolve design flaws which caused huge sections of glass to plummet to the pavement below. Fortunately, threatening panes signaled their intentions by changing color because of the enormous stress caused by the building's excessive deflection. This advance notice gave Boston Police time to safely clear the street of both pedestrian and vehicular traffic.

Fr. Foley greeted his friend with his trademark bear-hug. As the air was squeezed from his lungs, Santos caught a glimpse of a clock which assured him his reputation for punctuality was intact.

"How are you Michael, my old friend? Still saving souls?"

"I do my best, Eduardo, but I wish there were more good people in the world like you," the six foot-three, two hundred and fifty pound Roman Catholic priest gushed.

After Fr. Foley finished signing Mass cards his secretary had placed on his desk, the two men left the parochial house. They crossed Bennington Street and headed towards *Angelo's* for their monthly luncheon date. Before they reached the restaurant, Santos retrieved an envelope from inside his jacket and handed it to his friend.

"I'm going to Colombia on Sunday, so please put this on the plate for me."

"Thank you, Eduardo. I'll pray for your safe trip, and please give your saintly mother a big hug for me."

"No one gives hugs like you, but I'll do my best."

Later, in the privacy of his office, the parish priest opened the envelope and counted out ten, one hundred dollar bills. Every Sunday Eduardo Santos brought his wife and two year old son, Xavier, to Mass in East Boston, even though the family lived in the affluent suburb of Newton. St. Theresa's provided spiritual guidance to a proud working class parish and the weekly pilgrimage from Newton to East Boston accounted for more than half the money collected each week.

11:25AM –Friday June 3rd 1977
Boston, Massachusetts, USA

Eduardo Santos closed the bulky purchase and sale agreement for Marshall Builders and slid it back across the conference table to his attorney, Robert Grey.

"This is excellent, Robert. Everything we talked about is here." For some reason, despite having worked with his attorney for over six months, Santos still preferred the formality of Robert rather than Bob.

"Here's the construction contract for the nightclub," Grey responded. "Take your time and check it over. I don't expect Marshall for another twenty minutes."

The Colombian thumbed through the documents and complimented his attorney, not only for putting together the paperwork, but also for locating Marshall Builders. He had assigned Grey the task of finding an established general contractor that: used union labor; was struggling financially; and was an 'owner-operator' business. Frank Marshall had been approached by Robert Grey with an offer to purchase his construction company, but only after the attorney had completed extensive research. He was president and sole owner of Marshall Builders but his financial status was dire. The Boston based company had been started by his father when he returned from Europe after World War II. In 1972, an accident involving a snow plow on Route 128, took the life of Marshall Sr. forcing his son to take charge of the company, long before he was ready to assume such responsibility. Without influential friends in the Massachusetts State House, the twenty-eight year old soon found his construction company undercapitalized. He was two months behind in his residential mortgage payments when Robert Grey approached him with a plan that would make all his financial problems disappear. Marshall could not believe his good fortune.

When it came to laundering drug money, Santos understood the importance of diversification. Accordingly, rather than incorporate and form a new construction company, he opted to purchase a controlling interest in one that had already established a thirty year reputation. He needed a construction company to artificially inflate costs for Fr. Foley's proposed building project at St. Theresa's. He took control of Marshall Builders because it had signatory union agreements with several labor organizations, since building trade unions had a lock on most construction projects undertaken by the Roman Catholic Archdiocese of Boston. Owning a company, such as Marshall Builders, made sound business sense for his plans to launder money through the Parish Center construction project. His first job for the company, however, would be to build his new nightclub on Lansdowne Street. High profile city projects typically required union labor, but Santos had no personal preference when it came to that issue. He was more focused on laundering drug profits and Marshall Builders was perfectly positioned to help with that endeavor.

Eduardo Santos and Robert Grey had several meetings with Frank Marshall and subsequently made him an offer he could not refuse. In order to conceal the Colombian's involvement, Grey incorporated a holding company in the State of Wyoming called Marshall Holdings. In Wyoming, corporations do not have to reveal who owns their shares. They do, however, have to identify the officers and directors and Frank Marshall's name was used for that purpose. Santos wanted Frank to feel vested in the new venture, so he gave him 5% of the stock in Marshall Holdings and retained the rest for himself. The legal papers Grey had prepared also provided for Marshall Holdings to purchase 100% of the

Massachusetts stock of Marshall Builders for one dollar. In order to keep Frank Marshall focused on running the construction business, Grey arranged for Marshall Holdings to purchase the delinquent mortgage on the builder's home.

*****

As he signed the array of documents in front of him, Marshall reflected how his financial status had gone from 'zero to hero' in a few short weeks.

"From now on Frank, I want you to concentrate on managing the job sites," Santos instructed. "I'll appoint a comptroller to work with my accountants. He'll make sure the company's finances are kept in order."

Marshall understood that, in reality, he had become an employee in his own company. Although it was difficult for him to accept, the alternative would have been much worse. He would have had to close his family business; watch the bank foreclose on his home; and become an employee in someone else's company.

"I'm going out of town for a week," the Colombian continued, "When I return, we'll meet with the architect for my new nightclub, so you can get started on that project."

12:20PM - Sunday June 5th 1977
Logan Airport, Boston, Massachusetts, USA

As the Lockheed 10-11 climbed rapidly, Eduardo Santos peered out at the steeple of St.Theresa's. In three hours, he would board a flight in New York for Bogotá, Colombia. Klaudia carefully adjusted the pillow behind her head while Xavier colored with the crayons she had put into his backpack the previous evening.

"Does Fr. Foley have any idea what we've been able to do?" she asked.

"Definitely not! I spoke with the lawyers yesterday. They've already set up the charitable trust and acquired the land. I'll tell him when we get back, once I've confirmed everything is all set."

"Is Steffen okay with this?"

"Your brother likes the idea. It's a win-win for everyone. He's supposed to meet us later in the week. I want him to oversee construction and keep things running smoothly. With his Harvard MBA, I can't think of anyone better qualified."

11:05AM - Thursday June 9th 1977
Zipaquirá, COLOMBIA

Eduardo and Klaudia were delighted. Forty acres, immediately adjacent to the church on the outskirts of Zipaquirá, were now owned by their newly formed real estate trust. Fr. Foley's dream to build a 'twin school' in Colombia would soon be a reality. Steffen rolled out a set of construction plans on the hood of the car and the trio carefully reviewed the architect's design for the proposed structure.

"Where does Fr. Márquez think the money is coming from?" he asked.

"He thinks Eduardo's mining interests are paying for all this." Klaudia explained to her brother with a smile. "Once this project is finished, we're going to build a new parish center for Fr. Foley at St. Theresa's in East Boston. This will forge another legitimate link between the two countries for us to exploit. By no means will it conceal all our activities, but every bit helps. Once the school gets established, we can plan exchange programs and sporting trips that will provide a cover for narcotic shipments. It will also justify our travels back and forth. Having a couple of priests as chaperones will help deflect attention. The construction activities and school administration costs will also help conceal cash transfers in and out of the United States."

Their conversation was interrupted by a police car rolling to a stop beside them. Two officers stepped out and greeted the trio.

"Buenos días, Mañuel. How are you today?" Eduardo politely greeted the Zipaquirá Police Chief.

"Amigo. Welcome, and it's a pleasure to see you again Señora Santos." The older man turned and gestured in the direction of the other officer who had been driving the vehicle. "This is my right hand man, Sergeant Lopez."

"You're wrong, Mañuel." Eduardo interrupted. "Sergeant Lopez just got promoted. He's now the new Chief of Police."

The shock on Mañuel's face may have been caused by the unexpected news but, more likely, it was due to the speed with which Santos retrieved a revolver from his shoulder holster. The single shot left an incredibly neat hole in the Chief's forehead. The exit wound was catastrophic. He collapsed in a heap, the horrified expression frozen forever on his face.

"Congratulations, Chief Lopez! You're only on the job a few seconds and already you've got a major crime on your hands," Santos noted with a hearty laugh. "You can decide if this is going to be a murder investigation or a missing person case. How do you want to handle it?" Lopez was stunned. He made a concerted effort not to bring his right hand anywhere near his sidearm, lest he succumb to a similar fate.

"Your former boss was a greedy fuck. He wasn't content with the monthly thousand dollars I paid him to make sure our cocaine operation stayed under the radar in his jurisdiction. Not only did you just get promoted but you also got yourself a healthy pay raise. Here's your first month's pay along with an extra thousand dollars. Consider it a signing bonus."

"What am I going to do with him?" The new Chief asked.

"You'll think of something," Eduardo laughed, "That's why I'm paying you the big bucks. I have every confidence you're going to be a great asset to our operation in Zipaquirá. I'll not be here often, but Steffen Bremner here will be," he gestured, "and he'll take care of your monthly payments. Just remember not to get greedy like Mañuel. You'll get your regular Chief of Police salary, plus what we'll pay you. If you do a good job for us, you can expect additional bonuses."

The former sergeant appeared comfortable with his new role and patiently watched as Steffen and Eduardo wrapped Mañuel's body in polythene sheeting they had brought with them. It required his assistance to lift the lifeless lump into the police car.

"Here's a shovel," Santos instructed, tossing it into the trunk beside the body. "Why don't you take a long drive and dispose of this piece of shit. Also, don't go celebrating your promotion until I talk with the Mayor, and it gets officially announced."

"Si Señor! I understand, Señor!"

After the police car had left, the trio resumed the meeting to review the plans, as if there had never been an interruption. They paced out the perimeter of the proposed school and satisfied themselves the architect had orientated the building to take the best advantage of the topography.

"We need to get back to freshen up before dinner. Mama will be upset with us if we're late," Eduardo suggested.

12:50PM – Friday June 10th 1977
East Boston, Massachusetts, USA

Temptation was a vice Fr. Foley knew more about than he cared to admit. As a child he had been led to believe life was simple. None of the stories from the bible caused him concern. Adam and Eve eating apples in the Garden of Eden seemed benign. Four years at Boston College, however, and a further three studying in Rome, taught him there were more temptations in life than could be found in a grocery store.

He reached over and caressed Mrs. White's neck and moved his head closer to hers.

"You're beautiful," the priest whispered softly into her ear, as he gently ran his hand down the smooth curve of her back. With the warmth of her breath on his face, Fr. Foley gazed into her brown eyes, and tried to imagine what she was thinking.

"Take your hands off my girl!" Jennings joked.

"She's a beauty," the priest acknowledged. "I love horses and try to get over here whenever I can. I love to watch them work out."

"I know her trainer. Sometimes I'll help him by taking her out for an early gallop."

"Michael Foley," he replied as he shook the young man's hand. "I'm the Parish Priest at St.Theresa's in East Boston.

"Yes, I know who you are, Father! I'm Paul Jennings. I live in your parish, but I'd be telling lies if I told you I never miss Sunday Mass."

"Well, you're doing God's work here, Paul," the priest joked with a smile.

"Mrs. White has a race tomorrow. Would you say a little prayer for her?"

"I'd be delighted to do that." Foley said a short prayer which ended with the words, "and keep this beautiful creature and her jockey safe during every race." The young man thanked the cleric for his blessing.

"Is that a brogue I hear?"

"It is indeed, Father. I came over two years ago when I got the chance to work as an assistant trainer."

"What part of Ireland are you from?"

"I'm originally from Armagh but my parents moved to Salthill in County Galway soon after I was born."

"I know Galway well. I've gone over a couple of times for Race Week. I love the turf racing."

"Yeah. I had to adjust to conditions over here." Jennings acknowledged, as he mounted the filly. "Will you be able to come tomorrow and cheer us on?"

"I'd love to."

"I'll leave a pass for you at the ticket office, Father. Enjoy the rest of your day."

11:50AM - Sunday June 12th 1977
Zipaquirá, COLOMBIA

Nothing was allowed to upset the Sunday morning ritual at the Santos household. Mass at 11:00 was always followed by a visit to the grave of Hector Santos. Normally, Helena was only accompanied by Fernando, however, since they were visiting from Boston, Eduardo was also there with his family. Helena's character was tested when her husband was killed twenty years earlier. A faulty detonator caused gelignite to explode prematurely while he was setting charges in one of their mines. Eduardo and Fernando were young teenagers at the time, too young to be involved in managing the business. For twenty years, however, Helena had proved to be very much up to the challenge. Nevertheless, every week she visited her husband's resting place as if to update him on family affairs, as well as to offer a silent prayer.

"Papi, you never got to meet Xavier," she explained, as she squeezed her grandson's plump little hand. "He's your grandson. He came all the way from the United States of America to visit you."

Had Hector Santos been able to reply, he would surely have told young Xavier how proud he was of his grandmother. Since his fatal accident, Helena had not only taken over operation of the iron ore and silver mining business, but she had also quadrupled its production. Three out of every five men in the region were employed by Santos Mines. As a young boy, Fernando loved being in his father's presence. He grew up believing he had not done a day of honest work until his body was caked in sweat and grime. Ironically, the same sweat and grime inspired his younger brother to find an easier way to earn a living. The hands-on training and education Eduardo received in the family business taught him that more money could be made with a calculator than with a pick and shovel. He did not need to graduate from an elite business school to learn how a market economy worked, and he refused to allow morals to complicate his business operations. The commodity was inconsequential. He was only concerned with margins. If there was a market for a product, he focused on how efficiently he could satisfy the demand in order to maximize a return on his investment. Accordingly, he did not concern himself with the production of cocaine. Instead, he concentrated on its transportation. Bolivia was the best country in the world to cultivate the coca plant. The soils; the altitude; the climate; and the low cost of labor, made the Andes region perfect. The most lucrative marketplace was, however, 4,000 miles away in the United States. Eighty percent of the ore extracted from his family's mines was exported to America and he had been pivotal in managing that enterprise. Cocaine transportation seemed like a logical transition and his marriage to Klaudia had facilitated a perfect corporate merger. The Bremner twins already knew a marriage offered the perfect vehicle for memorializing the union of their business operations. The move to America enabled Eduardo to conceal his cocaine shipments amongst the many commodities he imported from South America through his shipping business in Boston. After he opened the *Cocoa Bean* nightclub, it became the perfect conduit to satisfy demand for the drug on the streets of that city and beyond.

Klaudia was familiar with the Sunday morning routine but it was her brother's first visit to the estate and he wanted to get an early start on his journey home. Neither Eduardo nor his mother would permit him to leave, insisting he stay for Sunday lunch. The twins appreciated the importance Helena placed on family and tradition. It reinforced the decision to trust the shipment of their cocaine to Eduardo. They were satisfied with the knowledge that, one day, Xavier would inherit both the production business and the shipping operation.

"I invited Fr. Márquez, our Parish Priest, to have lunch with us," Helena explained. "Anna is cooking his favorite dish, so we'd better not delay."

*****

"Fr. Márquez, would you like to say Grace?" Helena asked after Anna had placed an enormous roast beef in the middle of the table." It was the picture of a happy family enjoying a delicious Sunday meal. The air was filled with the sound of lively conversation punctuated with bursts of polite laughter. Eduardo decided to focus his attention on their guest, Fr. Márquez, and introduce his plan to build a new school adjacent to the church.

"My businesses are doing very well, Father, and I want to give back. I decided there was no better place to begin than here at home. The children in the area need a good education, but their parents may not appreciate how important this is. That's where we could use your help, Father. We'd like you to use the pulpit to stress this."

"It's a wonderful gesture, Eduardo. You can certainly count on my support."

"Well, you'll be working with someone you know. My Parish Priest in Boston is Fr. Michael Foley. He worked here as a missionary for two years after graduating from the seminary. He's helping me raise money for this school."

"Yes, I remember he said he wanted to do something to help our community. Does he still like to play fútbol, or, what do the Americans say, soccer?"

"I think he helps coach a team at Boston College."

"I remember he played goalkeeper. He was very good, so we used to call him, Our Saviour. Do you play football, or should I say soccer, Xavier?" the priest asked as he patted the young boy's head.

Xavier Santos only knew life in America where he was unaware of his financial status. In reality, not many people knew how wealthy his family really was. Helena Santos did not even know the extent of it. She had no idea her son's shipping business derived most of its profits from smuggling cocaine into the United States. Nor did she know her daughter-in-law, together with her twin brother, were Bolivia's largest cocaine producer and her son's primary source of the illicit drug.

"After lunch, Xavier is going on a horse ride with me and Uncle Fernando," Eduardo announced when everyone had finished eating and Fr. Márquez was about to leave. "His mother won't be able to come with us because she needs to bring Uncle Steffen to the airport."

Ironically, Eduardo recognized how important it was for Klaudia to see her brother on a regular basis. He made sure she visited Bolivia at least twice a year. When they needed to discuss their cocaine operations, he would arrange for the meetings to take place in Boston, so Steffen could stay with them at their Newton home.

Steffen's flight plans were flexible because he had made the trip in his own plane. They both shared their father's skill for flying although, of the two, Klaudia was the more expert. Their ability meant they were never dependent on major airlines so it was easier for them to evade law enforcement. They often joked it was impossible for the authorities to connect the dots, when there were no dots for them to connect!

3:25PM - Saturday July 25th 1977

Suffolk Downs Racecourse - East Boston, Massachusetts, USA

Michael Foley cringed when he spotted Paul Jennings heading towards him. He did not like meeting parishioners when he was at the racecourse, even if they rarely attended Mass.

"Who do you like in the next race, Father?" The priest had yet to back a winner that afternoon and hesitated before responding.

"Quincy Shore looks good."

"Sorry to disappoint you, but that's not going to happen. Did you put anything on him?"

"No, I was just about to. Do you have a tip?"

"Put your money on Mr. Sunshine."

Ten minutes later the two men watched the race leaders enter the home straight.

"Relax Father. Watch Mr. Sunshine turn it on." As if the horse had overheard their conversation, with a furlong to go, it glided effortlessly into first place and never looked back."

"Mr. Sunshine by a length over Quincy Shore and Dancing Star," announced the race commentator.

"You're always asking me what I do," Jennings joked, "and now you know! I help people and there's no need to worry about me blabbing around the parish. What happens at Suffolk Downs stays at Suffolk Downs. It's just like the confessional."

"Thank you, Paul. I appreciate that and also your tip. Listen, I've got to get out of here. I've got to say six o'clock Mass this evening."

Chapter 4

NORTHERN IRELAND - 1977

THE SELECTION PROCESS

4:10PM - Monday October 3rd 1977
Belfast, NORTHERN IRELAND

Peter Reid zipped up his jacket as he left the Ashby Institute on Stranmillis Road. The electrical engineering student had just met with his advisor to discuss his final year project and dissertation. He had recently returned to Belfast after spending the summer in Boston where he had worked for Wang Computers. The computer manufacturer planned to offer him a full-time position in their Limerick facility, subject to his June graduation from Queen's University.

Reid did not notice the driver of the Mini Cooper which was parked in front of his '73 Ford Capri. He had other things on his mind. On the fifth dead click of his ignition key, he noticed the headlight switch was set in the ON position. It did not take him long to determine why his car would not start. Just as quickly as he had identified the problem, he recognized the Mini would provide a solution. With its battery located in the rear, there was no better vehicle for jump-starting his car. Suddenly its engine started, so he needed to act quickly before it drove away.

His roadside assistance was provided by an attractive brunette in her early thirties. Together with a set of jumper cables it took only minutes to get his engine started. He thanked the young woman but since he had recently spent three months in Boston, her American accent escaped his attention. It was not the only thing he failed to notice. He never questioned he had, in fact, turned off his head-lights that morning. The distraction of an attractive female coming to his aid was, he considered, a stroke of good luck. Reid never suspected luck had absolutely nothing to do with what had just happened.

10:55AM - Friday October 7th 1977
Belfast, NORTHERN IRELAND

Maria Quintero finished her lecture on LCR circuits and gave the class her office number and teaching schedule. Every male student meticulously recorded the information. Reid also wrote it down but grinned. "Isn't it a small world," he thought to himself.

As she walked past him to exit the room, the professor caught his eye and commented with a smile,

"Well, if it isn't the electrical engineer with the flat battery! How ironic!" He wanted to reply with a smart quip, but she was gone before he could think of something impressive to say.

10:15AM - Friday November 11th 1977
Belfast, NORTHERN IRELAND

R eid believed his studies in Maria Quintero's class had being going well, so he was not alarmed when she asked him to stop by her office, later that afternoon, to collect a test paper. They agreed he would do so at 2:00PM. He hoped the meeting would be short since he had previously arranged to pick up his mother and younger sister from the Belfast City Hospital, at 3:30PM.

Peter's little sister, Catherine, was only eight years old. She knew she was sick, but her parents had been protecting and shielding her from the facts. Not that the eight year old knew what leukemia was, but like all children her age, a conversation on the topic was only going to generate questions no parent wants to answer.

3:50PM - Friday November 11th 1977
Belfast, NORTHERN IRELAND

A visit to the oncologist for their child is a harrowing experience for any parent. For the Reid family the stressful situation was intolerable because the hospital was not only undergoing major reconstruction, but it was also situated in the middle of a war zone.

The news Anne Reid received about her daughter that afternoon was not good. Little Catherine, however, had no idea about the seriousness of her condition. On the drive home, her mother and brother consciously avoided any mention of the doctor's grave prognosis.

6:55PM - Friday November 18th 1977
Belfast, NORTHERN IRELAND

The Troubles is the term used to describe the decades of sectarian conflict in Northern Ireland. On one side were predominantly Protestant 'Loyalist' and pro-British organizations, while on the other were predominantly Catholic 'Republican' pro-Irish nationalists. In 1969 the smoldering embers of their mutually destructive antagonism ignited once again. In response, the British government marshaled: the Province's police force, the Royal Ulster Constabulary (RUC); a part time, quasi auxiliary police force called the RUC Reserve; British Army troops from mainland Britain; and an army regiment recruited in Northern Ireland called the Ulster Defence Regiment (UDR). It was normal for Reid, and everyone who lived there, to expect daily interaction with one, if not all, of these armed forces. Due to the bombing campaign, cars were excluded from city and town centers, prompting the proliferation of 'pedestrian precincts' which have since become common in modern urban environments. The 'precincts' were established by constructing steel barricades around specified perimeters. These zones were manned by security personnel who frisked civilians, and searched delivery trucks accessing the restricted areas. In addition, stores and offices employed their own private security staff, who repeated the 'search' process on individuals entering their premises. Despite all efforts, however, a day without an explosion, or at least a bomb scare, was the exception rather than the rule.

Contrary to the image portrayed in media headlines, people tried to live a normal life. The feuding tribal factions made sensational news but children went to school, and people went to work, just like everywhere else. Unfortunately, sometimes innocent victims happened to be in the wrong place at the wrong time and neither bombs nor bullets discriminated.

In Northern Ireland civilians routinely encountered vehicle 'spot' check points that were jointly manned by armed Police and the British Army. That evening, however, Reid's security encounters would also have an international dimension. He had been invited to attend a cocktail party at the Consulate General of the United States, so he would be subject to the scrutiny of United States Marines posted at the entrance of the building.

When Maria Quintero invited him to the function she explained he would meet executives from American companies based in Northern Ireland. The Consul General had extended invitations to them for a pre-Thanksgiving event because most would be returning to the United States for the holiday. Since Reid had worked for Wang, in Boston, during his summer vacation, she wanted to introduce him to their Director of European Operations. As appreciative as he was for the opportunity to meet these industry leaders, the young man was distracted by his sister's medical situation. To further complicate matters, his father was in the middle of an eight week assignment on a *BP* oil tanker, so Peter knew much would be expected of him at home, to support both his mother and Catherine.

11:45PM - Tuesday January 24th 1978
Belfast, NORTHERN IRELAND

Reid spent the entire morning working on a computer programming assignment. The result of three hours work had been punched onto a four inch thick bundle of Hollerith cards which he dropped off at the service desk of the computer center.

"Hi there, Peter. I've been meaning to talk to you about something. Do you've time to grab a cup of coffee?" a familiar voice with the twang of an American accent inquired. "Come on," she insisted, "There's a new coffee shop on Botanic Avenue I want to try out."

*****

The waitress returned with one cup of coffee and one cup of tea.

"Even if you solve *The Troubles*," Maria lamented, "There's no hope for Northern Ireland until you guys learn how to make a decent cup of coffee." Reid smiled and sipped his tea.

"I'm going to share some information with you but it is for you, and only you. It can't be shared with anyone else. Do I have your word on that?" his professor requested. Peter nodded affirmatively and she continued. "It wasn't a coincidence I invited you to the function at the Consulate before Thanksgiving. One of the duties of my posting here is to recognize academic talent for US corporations. It's my job to identify individuals who could make positive contributions to American commerce. With your permission, Peter, I'd like to submit your name to the Committee."

"The Committee?" he repeated.

"Yes. Its membership is a blend of industry professionals, academics, and US government representatives. If you pass their scrutiny, your life will never be the same. This is truly the offer of a lifetime." Maria paused and studied the young man's eyes. "It's probably something you'll want to think about before giving me an answer."

"No it's not," he exclaimed without even a moment's hesitation. "Look around. What's this place got to offer me when I graduate?"

His plans had always been to finish his degree and return to the United States where he hoped life would offer more than war-weary Northern Ireland. His first trip to Boston had been July 2nd 1976. He arrived on a Friday evening and spent Saturday recovering from jet lag. Sunday was spent with his cousins celebrating the Bi-Centennial holiday. The United States was two hundred years old and he had arrived just in time for the massive party. It was a spectacular introduction to life in America.

"I can't believe you're considering me for something like this," Reid responded. "Is there an application process? What do I need to do?"

"Nothing for now because I've access to your academic file at the university. These people are very discreet. Once I put your name forward, all communications will be through me. An interview panel will be convened, and if you pass its review, you'll be assigned an employer and offered a position. All you have to do is pass your final exams and graduate in June."

"Where will I be working?"

"You could be posted anywhere in the world. The only requirement is that you do not discuss this with anyone, not even your family. The job will come with a very generous salary and benefit package, but it also comes with a high level of confidentiality. No one must know your employer's business. So, Peter, what's it going to be? Do you want me to put your name forward?"

"Absolutely!"

Maria Quintero had been economical with the truth about the hiring process. Reid had already been vetted and the decision had been made to offer him a position. His fingerprints had been taken off a glass he used in November at the party at the American Consulate. Immigration and Naturalization Service (INS) and U.S. Customs records from his earlier trips to Boston had been collated and analyzed. Maria was merely going through the motions to confirm Peter Reid was interested.

"I'll have more information in two weeks," she advised as she pushed away her barely touched cup of coffee. "I've taken enough of your time and I've got a freshman tutorial in twenty minutes."

10:30AM – Saturday February 11th 1978
Dublin, REPUBLIC OF IRELAND

As the Belfast train pulled slowly into Dublin's Connolly Station, Maria and Peter stood up to stretch their legs.

"You'll do fine," she coached. "You've got a super academic record and the folks at Wang Computer gave you a high recommendation. I know they're going to love you and I wouldn't say that if I didn't believe it. You're here because I chose you and that goes a long way with these people. Now relax."

Peter was scheduled for interview at 2:00PM in a suite at Jury's Hotel on St. Stephen's Green. Prior to catching the 8:00PM return train to Belfast, their agenda included an early dinner with an American, George Mulligan, who was on sabbatical at Trinity College. Apparently George was a close family friend of Maria's from New York City, having been in the same high school grade as her older brother.

4:55PM – Saturday February 11th 1978
Dublin, REPUBLIC OF IRELAND

I t was almost two hours into the interview and Reid could not believe how few questions had been asked about his electrical engineering background. It completely baffled him. John Smith prefaced the interview process by explaining how redundant such questions would be because they had access to college transcripts from Queen's University, as well as high school report cards from St. Patrick's College that included O-Level and A-Level grades. "They must have more than my academic records," he thought to himself, as he observed the thick files in front of the three man panel. "Mr. Smith, Mr. Brown, and Mr. Fox; are these even their real names?" During the two weeks since Maria Quintero had asked if he wanted to be considered as a candidate for this employment opportunity, Reid had found himself to be overthinking aspects of the process.

Most of their questions focused on his political views. Ironically, despite the fact he had grown up in the cauldron of Northern Ireland's contentious culture, Reid was ambivalent about politics. He was an engineer. Things either worked or they did not. A bridge either withstood a load or it collapsed. An engine either fired on all cylinders or it did not. Politics barely registered on his radar. Of course he was aware of it, but despite all the rhetoric, he never saw politicians going to prison for their cause. On the other hand, the court system was stretched to its limits with people who responded to their provocation. Unfortunately, hospitals and morgues also had to deal with the atrocious consequences of the festering evil that propagated and thrived in Northern Ireland's political climate.

Reid was unaware that political apathy was exactly what Smith,

Brown and Fox wanted to hear. They also questioned him at length to understand the extent of his knowledge of car maintenance because his school transcripts were lacking in such detail. His mechanical aptitude coupled with his scientific background and apparent disconnect with politics, was a perfect blend. The panel could not have been more pleased with Maria Quintero. She had presented them with a very worthy candidate.

5:10PM – Saturday February 11th 1978
Dublin, REPUBLIC OF IRELAND

When Reid finished his interview, he met Maria in the hotel lounge and learned their plans to catch the last train to Belfast had literally been derailed by several suspicious explosive devices which had been placed on the railway tracks earlier that afternoon. The line had been shut down, forcing Northern Ireland Rail Service to ferry passengers by bus between Newry and Belfast, while British Army bomb disposal engineers worked to neutralize the devices. Consequently, Maria opted to book two rooms at the hotel so she and Peter could relax and enjoy the evening with George Mulligan. On Sunday they would return to Belfast, once the bombs had either been defused or detonated in a controlled manner.

"I called Professor Mulligan and put back our dinner reservation until 7:00PM so we can get some overnight items. Let's get you a couple of nice shirts before the stores close. I've got an expense account for situations like this."

"… for situations like this?" Reid thought to himself.

12:45PM – Sunday February 12th 1978
Dublin, REPUBLIC OF IRELAND

The pair got to the train station early to make sure they would be able to get a seat, since train services had been disrupted the previous day.

"I get the feeling something's bothering you," Quintero probed, when they settled, "Aren't you pleased with your interview?"

"Yes, I'm pleased but it's not that. It's nothing to do with any of this."

"A problem shared is a problem halved."

"I wish it were that simple," he replied, "But it doesn't look like anyone's going to be able to solve this problem. My eight year old sister has been diagnosed with leukemia."

"Oh no! I'm so sorry, Peter."

"Last week my father went back for another eight week shift on an oil tanker for *BP*. That leaves me and my mother to look after her. Things aren't too bad at the moment, but the future isn't good. If I could trade places with her, I'd do it in a heart beat."

"I thought you had an older brother. Can't he help a little?"

"I do, but he just started a new job working for a bank in London. I just don't know what to do!"

7:50AM – Monday February 13th 1978
CIA Headquarters - Langley, Virginia, USA

S cott Hamilton was about to bite into an almond croissant when his secretary interrupted.

"Maria Quintero is on line One. She hasn't been able to contact George Mulligan and asked to speak with you."

The senior intelligence officer wiped away tiny pastry flakes from his fingers before lifting the receiver.

"What's up, Maria? Is there a problem?"

"I need your permission to close the deal with Reid. I think I've got what we need. His eight year old sister has been diagnosed with leukemia. Who do we know on the east coast who can help with this? Surely there's someone in Boston?"

"The Faber Institute is an option and we've also got good people in New York. Sounds like it's something you'll need to act on immediately. Give Mulligan all the details so he can get a copy of her medical files. Reid doesn't need to know anything until we have a diagnosis and an opinion."

1:10PM – Wednesday February 15th 1978
Belfast, NORTHERN IRELAND

Maria Quintero knew Peter Reid was very concerned about his sister's illness. Two days had passed since she had spoken with Scott Hamilton so she was relieved to hear her boss' voice when she answered the phone.

"If they're going to do anything for the sister, they'll need to see the girl immediately. They're pretty confident but don't want you to commit to odds of anything better than 70%. They did say that if she stays in Belfast, prayers are her only hope."

"I'll get back to you once I've talked to him. My guess is he'll sign up."

"You've done a good job, Maria. Dublin is very impressed, especially Mulligan," Hamilton acknowledged and promptly ended the call.

3:05PM – Thursday February 16th 1978
Belfast, NORTHERN IRELAND

When he arrived for his meeting with Maria Quintero, Reid was surprised to also see Professor Mulligan.

"Come on in, Peter," invited the older man. "Good to see you again." He sat down as George Mulligan cleared his throat to begin a speech he had made on many occasions during his career. "Maria and I have been authorized to extend an invitation to you. There is, however, a stipulation. We need you to sign a confidentiality agreement before the offer is presented. Regardless of whether you accept or decline, you cannot discuss details of this conversation with anyone."

"This sounds serious," Reid quipped nervously, as an affidavit was placed in front of him to read and sign. "Is there a copy for me to keep?" he questioned then signed and returned the document. He realized immediately he had asked a foolish question which was confirmed by the expression on Mulligan's face.

Maria continued, "Should you decide not to accept our offer the matter will be closed for ever, unless you discuss this conversation outside this office. Please don't bring a problem like that upon yourself." The young man sat up straighter and readied himself for what Mulligan was about to say.

Details of the job offer were meticulously explained to the young engineer.

"We are giving you the opportunity to join a very select group of professionals. You will never be assigned a task unless you are properly trained and furnished with the equipment, and back-up, to ensure its success. In return for furthering the goals of the United States of America, you will be compensated very well."

"This is a lot to take in," Reid acknowledged, "I'm flattered."
Mulligan retrieved another document from his briefcase and slid it across
the table.

"This is an employment contract for one of our subsidiaries,
National Semiconductor. Paragraph 6 identifies a signing bonus of five
thousand pounds, which I have here, in cash," he continued, as he placed
a bulky envelope on the table.

"Everyone likes to make fun of government bureaucracy," Maria
mocked and opened the envelope to reveal its bulky contents. "But our
mandate permits us to operate without having to comply with tedious
administrative details."

Reid picked up the pen, which Mulligan had placed before him,
and signed the employment contract.

"You guys don't mess around and I can't imagine anyone match-
ing this salary." The young man was a quick learner and knew better than
to ask for a copy of the contract for his records.

"Welcome aboard, Peter," Maria responded with a huge smile.

"You're always going to know this was the day your life changed
for ever. George has something else to tell you."

"Indeed. We've been observing you since last July when you
worked at Wang computers. We also know about your family. Your
sister's prognosis is not good unless we get her to the *Faber Center* in
Boston. We've already had cancer specialists review her medical records
and they're confident her chances of beating the leukemia are 70%, provided they can treat her immediately. If she remains here in Belfast ..."
Mulligan stopped short. There was no need for him to finish the sentence.
Reid was stunned.

"Her doctors never mentioned this option," he finally muttered.

"That's because they know nothing about it. Our people recovered copies of Catherine's records without her doctors' knowledge. We are goal orientated. If we can help your sister, we know you'll be more focused on completing your assignments."

"When you signed the contract," Maria interjected, "I was relieved because I know what it means for your sister. We're going to do whatever we can for her. Tomorrow you need to get photographs of her and your Mom because George has made arrangements with our friends in Dublin to get them passports. They're scheduled to fly out on Tuesday morning. Time is Catherine's biggest enemy. We need to get her to Boston ASAP."

Reid's head flipped back and forth as the two Americans tag-teamed him with instructions and information.

"Maria will be your primary point of contact," George continued. "We need you to focus on graduating in June. Remember, no one must know about this. Your salary will be deposited directly into your bank account, starting next Friday. An apartment has been leased in Brookline, three blocks from the hospital. Fighting cancer requires everyone to focus 100% on the battle. Your family and friends need to be told a convincing story. Tell them Catherine has volunteered to participate in a treatment trial requiring complete isolation for her and her mom. Say she'll be getting blood transfusions from her mother and neither can risk getting an infection or virus. That should explain their absence from your neighborhood."

"How long will they need to stay in Boston?" Reid asked, partly in disbelief that he was having such a conversation.

"At least three months," Mulligan continued. "Catherine's reaction to the treatment will dictate what happens next. With luck, she'll regain strength, return home and put this all behind her."

"This will take a lot of explaining to my mother and Catherine."

"No it won't," Maria interrupted. "They're going to get a phone call in ten minutes from Belfast City Hospital explaining Catherine's case has been selected for an experimental treatment program, and the expenses will be covered by an American benefactor who wishes to remain anonymous. They won't know you're involved. It's better that way. All you need to do is make sure they get their photographs taken tomorrow morning, and complete their passport applications. Tell them time is of the essence and you're going to deliver the applications to the passport office yourself, but bring them here to me instead. The passports will be ready anytime after 3:00PM on Monday, in Dublin, but they'll have to pick them up in person. You'll need to drive your mom and sister there on Monday, and stay overnight. Then they'll fly to Boston on Tuesday morning. They'll be met at Logan Airport and brought to the apartment in Brookline. Catherine has an 8:30AM appointment on Wednesday. All the details are in this envelope. Let me know immediately if there are any problems."

*****

One hour later, Peter's mother relayed to him the wonderful news she had just received from the City Hospital. Apparently a pioneering team of doctors in Boston wanted to treat his sister. She would need his help getting their passport applications couriered to Dublin because everything was in place for them to fly out on Tuesday morning.

"The doctors want to see Catherine ASAP," she explained to her son, who gave a very convincing performance as someone taken completely by surprise.

4:10PM – Friday March 17th 1978
Belfast, NORTHERN IRELAND

R eid hung up the phone and sighed with relief. One month into Catherine's treatment and his mother was ecstatic about the results, as were the doctors. His sister was getting healthy and so was his bank account. In two months he would sit his final examinations and say goodbye to university life.

His feet hardly touched the stairs as he ran up to the bathroom to get ready for the evening. Maria Quintero had been invited to a small 'St. Patrick's Day' party at the home of the American Consul General, Andrew Johnson, and she had invited Peter to be her "+1." In the shower he found himself wondering what she and Mulligan planned for him after he had graduated. Later that evening, he found out!

*****

Reid enjoyed the party, except for the corned beef and cabbage the caterers had been instructed to serve.

"Thanks for driving this evening. I love your country, except driving in it," Maria teased. "Everyone drives so fast. The cars are tiny, they're all standard shift, and everything is on the opposite side."

"It's no problem especially after the news I got from Boston this afternoon."

"Your mom must be thrilled with Catherine's prognosis. By the way, George called me earlier. He's been putting together some things for after your graduation. He has arranged for you to work in *National Semiconductor*'s HQ in Waltham, Massachusetts. The majority of their work involves defense contracts for the US Navy. You won't start until August 1st, but we want you to fly to Boston after you graduate. If Catherine continues to make this sort of progress, all three of you will be able to spend July together. After that, they'll return home and you can remain at the Brookline apartment."

"Thank you. How will I ever repay you?" Maria simply smiled but he saw something in her expression that told him she already knew the answer to his question.

4:20PM – Sunday July 9th 1978
Logan Airport – Boston, Massachusetts, USA

Peter Reid pushed his luggage cart out into Boston's intense summer heat and humidity. Most new graduates would have looked for a bus but since February, when he signed his employment contact with the CIA, his finances had been better than he could ever have imagined.

The taxi dropped him outside the Walnut Street apartment in Brookline. He planned to meet his mother and accompany her to the hospital to see Catherine. The girls, however, had another plan. Due to her progress and improvement, his sister was in treatment as an out-patient but they managed to keep the news a surprise for him. He could not remember the last time he had seen either of them looking so healthy and happy. When his father also joined the familial festivities, Peter was truly caught off-guard.

"Your Dad was able to reschedule his leave so we could all be together for a few weeks," his mother explained. Before he could say anything, Catherine chimed in with her own exciting news. The doctors had cleared her to return home to Belfast.

7:05AM – Monday July 10th 1978
CIA Headquarters - Langley, Virginia, USA

Scott Hamilton remained seated at his desk as Maria Quintero entered his office. It was an ordinary space but photographs, diplomas, and letters of commendation on the walls indicated Scott Hamilton was not an ordinary man.

"How was your 4th, Maria?" Social etiquette inspired the question rather than genuine interest.

"Good, thanks. How was yours?"

"Busy. We've got all sorts of crap going on in South America. Practically every country down there has issues. The FARC guerrillas in Colombia are giving us cause for concern and Central America is a shit storm too. The President believes cocaine trafficking is funding a lot of these revolutionary groups."

"I don't envy those DEA guys over at 1405. It sure sounded great in '73 when Nixon set up the Agency, but it was like giving a plumber a mop and bucket and telling him to go fix the leaking pipes."

"Well, Maria, they keep giving them bigger mops and bigger buckets, but you and I know the problem needs to be solved at its source. That's where you two come in."

"What do you mean by, 'you two'?"

"You and your boy, Peter Reid."

"Jesus, Scott. He hasn't had any training, and he's an electrical engineering graduate from Belfast. Let's be realistic. Do you have any idea how hard it was to recruit a candidate like him?"

"I've read his file and he's just what we need. He speaks a little Spanish, and everyone loves the Irish. He'll fit in no matter where we send him. Besides, it's time we started to get a return on our investment."

"I know more than anyone he has potential, but I'd hate to see everything get screwed up because we threw him in over his head."

"Don't worry about it. We'll start him off slow. I'll not let anything bad happen to him," Hamilton insisted. "I'm pulling you out of Belfast so you can oversee his training. He's got some serious medical bills to pay off!"

11:05AM – Wednesday July 12th 1978
Boston, Massachusetts, USA

T he Irish family walked around the observation deck of the Prudential Building and marveled at the magnificent, panoramic vista of
Boston. When their children were growing up in Belfast, the Reid parents
made sure to vacation in Dublin every year in order to avoid the Loyalist
parades and violence, synonymous with the July 12th holiday. Although
the Reids were Roman Catholic, their home was situated in Dundonald,
in East Belfast. It was a middle class suburb where the residents were
predominantly Protestant, and pro-British.

The sectarian conflict that overshadows Northern Ireland fol-
lows a cyclical pattern. The summer months are known as the *Marching Season*, because the Orange Order and other Loyalist organizations
pledging allegiance to Britain, hold parades to commemorate battles and
events, which date back to the 1600s.

The main event takes place on July 12th or, *The Twelfth*, as it is
known colloquially, when Orangemen and their marching bands parade
through streets and towns. During the previous weeks and months,
material such as wooden pallets and old furniture, is collected to build
bonfires on abandoned open lots throughout the Province. Prior to July
12th, the rubbish heaps are protected from Catholic youths, who, given
the opportunity, would ignite them prematurely. Despite warnings from
the fire department, the bonfires are often built to a height in excess of
thirty feet. Traditionally they are lit at dusk on July 11th, or *Eleventh
Night*, but not before effigies of the Pope are placed on top. Drinking,
partying and the singing of sectarian songs continue into the early hours
of the morning often causing Orangemen, and some band members, to

miss the parades the following day.

For Catholics living in Northern Ireland this is always a tense time since these activities celebrate the Loyalist, Protestant heritage. In 1534, King Henry VIII proclaimed himself Head of the Church of England and severed all ties with the Vatican. Five hundred years later, Northern Ireland's politics and culture continue to be impacted by these historical events. Peter Reid's parents had little time for such matters. They had wonderful Protestant neighbors and neither politics nor religion was ever discussed. Nevertheless, they always rented a cottage for the month of July in the coastal town of Rush, located fifteen miles north of Dublin. When Peter was a young boy, and before he understood the significance of *The Twelfth* celebrations, he thought it was simply bad luck his family missed them when they vacationed in the Republic of Ireland. Back then he had no idea why his uncles and aunts were amused by his desire to be an Orangeman. By the time the modern conflict erupted in 1969, he no longer had this unrealistic desire.

Just like in previous years, Peter and his parents were happy to be out of Northern Ireland during *The Twelfth* activities. He glanced at his little sister clutching her father's hand and marveled how much their lives had improved in recent months.

Friday July 14th 1978
Boston, Massachusetts, USA

R eid had run one mile and his breathing had settled down as his body adjusted to the pace. He liked to run five miles at least two or three times a week. Since arriving in Boston, however, he managed to run every morning, rising early to avoid the muggy heat that smothered New Englanders in the summer.

At first, he dismissed the feeling and resisted the urge to look behind. By the time he realized he was being followed, Maria Quintero was already running by his side.

"Come on, let's pick up the pace," she teased. His facial expression failed to conceal his shock.

"When did you get into town?"

"Yesterday, but I've been in D.C. for the past week." He rarely maintained an eight minute pace, so when they completed five miles in thirty-six minutes he was wheezing and gasping. They stopped a block from his apartment to rest and catch their breath.

"We've got to get you out here more often; not only to get you fitter, but also to get some color on those legs!" Reid smiled, nodding in tacit agreement. "I'm taking some heat from my boss. We need to get you ready for your first assignment. Your family is returning to Belfast next Friday and you'll start at *National Semiconductor* the following Monday. Enjoy this time with them because you'll soon be on a heavy schedule."

"Can you tell me anything about what you want me to do?" the young Irishman inquired with trepidation. He was excited but also fearful about her response.

"We need you to join the Irish National Republican Army."

"The INRA? Are you fucking crazy? You say it like you want me join the local library. Those guys are ruthless. They split from the Provisional IRA because they felt Sinn Féin and everyone else was holding them back."

"We don't mess around either, Peter. I'm letting you know what's ahead of you because I need you to focus on your training. For the next three months, every minute not working for *National Semi'* will be spent preparing for this assignment. And I mean every minute. When your family leaves next week, I'll be moving into the apartment above yours."

"This is insane!" he protested, pacing back and forth. "It's absolutely insane. I'm not doing that, no fucking way."

"Stop it. Everything will be fine. When you go back to your apartment, look at your sister and ask yourself if we know what we're doing. We're not going to let anything happen to you. We only care about success. I know it sounds corny, but failure is not an option. You'll be very well trained with a support network that's second to none."

"I'm sorry, Maria. This morning when I left the house I thought I was going for a gentle jog around the neighborhood. Instead, you run my ass off and then drop this shit on me."

"Well, there's one more thing I've got to tell you. There was an incident at your home in Belfast last night. Two incendiary bombs were thrown at it."

"Jesus! Thank God we were all here, but how do you know about it?"

"Because we did it."

"What the fuck! This just gets crazier and crazier!"

"Relax. We knew no one was there. Your neighbors called the

fire department. We just wanted to send a message. We had one device fall short and the second one only did superficial damage. Your story needs credibility and your family's cloistered, middle class life in East Belfast, doesn't fit the demographic for INRA recruitment."

"Listen Maria, please don't get me wrong. I couldn't be more grateful for everything you've done for Catherine, but things are happening much faster than I expected."

"I could've bull-shitted you and let you believe Protestant para-militaries did it. Nothing happened money can't fix and you know we're not stingy when it comes to that. In a few weeks, your family will be in a nice house in West Belfast with less chance of neighbors questioning how Catherine made her miraculous recovery. You'll also have a cred-ible reason for relocating." Reid conceded by silently shaking his head. "Your father is a smart guy and we'll make sure the insurance company takes real good care of his claim. We'll also have a real estate broker find him an incredible deal. Your folks need to enjoy their last week in Boston, so put a smile on that face of yours. Relax. It's all going to be fine."

5:20PM – Friday July 21st 1978
Logan Airport - Boston, Massachusetts, USA

Not being allowed to tell his father about the firebombing of their home weighed heavily on Peter's mind, but in his heart he knew it was for the best. He thought back to the interview with Messrs. Smith, Brown and Fox when he signed the papers for George Mulligan and accepted the employment offer with the CIA. When Catherine's treatment was arranged in Boston, he knew he had made the right decision regardless of his uneasiness about his nebulous new employer.

"I'm not sure how long I'll be here, Dad. *National Semiconductor* has a facility in Limerick and it also has some contracts with clients in Northern Ireland. There's a good chance I'll be back home before Christmas."

"Well, you look after yourself, son. I've another six weeks leave before I head back to work. No doubt your mother has a few jobs around the house for me to do."

He avoided further eye contact with his father by turning to hug his mother and sister. "You'll all have plenty to do," he thought to himself as his family disappeared down the ramp towards an Aer Lingus 747 jet.

5:10AM – Saturday July 22nd 1978
Boston, Massachusetts, USA

Perhaps it was due to the noise from the window fan, but Reid did not hear the intruder enter his bedroom. He was in a deep sleep, dreaming he was playing for Manchester United with his compatriot, George Best. He attributed the initial poke in his back to a hard tackle, but the second one woke him immediately. Instinctively, he turned and sat up in one motion.

"It's not just your legs that need color," Maria Quintero mocked.

"How the hell did you get in?"

"I used my key. This is an Agency apartment, you know!" He awkwardly reached down and tried to pull up the bed sheet.

"Come on, we've got a lot to do today. I'll wait for you outside. We're running ten miles this morning. Vacation is over!" she announced with a friendly facial expression that was somewhere between a sneer and a smile.

Peter shook his head and wished he was still dreaming. As he dressed, he glanced out the bedroom window. Maria was pushing against a utility pole, diligently stretching her hamstrings. "What the fuck did I sign myself up for?" he sighed.

8:25AM – Monday July 24th 1978
Waltham, Massachusetts, USA

❝Tonight after work, we need to go car shopping. I'm not going to drive you to work every day," Maria chided as she stopped outside the main door of *National Semiconductor*. "I'll pick you up at five."

"Are you going to cook something nice for dinner, Honey?" Reid joked.

"Don't push your luck, smart-ass."

The first day went by in a flash. Most of his time was spent completing forms for everything from health insurance to affidavits regarding non-disclosure of intellectual property. Reid was legally allowed to work in the United States because he had been issued a prestigious H-1 Visa, but there were also documents requiring additional FBI background checks since some of the company's work involved defense contracts.

Later that afternoon, he learned about his designated project. *National Semiconductor* had a contract with a robotics company that developed equipment for production line automation. He had been assigned to a team of engineers who would be calibrating the electronic controls for a car manufacturer.

After work Maria gave him a thousand dollars in cash for the deposit on a new *Ford Mustang* and they arranged to pick it up the following day.

"Normally the company would provide transportation," she explained as they drove back to Brookline. "But if someone decides to do a background check, you need to have a credit history. You'll get reimbursed for the car payments, registration and insurance."

"Understood, but the job seems to have nothing to do with joining the INRA."

"It might look that way now but these things can't be rushed. It would be better if the INRA came looking for you. With the training you're getting at *National Semi'*, plus the material I'll be getting for you from Langley, no one will be more qualified on the use of remote detonators. We'll also get you set up with contacts for sourcing materials. For the next three months, we're going to focus on training and getting your face known around specific Irish bars and clubs. Our goal is to send you back to Belfast next year when, hopefully, the INRA will recruit you. Your cover will be the contract *National Semi'* has with *DeLorean Motor Company* or *DMC*. John DeLorean plans to build his new sports car in Belfast. Construction on the factory is scheduled to start in October. You'll be going over next year to work on controls for the assembly line equipment."

"You people have it all worked out."

"We don't like surprises. That's why we put so much time and effort into planning our operations. By the time you're in the field, everything will be second nature to you. You won't be acting or pretending to be anyone. You'll actually be that person. We're going to mold you into the man you need to be."

As Maria merged onto I93 North to head back into Boston, she turned up the volume on the *KISS 108* radio station so she could duet with Donna Summer.

"Last Dance …. Last Dance …."

"Don't give up your day job," Reid cringed.

"Hey, I'm only trying to educate you about this great city. You're not just listening to Donna Summer, you're listening to 'Dorchester's own' Donna Summer. There's probably no better time than the present to broaden your education. I think we'll get off 93 and cut through

Dorchester. Last Dance! Last Dance!"

Ten minutes later Maria parked outside *The Patriot* on Dorchester Avenue.

"For putting up with my singing, I'm going to buy you a pint of *Guinness*."

"Now that's music to my ears. Disco is wasted on the likes of me. We Irish boys have no rhythm."

"Keep your eyes and ears open when we go in here. Dorchester has a large Irish community and *The Patriot* is appropriately named. I'm taking you in here for a reason."

"Here I am, thinking you wanted to be nice and buy me a pint, but instead, we're back on the clock."

"We're always on the clock, Peter. That'll never change, but there's no reason we can't enjoy ourselves at the same time."

The Patriot's ambiance was dark, verging on grim, but that did not seem to bother its patrons who were watching Carl Yastrzemski take a count of 2 and 0 from the home plate umpire. Reid grabbed a stool beside an elderly gentleman wearing a Boston Edison hat, who clutched his pint of *Guinness* as if it were a utility pole he used to climb.

"Three pints of *Guinness*," Reid ordered in response to the barman tossing two coasters on the bar.

"Who are you expecting?" Maria whispered in his ear.

"You said I needed to start blending into the Irish community," he responded surreptitiously. "I think I've found a new best friend and fellow electrical engineer."

As the barman placed the drinks in front of his newest customers, Yaz finished his run around the bases. A dejected Orioles pitcher watched as his manager walked in the direction of the mound. Peter paid for the beers and slid one over to the retired lineman.

"There you go boss. Thanks for keeping the lights on." The old man raised his glass.

"Up the IRA."

"Up the IRA," Reid echoed with a smile.

Two hours later, Maria and he knew everything about the life of a lineman in Boston, especially the part about how lucky Patrick Collins was to have retired before the Blizzard of '78.

"We've got to go," Peter announced and patted him affectionately on his back.

"Put something in there before you go," the old man instructed, as he motioned towards a collection box on the bar. Reid made sure both the 'old timer' and the bartender saw him place two, ten dollar bills into the tin can labeled, "SUPPORT THE FAMILIES OF IRISH REPUBLICAN PRISONERS."

"I never tasted *Guinness* before," Maria confessed, as she started the car. "Now I know why you Irish never had an empire. Your beer is too good."

"We're trying to level the playing field with an aggressive export campaign," Peter joked.

"I wish it were that easy, otherwise I'd recommend we start shipping it to Tehran. The natives there have gone crazy and they're wise to your plan. Alcohol is banned."

"Everywhere is a mess. Belfast, Tehran, South America. ..."

"I'll probably be going back to Langley for a few days at the end of the week."

"What's up?"

"I've got to help review intelligence from Iran. I spent two years there in '74 and '75. I taught science at a private school for the children of ex-pats."

"I'm sure you did more than teach science."

"You're right. Iran is a beautiful country. It's a shame what's happening over there." As he unlocked the apartment's door, Maria announced she had another surprise for him.

"It's for the reading material you'll be getting," she explained, as she turned the dial on the door of a safe.

"How the hell did they get this up the stairs?"

"It wasn't easy. They've set the combination to match the digits on your phone number in Belfast. When you're not reading the material they send you from Langley, it's to be locked in here. I've arranged for a crew to build a closet around it. We don't need casual visitors eyeballing this monster."

5:35PM – Saturday July 29th 1978
Boston, Massachusetts, USA

R eid finished the call with his father and hung up the phone. As Maria had promised, the fire damage to their home had been relatively minor, but his mother no longer felt safe living in Dundonald. They had engaged an estate agent to look for properties in West Belfast, while they stayed in a hotel off the Ormeau Road. He was relieved it had happened while his father was on shore leave. Compensation claims for the property damage had to be filed with both their insurance company and the Northern Ireland Office (NIO) which was the British Government department responsible for all matters concerning Northern Ireland. Consequently, one of its duties was to evaluate and, subsequently, compensate property owners for losses related to the sectarian conflict.

It had been a hectic week for Reid and he struggled to keep up with the demands of his new job. When he returned from work each evening he discovered his safe had been stocked with new reading material which he was expected to study, in addition to his regular work assignments at *National Semiconductor*. He tried to keep in touch with his family in Belfast, but this proved difficult because of the time difference as well as his heavy workload. Maria stayed in contact from Langley where she was reviewing intelligence reports from Iran. Since February, when the Shah had been overthrown, matters appeared to have gone from bad to worse. American interests in the region were being seriously undermined and news from the embassy got worse as each day passed.

He cranked closed the handle of the safe and spun the combination dial. Initially, he thought the safe was merely a cautious overreaction to paranoia, but that was before he read the material from Maria. There was documentation about bomb making as well as information about members of the INRA. There were also notes on other paramilitary groups in Northern Ireland, both Republican and Loyalist, along with their affiliations in the United States and Canada. There were pages and pages of organizational trees, photographs, and intelligence reports. He marveled at the minuscule and mundane detail which included: favorite beer; favorite soccer team; girl and boy friends including those of men who were married.

The only aspect of his training which he could not fathom was the Spanish conversation class he was ordered to take at Boston University. It had been five years since he had studied the language but unbeknownst to him, his basic knowledge of Spanish was one of the reasons he had been targeted by Maria Quintero and George Mulligan.

Since he had recently put so much effort into both his job and training, Peter decided to reward himself with what he considered to be a well deserved night on the town. He returned to *The Patriot* for a few beers with the intention of ending the evening at a nightclub. That was the plan but eight pints of *Guinness* later he had, in fact, spent the entire evening subjected to casual interrogation by Paddy Lynch. Lynch had owned the bar for several years and always made a point of getting to know his customers, especially those with a Belfast accent.

"What're you doin' tomorrow evening?" he asked as the young man slid off a bar stool and emptied the last inch of beer from his glass.

"I don't have anything planned."

"I've got an extra ticket for a benefit tomorrow evening, if you're interested."

"Why not. I've got to eat dinner at some stage."

Lynch reached up to a shelf above the cash register and retrieved an envelope. "It's at Concannon's in Norwood at 7:00PM. The directions are in here with the ticket."

"How much do I owe you?" Reid asked.

"Don't worry about it, Peter. You can buy me a drink tomorrow night."

The function was a benefit to raise money for NORAID, a charity that, amongst other things, provided financial assistance for families of Irish Republican prisoners. The term "amongst other things," was code for the tacit support of anti-British paramilitary groups in Northern Ireland.

Reid staggered out of the bar, pleased with the progress he had made to establish himself in the Irish community. He wisely decided against driving his new Mustang, opting instead to flag down a passing cab. Twenty minutes later he was stretched out on his bed, fast asleep.

7:10PM – Sunday July 30th 1978
Norwood, Massachusetts, USA

As Peter walked from his car towards the function hall, the pounding beat of rousing Irish rebel songs confirmed he was at the right location. Paddy Lynch spotted him and waved as soon as he walked inside.

"You made it," Lynch acknowledged as Reid approached a table with an elevated ornate sign that read, *"The Patriot – Dorchester, MA."* Lynch stood up and gestured for him to sit in the last empty seat. The younger Irishman concentrated as names of the other guests were fired at him.

"So now you know everyone, Peter. You're in good company." Lynch had brought his wife, Geraldine. Other guests at the table were all couples in their forties, with one exception. She had been introduced as Lynch's niece, Nuala Mallon. It was instantly clear why he had been given the last ticket and that Paddy had manipulated seating arrangements so the two youngest guests could sit beside one another.

"I grew up in the Short Strand," Nuala replied, when he immediately acknowledged her Belfast accent. "My Uncle Paddy helped get me a visa and fixed me up with a job at *The Patriot.*"

"I've only been in your uncle's bar once or twice, but I've never seen you. I would've remembered," he remarked with a grin.

"I was home in Belfast for two weeks," the attractive red head added. "I only got back yesterday."

Still feeling the effects of Saturday night's *Guinness*, Reid made a point of sticking to ginger ale for the evening.

"I've got an early start tomorrow morning," he responded to Lynch's insistence he take a shot of whiskey. "It's okay for you. You're the boss, and Nuala doesn't have to open the bar until 10:00 tomorrow morning." His real fear was the knowledge Maria Quintero was due back from Virginia later that night which meant his Monday would begin at 5:00AM with a five-mile run.

When the entertainment was interrupted to hold a collection for *The Cause*, he made sure he was seen making a generous contribution to the NORAID charity. Lynch was suitably impressed and privately praised himself for having the ingenuity to invite the young Irishman. He had no idea Reid would be reimbursed, once Maria Quintero received his expense report.

Chapter 5

BOSTON - 1978

OFF TO THE RACES

2:55PM - Saturday August 5th 1978
St.Theresa's Church, East Boston, Massachusetts, USA

F r. Michael Foley could not believe his bad luck. When he realized
what the parish secretary had done, it was too late. A month had
passed and wedding invitations had already been sent. Originally, the
young couple had arranged their wedding for 11:00AM. The priest
recalled that the proposed time of the wedding service was practically
the only thing they had agreed upon. He was out of the office when
the bride-to-be rescheduled the ceremony for 3:00PM. The secretary,
unfortunately, did not appreciate the consequences of accommodating
the request. Instead, she checked the calendar, confirmed there was no
conflict, and made the change. She was completely unaware of Fr. Foley's
plans to go to Suffolk Downs for his annual pilgrimage to the historic
MassCap horse race at 3:00PM. No one in the congregation knew about
his interest in the Sport of Kings. No one, that is, except for Paul Jennings who had given him a hot tip.

"Big John Taylor, Big John Taylor," Foley repeated in a lame
effort to mimic the congenial Irishman's accent. The frustrated cleric
adjusted the tuner slightly on the transistor radio and set it back on the
window sill of the vestry bathroom. Never was he more tolerant of a bride
being late. The race would take two minutes, so by 3:02 he would know
if Paul's flawless record was still intact. The wedding had cost him the
opportunity to place a bet, but he was still intrigued about the outcome
of the race.

The limousine arrived at the church as Big John Taylor glided
across the finish line to claim his place in history alongside legends such
as the great Seabiscuit. As he hastily turned off the radio and exited the

bathroom, he envisioned Jennings pumping his fist in the air with a huge grin on his face.

Fr. Foley caught a glimpse of the groom's expression just as the bride crossed the threshold. "Jennings is probably looking as happy as that guy," he thought to himself.

11:40PM - Sunday August 6th 1978
East Boston, Massachusetts, USA

Parishioners squinted as they exited St. Theresa's Church after eleven o'clock Mass. Fr. Foley shook as many hands as he could and acknowledged others with a friendly smile. As usual, the last to leave were the altar boys who had to put away the cruets, extinguish the altar candles and change out of their surplices.

"What do you two have planned for this fine day?" the parish priest asked the Pasquale brothers, as they were leaving the sacristy.

"We're going to the Red Sox game this afternoon, Father."

"Great! Well, have fun, and bring your gloves in case Yaz hits a home run towards you!"

After they left, Foley was about to take off his vestments when he thought he heard a noise. To satisfy his curiosity, he went back into the sanctuary to see if someone was there.

"Hi Father," Jennings greeted.

"Paul. What are you doing here? Is everything okay?"

"Things couldn't be better. That's why I'm here," the young man continued. "I felt bad for you yesterday that you couldn't get to watch the race."

"I got to hear it on the radio. Your tip was right on. 'Big John Taylor' came through for you. Good job, Paul."

"I know if you'd been there, you'd have placed a little wager on the horse, so I did it for you," he explained and passed an envelope to the cleric. Fr. Foley was a little confused, but took it, not really knowing if it was appropriate to look inside. "I'm sure you'll put the money to good use."

"I can't accept this," the priest protested when he realized what was going on.

"And neither can I," Jennings responded, stepping back to avoid touching the envelope which the cleric was trying to return. "When I placed that bet, it was on your behalf and after that, everything was in God's hands. That money belongs to you Father."

"How much did you win?"

"Don't you mean, how much did you win? You won a little over four thousand dollars!"

"Good Lord, Paul, this is amazing. We've started a building fund for a new community center. This will certainly help!"

"Keep something for yourself. I can't be making all your bets for you," Jennings joked.

As the young man turned to leave, Fr. Foley raised his arm and blessed him.

"You're a good man, Paul Jennings. I don't know how you manage to pick these winners, but whatever you're doing, please keep it up. Every one of your tips has paid out. It's incredible!"

"Don't forget, Father. Not a word to anyone. Nobody needs to know our business. I don't want to read any announcements in the parish bulletin. If you're happy with this arrangement, we'll get more donations for your building fund."

"You have my word, Paul."

The heavy main door of the church closed gently behind the young Irishman leaving an elated Foley to marvel at his good fortune. For months the building fund had been underwriting losses from his gambling habit. Weekly cash donations by Eduardo Santos had been too much temptation. The timely windfall from Jennings would cancel out some, but not all, of his debt. His problem was not so much with the horses, but with the dogs. During winter months, when the horse track closed down, Foley would go to the greyhound track in Raynham, Massachusetts. The Wonderland track was closer, but he preferred Raynham since he was less likely to meet a parishioner.

The priest slipped the envelope into his pocket, knelt at the altar rail and made the sign of the cross.

"Thank you, Lord, for sending Paul to assist me with your work at St. Theresa's. I'm not proud about borrowing from the building fund, but if sending Paul is part of your plan, I offer you my most humble thanks."

6:40PM – Sunday September 3rd 1978
Scituate, Massachusetts, USA

Every Labor Day weekend, Paddy Lynch hosted a barbecue at his Scituate home. Reid had been invited because he had continued to frequent *The Patriot* bar, where he continued to foster a relationship with Lynch. He also attended Gaelic Athletic Association (GAA) games and other events where he thought either Lynch, or his patrons, would be present. He had even signed up to play GAA football for a team sponsored by *The Patriot*. The problem he had not anticipated, however, was Nuala Mallon's amorous interest in him. His desire to infiltrate *The Patriot* meant he could not avoid seeing her, but while he appreciated she could complicate his mission, he also knew she had, as Lynch's niece, the potential to enhance it. He had managed to contrive plausible reasons why he could not go on a date with her, but as the afternoon progressed and the inhibitions of the twenty-two year old were lowered by her alcohol consumption, Peter found himself, once again, the target of her affections.

"I think you're afraid of my Uncle Paddy," she whispered scornfully.

"Why would you say that?" he replied, checking to see if anyone was within ear-shot.

"It's why you won't ask me out."

"I'm not afraid of him," he replied indignantly, before realizing his bravado was getting him deeper into a conversation he had spent weeks avoiding.

"Prove it." There was a pause. "Ask me out," she challenged. "You're not gay, are you?

"Okay then, I'll ask you out. What night works for you?"

"I don't know. We can talk about it while you're driving me home. I'll tell my uncle I've got a ride."

Her long red hair brushed his shoulder as she turned and set off in the direction of Paddy Lynch. He smiled and consoled himself with the knowledge he was doing what Maria had asked him to do; infiltrate *The Patriot*.

Mallon shared an apartment with two other girls in the Boston suburb of Brighton. On the ride home, Reid learned that Paddy Lynch was not really her uncle, but had actually been a close friend of her father who was killed in *The Troubles* in Belfast, when she was sixteen.

"Paddy left Belfast and came to Boston soon after my father got shot. He always kept in touch and helped me get a visa when I left high school. It was tough on my mum, but she knew, more than anyone, that I'd be better off away from Northern Ireland."

While she gave the impression Lynch was a father figure, Nuala Mallon neglected to tell Reid her deepest secret. She did not share that her father's murdered body was found dumped on the edge of the road, three miles outside Belfast. He had been held and tortured, for three days and nights, by the INRA. More importantly, she failed to mention she knew it was Paddy Lynch who had led Brian Mallon's interrogation before finally executing his friend. She also did not think Reid needed to know she was, in fact, a paid informer for MI6 of the British Secret Service.

Nuala had been living in Boston for almost two years when she was approached by Clive Noakes. He introduced himself as an Assistant Trade and Industry Secretary assigned to the British Consulate General in Cambridge, Massachusetts. Despite the fact she had never met the man, he had known all about her. He had also known about Paddy Lynch. He knew about his fund raising activities with NORAID and that he had been Quartermaster of a Brigade of the INRA from 1970 until he left Northern Ireland in 1973. Noakes had wanted to recruit a mole within Paddy Lynch's operation, so he waited until he felt Nuala was well established in *The Patriot* before he made his move. He had been able to show her irrefutable proof, with the aid of photographs and audio tapes, that Paddy Lynch was behind the murder of her father. He could even have played a recording of the last minutes of Brian Mallon's life, but chose not to do so. There was no need. She had heard enough from earlier in the interrogation to identify her father's voice as well as that of his murderer. For more than a year, the young woman had been providing Noakes with information about everyone who came into contact with Paddy Lynch.

"Are you in a hurry, Peter?"

"No. Why do you ask?"

"I've to see someone near Kenmore Square. It won't take a second. If it's a problem, I can let it go."

"It's not. What's the address?"

"The *Cocoa Bean* on Lansdowne Street. I need to see a DJ there."

Nuala was true to her word. It took no more than two minutes for her to purchase fifty dollars worth of fine Bolivian cocaine from the DJ who supplemented his gig by moving product for his employer.

"Thanks. You're an angel." She smiled as she fixed her skirt and sat back in the passenger seat, subtly making sure her driver was distracted by her long slender legs.

Minutes later Reid stopped the car in front of her apartment. He had barely put the gear lever into the PARK position when Nuala reached over and landed an incredibly sensual kiss on his lips. Her tongue disappeared down his throat, wriggling and investigating everything it touched. As her mouth moved round to the side of his neck her long red hair enveloped and caressed his face.

"Come inside and show me how much you're not afraid of Paddy Lynch," she invited as she opened the passenger door and exited the vehicle.   "James Bond probably encounters this situation every day," Peter chuckled silently to himself. "I can't believe this is part of my job!"

She led the way to the door and then into her apartment. Without speaking, she guided him backwards in the direction of her bed where she pushed him down and immediately threw herself on top of his firm body.

*****

Having lost all track of time, Reid lay exhausted and stared at the ceiling, while Nuala panted and perspired beside him. She reached over and opened the drawer in her bed-side table and recovered one of the small folded paper packages the DJ had given her when she stopped at the *Cocoa Bean*.

"Is that all you've got Belfast Boy?" she teased, as she sat up and leaned against the headboard.

"I'm just being polite," Reid joked.

"This will help you." She sprinkled the fine cocaine powder onto a small vanity mirror and began to chop it with a razor blade.

"I don't want to be a party-pooper, but I'm not a big fan of recreational drugs."

"I understand. No one's going to force you, but 'a girl's gotta do what a girl's gotta do'," she smirked and turned her naked body towards him. He arched his neck with pleasure as she literally took matters into her own hands. She strategically sprinkled the white powder, evoking the desired and necessary effect to resume their sexual activity once again.

It was a little after midnight when he announced he would shower and get on his way.

"Are we going to get together again?" she asked nonchalantly.

"Sure. What nights do you have off?"

9:25AM – Friday October 27th 1978
New England Aquarium, Boston, Massachusetts, USA

Nuala was unaware a British agent had been following her. Clive Noakes usually scheduled their meetings for the morning so he could have her followed from the time she left her apartment until she arrived at their agreed meeting place. Only when he was certain she had not been followed, by anyone else, did he proceed as scheduled. Noakes also made sure he had not been followed. Mallon's intelligence reports made her one of MI6's most valuable confidential informants.

Although the United States and Great Britain were close political allies, Boston and its suburban hinterland had deep Irish roots with strong anti-British sentiment about the Northern Ireland conflict. Over the years the Boston media had given extensive coverage to *The Troubles* and the Republican prisoners in Long Kesh Prison. The transition from the 'Blanket Protest' to the 'Dirty Protest' put matters firmly in the public eye. Prior to 1976, prisoners in Northern Ireland whose convictions related to the sectarian conflict were classified as 'Political Prisoners.' Consequently, they were granted 'Special Category Status'. Privileges included the right to wear clothing of their own choice rather than prison uniforms. After the British government took away these rights, in 1976, many Republican prisoners refused to wear uniforms, choosing instead to wrap themselves in a blanket. Tensions increased in the prisons, including Long Kesh's notorious 'H-Block' wings where some Republican prisoners staged a 'Dirty Protest' by smearing excrement on the walls of their cells. The deterioration in their living conditions had a similar effect on working conditions for prison guards. It also meant news editors in the United States maintained an interest in the Northern

Ireland conflict.

"What's going on with Paddy's gang these days?" Noakes inquired, as he and Nuala watched a giant turtle glide effortlessly past two sea horses that appeared to be kissing.

"There's a new man on the scene. He and Paddy seem to be getting very friendly, and I think I know why. He's an electronics engineer."

"You're going to have to keep an eye on him."

"No need to worry, Mr. Noakes. I'm on top of it!" Nuala assured him with a grin.

She proceeded to provide the British agent with details about Reid's involvement with her 'uncle.' In return for her regular monthly report, she was discreetly given an envelope containing five hundred dollars. Noakes, of course, knew about her cocaine habit and how much it cost the British tax-payer to keep her focused on providing solid intelligence. From MI6's perspective, her habit was little more than a recreational indulgence. Considering the quality of her information, it was cheap at the price. The Service was so impressed it wanted more, so Noakes was instructed to give her a modified lipstick which contained a miniature camera.

"The camera in this lipstick can take twelve pictures," he demonstrated.

"I need photographs of Lynch and his crew, as well as their vehicles' license plates and any information you think would be of interest. The next time we meet I'll have some recording equipment for you so we can also listen to their meetings."

6:05AM – Saturday October 28th 1978
Boston, Massachusetts, USA

Peter and Maria had been running for four miles when she told him about her most recent phone conversation with Scott Hamilton.

"We've got to kick it up a notch and get you more involved with Lynch."

"I'm not sure how I can force the issue. I know he likes me, but that doesn't mean he's going to invite me into his inner circle."

"Let's head back to my apartment and I'll fill you in over breakfast. Opportunities are presenting themselves and we need to act sooner than we originally planned."

He sat attentively in Maria's kitchen and watched her toast bagels as they waited for coffee to brew.

"I need to tell you why you have to infiltrate the INRA for us. It's actually not our primary target. We want to use it as a stepping stone to Fuerzas Armadas Revolucionarias de Colombia a.k.a. FARC. It's a revolutionary Colombian guerrilla terrorist group."

"Jesus, Maria. This just gets fucking crazier and crazier."

"Relax, Peter, you're not doing this by yourself. There's a plan and a team. Remember, it's no ordinary team. We focus on winning. Anything short of that is not an option." He opted to lather cream cheese on his bagel and just listen while she talked. "Everything we've done has been calculated to ingratiate you with Lynch. Initially, we chose you because of your electrical engineering background. Fire bombing your family's home was a necessary evil, but one that has made your story more credible. We both know where your folks lived in East Belfast could hardly be described as a hotbed of Irish Republicanism. Lynch is becoming more comfortable about you every day and must be pretty damned excited at the thought of recruiting an electronics expert for *The Cause*. Arranging a job for you at *National Semi'* was specifically designed to elevate your stock in his eyes. You've access to technology and components that, until now, the INRA could only have dreamed about. Recruiting you will catapult its bomb making expertise to a new level."

Peter would have found Maria's scheme to be both fascinating and stimulating but for the fact it was his life she was putting in danger. Although her people had shown themselves to be very capable, he reminded himself they could not predict the future.

"We're going to force his hand a little," she continued.

"I'm afraid to ask. What does that mean?"

"Construction just started on the DeLorean factory in Belfast. You're going to inform Lynch that *National Semiconductor* has been awarded a contract with DeLorean Motors which means you'll be spending time in Belfast, on a regular basis. This news is going to force him to make a play to see if you're ready to step up and join the INRA. You'll have access to an infinite range of electronic components and you'll have a legitimate cover to justify your travel itinerary and involvement with such items. Our goal is to make you the INRA's number one electronics expert with respect to both bomb detonation and radio communications. Once that's established, we expect you'll get onto FARC's radar because they'll also want you to teach them everything you know."

"So you want me to infiltrate the INRA, ...who could kill me, and penetrate the FARC Colombians, ...who could kill me. Are you fucking kidding me? Nobody said anything last February about me getting fucking murdered. We're talking about my fucking life here!"

"What do you want me to say, Peter? There's no risk? I'm not going to sit here and tell you lies. You deserve the truth." He slumped over the table and pushed the palms of his hands against his temples. He took a deep breath then exhaled a long dejected sigh. Maria gave him a few minutes and then continued.

"We'll be investing millions of dollars in this mission and we'll do everything humanly possible to make it succeed. We have extensive political and economic interests in South America and the FARC guerrilla movement in Colombia is a serious threat to them. We don't have much reliable intelligence so we see this as our best opportunity to get someone deep inside their organization."

"And that 'someone' would be me." Reid sounded resigned to the idea. "I really appreciate everything you've done for me and my family and I'm a man of my word. It's not going to be easy but your team was there for my family, so now I'm here for you."

"Right answer," Quintero acknowledged with a smile, as she reached over and took the last piece of his bagel and placed it in her mouth. She was suddenly staring straight at him. Perhaps it was tension from what he had just heard. Perhaps it was because he was so close to her perfect face but, in that instant, he was conscious of her warm breath against his cheek, and oblivious to everything except the look in her eyes. Maria was also caught off guard by the moment and maintained his gaze, motionless. They stared at each other for several seconds until she walked around the table and inserted herself between his legs. Slowly, she unbuttoned her blouse and leaned forward to gently caress the back of his head as she drew it towards her breasts. Peter moved forward in the chair as his right hand glided up her spine to the back of her bra strap. His left arm reached around the back of her jeans guiding her gently down onto his lap.

"You've a lot to learn before we send you into the field," she whispered softly as she removed his sweat shirt. "This is a front fasten-ing bra."

"You're right," he joked. "I need a lot more hands on training in this area."

Maria's long hair brushed against him as the couple kissed for the first time. Her firm breasts pressed against his chest. He grasped her thighs, stood up, and lifted her without interrupting their kiss. As he placed her on the bed, she arched upwards and backwards, causing flowing brunette locks to cascade across the pillow.

For the next hour he would learn that Maria was every bit as demanding in the bedroom as she was on their training runs.

"You're actually the first Irishman I've had."

"Did I live up to your expectations? Suddenly I feel like I've got the reputation of an entire nation on my shoulders."

"We've got to get that Irish Catholic guilt knocked out of you. I can't have emotions messing up the mission. You're going to meet a lot of Nuala Mallons during the course of your work and its important not to let the sexual aspect of these relationships cloud your judgment."

"So this was just another lesson in the training manual?"

"Pretty much, but a fun one, don't you think? A lot's going to be expected of you and I don't want you to think we don't appreciate it. I only know one way to demonstrate that sleeping with the likes of Nuala is something you'll be forced to do from time to time. It's important you keep it in perspective. This is one lesson where 'hands on education' is better than anything you could read in a text book. At least that's the way I feel."

Maria glanced behind her and smiled as she skipped towards the bathroom.

"If this wasn't part of your training program, we'd both be in this shower making plans to spend the day together. Sadly, I've got a lot to do today, so you'll have to see yourself out."

10:10PM – Saturday October 28th 1978
Boston, Massachusetts, USA

❝ What do you mean, you're heading home?" Nuala asked. "It's just ten o'clock and you've only had two beers!"

"I had to work today and I could do with an early night." Peter explained. "I'll give you a call tomorrow. Maybe we can go see '*The Boys from Brazil*.' I hear it's a pretty good movie."

3:20PM – Tuesday November 21st 1978
Boston, Massachusetts, USA

T he meeting with his boss at *National Semiconductor* went just as Reid had been led to expect. Maria and her associates had been able to manipulate events to suit their agenda. Obviously her team had an agent, or agents, in his workplace, but if he were to concern himself with such details, it could be at a cost to the mission or possibly his life! He was part of a team and he resigned himself to concentrating on his own responsibilities. For his legend or cover to work, he needed to have a thorough understanding of the computerized controls of the *DeLorean* production line. Arrangements had been made for him to make several visits to Belfast before relocating there in March 1979. The engineers at his company anticipated it would take a full year to install the computerized assembly controls and then calibrate them. Maria felt that would give him enough time to gain the confidence of high ranking operatives in the INRA.

The British Government's investment in *DeLorean Motor Company* was part of an economic policy designed to counter social conditions which fueled the conflict in the troubled Province. The factory's location was carefully selected so it would span both Catholic and Protestant neighborhoods. It was hoped the community, which had been torn apart by sectarian violence, could work together to produce an iconic sports car: the *DMC-12*. In October 1978 the dream to build the most sophisticated assembly plant in the world was born in a green field, with a set of construction plans. Northern Ireland's Industrial Development Board (IDB) was the government agency charged with promoting foreign investment in the six counties of Ireland under British

rule. John DeLorean's decision to build there was influenced by the huge
financial investment the British Government would make in his company. Nevertheless, there were other favorable factors. Northern Ireland
had an established, educated, English speaking workforce with a sound
mechanical engineering history. *Harland and Wolff Shipyard, James
Mackie & Son Engineering Works*, and *Short Brothers* aircraft factory,
were all pioneers and leaders in their respective fields. Queen's University
Belfast and Ulster University, each had mechanical engineering, electrical engineering and computer science faculties, which produced highly
qualified talent for the global marketplace. *Ford* and *General Motors*
already had assembly plants in the Province and, despite the sectarian
violence, had maintained productivity and profitability records on par
with other plants in their respective companies. Northern Ireland's scientists and engineers, such as Dunlop and Ferguson were synonymous
with advances in automobile and combustion engine technology. Even
in the midst of *The Troubles*, Professor Blair of Queen's University
worked with *Yamaha* to invent 'the expansion box' in the early 1970s.
With a population of 500,000, and located within a one hour flight from
London, Northern Ireland was an ideal location for John DeLorean to
establish his new factory.

After work Maria provided Peter with a file containing information about INRA operatives in Belfast who were known associates
of Paddy Lynch. She hoped Lynch would facilitate an introduction to
them once he discovered Reid would be returning to Northern Ireland.
Since the first trip was imminent, she told him to embellish the fact that
his family had been burned out of their home and to convey a desire
for retaliation. She stressed the importance of not appearing too asser-
tive. They wanted the INRA to take the initiative and suggest the young
engineer could do something for *The Cause*. The stage was unwittingly

set by Nuala when she asked 'her uncle' to invite Reid for Thanksgiving
dinner.

7:10PM – Thursday November 23rd 1978
Boston, Massachusetts, USA

Paddy's wife chased her husband and their young guest from the Thanksgiving table and Nuala offered to load the dishwasher. Both men had eaten much more than they should, and were glad to have landed in the soft leather reclining chairs in Lynch's den.

"It's ironic. There'd be no America and no Thanksgiving had it not been for religious persecution," Reid remarked. "Do you think Northern Ireland has a similar future ahead?"

"Who knows lad, but freedom isn't free. Sometimes you have to fight for it. Maybe I'm wrong," the older man reflected, pausing for effect, "and way off base, but I get the impression there are times you wish you could do more?"

"I feel guilty, Paddy. I'm doing okay, but my house in Belfast gets fire bombed and my folks get told where they can or can't live. It doesn't seem right. I wish there was something more I could do."

"There is, but it's not a decision to be taken lightly. The people who burned your family home have a sense of entitlement that comes from the British occupation of Northern Ireland. So long as there's a British presence, you and your family are going to be second class citizens."

"You're right. America has never looked back since it took control of its own country and as long as Britain is committed to staying in Northern Ireland, there'll always be a problem."

"You have skills that could help bring an end to British rule."

"What are you suggesting Paddy?"

"I know people who could benefit from your knowledge, but only if you are committed to their cause, and genuinely believe Ireland should be free of British oppression."

"I'd be interested," the younger man acknowledged, trying to conceal he felt his heart had become lodged in his throat and was beating at an alarming rate.

"Why don't we talk in a week and if you still want me to make an introduction, then I'll see what I can do. Once you join this organization, there's no turning back. It's not like joining a gym. You're either involved 100% or you're a liability."

"Who are we talking about?"

"Committed Patriots, Peter! That's all you need to know. Committed Patriots."

5:10PM – Monday December 4th 1978
Boston, Massachusetts, USA

Peter and Maria removed all sensitive files from the safe in his bedroom and replaced them with technical material from his work at *National Semiconductor.*

"It looks like Lynch will introduce you to his INRA contact this evening, so from this point on, you can't do anything that could blow your cover. Also, you and I will no longer meet in this apartment. We can't risk them 'bugging' it, and if they do, we won't remove it. We'll let them hear exactly what we want them to hear," she continued with a grin.

"I won't be in Boston much longer, but I'll still have the use of the apartment upstairs so we'll have somewhere when we need to communicate in private. When I'm in Boston and need to speak with you, I'll slip a Chinese take-out menu under your door to let you know I'm upstairs. If discussions are too sensitive for the telephone, we'll either notify you of a recall on your *Mustang* or you can call this 800 number to schedule a service at the dealership we use as a cover. We've got a dental office too, so don't be surprised if you get a call from them. If I can't meet you, George Mulligan will. He's joining the faculty at MIT in January. Until we advise otherwise, we will be the only two people with authorization to either contact you, or respond to a communication from you. If Paddy Lynch takes the bait tonight and introduces you to his INRA colleagues, this whole operation goes to a new level."

"Got it," Peter declared. "But there's one part of my training where I think I need more coaching." He tilted his head slightly to the side, flashing the infamous grin that had rescued him from many awkward situations in the past.

Maria was caught off guard. He leaned forward, pulling her towards him, and passionately kissed her warm, moist lips.

"I'd like to have more practice at this." Maria did not resist. Instead, she lay back on his bed in the sudden realization that the pupil had become the teacher.

9:25PM – Monday December 4th 1978
Boston, Massachusetts, USA

Reid had been forty-five minutes late for his Spanish conversation class at Boston University and paid little attention to what the teacher had to say. Nevertheless, he had agreed to maintain his schedule in case the INRA already had him under surveillance. The fact that two INRA operatives were searching his apartment while he was in class, vindicated the need for caution. Despite Maria's assurances as to his readiness, Peter was consumed with anxiety about how the evening would unfold. The drive from Boston University to *The Patriot* was another blur. "What the fuck!" he chastised himself as he parked his *Mustang* outside the bar. "Get your head back in the game, man, or this mission will turn to shit!"

Only Lynch was working when he entered the premises. It had been a slow night and the six remaining patrons were Local 103 electricians watching the final minutes of a Bruins game in New York. He settled on a stool at the end of the bar and nodded approvingly as Paddy held a pint glass above the *Guinness* tap.

"My guys want to meet," Lynch confided in a low tone. "They might stop by tonight."

An hour later, no one was left except the two Northern Irishmen who spent the time talking politics and European soccer. When it was clear there would be no more customers that evening, Lynch reached to the top shelf for a bottle which had no label.

"Uisce Beatha," He announced and proudly placed two glasses on the counter. "You can't buy this in a liquor store, either here or in Ireland. I get this poteen from a good friend in Recess, County Galway.

It's better than any single malt on that shelf."

"To a United Ireland!" They toasted as their glasses touched.

"We'll try again another night. Something must've come up."

As he drove home, Reid had mixed feelings about the night. He was disappointed his and Maria's efforts had failed to yield the result they had anticipated. Three pints of Guinness, however, and two shots of poteen helped him forget his evening at *The Patriot*. He carelessly tossed his jacket onto the couch and kicked off his shoes. On further reflection he was relieved Lynch's INRA contacts had decided not to meet. He rationalized he probably already knew some of its members from his visits to *The Patriot* so he tried to persuade himself everything would be fine. He tossed and turned in an effort to get his neck comfortable on his pillow and wondered if Lynch's colleagues still had an interest in meeting. As he began to second guess the plan, he gently drifted off to sleep.

Initially, it seemed like a nightmare. He could neither open his eyes, nor mouth. He estimated there were at least five assailants. While each arm and leg was restrained, the fifth person had taped his eyes and mouth, leaving him silenced and disoriented. Attempts to struggle free were futile. He reluctantly complied with the hushed instructions of, "Shut the fuck up." The familiar accent told him he was in the process of meeting the INRA operatives, but under circumstances he had never envisioned. It was not their verbal instructions that conveyed the seriousness of the situation, but rather an ominous "click" beside his ear. Compliance was the only option. His 'visitors' placed him at the kitchen table and bound his hands behind his back, then taped them to the chair. They also taped his ankles to its front legs. They left him there, unable to move and unable to see. For added suspense, nobody spoke.

At last, after what felt like an eternity, one of the intruders approached him. Every muscle in his terrorized body tensed with fear. Would it be blows to the stomach, groin or face? A 'kneecapping' with a power drill to one or both legs? Or would it be a quick shot to the back of his head? Reid was more terrified than he had ever been in his entire life. He winced as he felt the gloved hand on his face, tugging on the tape covering his eyes. In an instant it was off pulling hairs from his eyebrows and lashes. His eyes were hot and painful but he could see. He had been correct in his estimate of five assailants but he could identify no one since each wore a ski mask, as well as black leather gloves.

"We've got some questions for you so we're goin' to remove this tape," a strong Belfast accent barked. "If you even think of doin' anything stupid, I promise you'll not hear the shot that kills you." The familiar "click" at his ear sounded again as tape was pulled from his mouth. "If we don't get a satisfactory answer to the first question, there won't be any more. Do you understand?" Peter tried to acknowledge he understood, but no words came out. "We need the combination for the safe."

"The things in there belong to my employer," he eventually mumbled. "They're just electronic specifications."

"I didn't ask what was in the fuckin' safe. I asked for the combination." The muzzle of a gun pressed menacingly into the side of his temple forced him to recite the combination. He could not believe how fortuitous it was Maria had thought to remove the sensitive material.

'Mr. Tall', as Peter mentally named him, returned and tossed a pile of files and blue line prints on the kitchen table. He pulled up a chair, and stared through the slits in his ski mask.

"What do we have here?" he asked as he shuffled through the heap. Knowing 'Mr. Tall' and his crew had embarked on a useless search gave Reid a small sense of satisfaction.

"I work for *National Semiconductor* and those are electrical plans and specifications for a project I'm working on. The company is very cautious about its designs and insists they're kept locked up when I'm not working on them."

'Mr. Tall' was not willing to take him at his word. Without saying anything, he signaled for one of the crew to study the documents. At the same time, he stared at his captive searching for a sign in the young engineer's eyes that would reveal more than the papers on the table. Peter was adamant he was not going to blink. He managed to hold the stare until the accomplice finally confirmed everything was as he had represented. His captor was still not satisfied. He fired a barrage of questions that probed into Reid's family and life in Belfast: where he went to high school; why he chose to study electrical engineering; where his parents worked? The only time he was caught off guard was when he was asked why he had not been involved with political groups at university. It was then he realized the major flaw in his legend. Maria and her team had asked him to portray someone who wanted to join the INRA, yet, as a student, he had neither voted in an election, nor attended a political meeting. He needed to think of a plausible reason if he was going to satisfy the intruders, and he needed to do it immediately.

"I can tell from your accent you grew up in Belfast, but your question tells me you didn't grow up in my neighborhood." 'Mr. Tall' was intrigued by the answer. "I grew up in East Belfast where Catholic families were outnumbered five hundred to one. Involvement in politics seemed pretty fucking futile to me. And with my engineering schedule at Queen's, there was no fucking time for anything else." He was relieved he had responded so quickly under pressure. "I knew there wouldn't be a job for me in the shipyard and I'm surprised it took this long for our family to be burned out of our home." The masked man considered the remark for several minutes then took a jackknife from his pocket, opened it carefully and placed it on the table.

"A word of warning before you decide if you want to join us in our struggle to free Ireland. We've done our fuckin' homework. We know all about your family in Belfast, as well as your brother in London. If you utter a word about who you saw or what was said tonight, we'll kill you, but not until you watch us kill your family. We don't fuck around. Don't make the mistake of making us prove it." Peter nodded and 'Mr. Tall' continued. "We're committed to freeing Ireland from her British oppressors and to the eradication of imperialism, anywhere in the world, where it tramples on the backs of the working class. We've fostered contacts with Republican paramilitaries in Northern Ireland and support them in their armed struggle against the British Army. We believe your skills and knowledge will be a game changer. If you take the oath you'll be assigned to an active cell. In your case it will be in Belfast. How you contact this cell will be conveyed to you at another time." Without hesitation Peter acknowledged he was ready to take the oath, so 'Mr. Tall' cut loose his wrists and ankles. One of the men draped a Starry Plough flag over the kitchen table. A volume of Marx's 'Das Kapital' was placed in front of him and he repeated the oath his captor recited.

"Congratulations, Volunteer!" 'Mr. Tall' announced, as he reached out to shake the newest member's hand. "Until things are set up with your cell in Belfast, you'll report to me. He turned to face his cohorts who had already made the room look like nothing had happened. "Right boys, you're dismissed. I need a few words in private with our new Volunteer. I'll be in touch."

The four men stood to attention, saluted and left the room without removing their masks. 'Mr. Tall' then removed his ski mask and formally introduced himself, "Captain Joseph Lagan. I'm not supposed to reveal personal information but the rules are stricter at home where the Brits, and RUC, are always 'lifting' people for questioning. We'll need to get together before you head to Belfast," he continued. "If you're half as good as Paddy Lynch says, we'll want you to work on developing timers and remote detonators. With a bit of luck, it won't be long before we get the upper hand on the Brits!"

Reid reached up to a shelf above the refrigerator and lifted down a bottle of Irish whiskey and two cofffee mugs. There was no further interaction. As soon as the drinks were finished, plans were made for him to meet Captain Lagan the following evening.

3:55PM – Tuesday December 5th 1978
Waltham, Massachusetts, USA

Reid spent most of the day in a test lab at *National Semiconduc-tor* where he had his own work station for testing components and modifying designs for the *DeLorean* project. He was pleased with what he had managed to assemble for his meeting with Captain Lagan, which was scheduled for later that evening. The design was basic and somewhat bulky, but it would clearly demonstrate that, by using a coded radio signal, the INRA would be able to remotely detonate bombs from a distance of a quarter mile. For the purpose of the demonstration, he had soldered a small buzzer onto the circuit board to take the place of a detonator and added two mercury tilt switches to show Lagan how the bomb would detonate, should an attempt be made to defuse it. He had also designed an encrypted component signal to ensure the bomb would only detonate when the INRA operator's radio transmission was received. It would be more effective than previous attempts Lagan and his colleagues had made. His "safety feature," a term he thought both unfortunate and inappropriate, would prevent the British Army from detonating the device prematurely by randomly broadcasting signals. The new feature was created by incorporating a *Texas Instruments* hand calculator within the circuitry of both the receiver and transmitter. He then programmed the calculators so the transmitter would send a precise series of pulses that were separated by specifically determined time gaps, measured to the nearest one hundredth of a second. Since only the bomb's receiver had been programmed to recognize the signal, it would be immune to British Army attempts to remotely detonate it.

Peter had been engrossed in his INRA project for Captain Lagan

so he completely lost track of time. To make matters worse, his commute home would be hampered by snow that had been falling for hours,
totally blanketing his car. As he set the box containing the detonator
components into the trunk of his *Mustang*, he felt relieved there was no
real bomb attached. Driving home, he appreciated how refreshing it was
to live stress free in Boston, far from the sectarian conflict of Northern
Ireland. In two days, however, he would be back in Belfast as a member
of the INRA which would place him at more risk than he could ever have
imagined. Furthermore, the whole point of the mission was, ultimately, to
use his membership in the INRA to infiltrate the Colombian paramilitary
guerrillas, FARC. Yet, despite everything, his most urgent problem was
to get to *The Patriot* before six o'clock when Nuala's shift would finish.
They had planned to go to an expensive restaurant for dinner and then
see a movie, but that was not going to happen because he had to meet
with Joseph Lagan instead.

When he walked into the bar Nuala was delighted to see him,
erroneously thinking he had arrived for their date. When she realized
the extent of their evening would only be fast food then home, she was
not happy. Evasive responses to her questions made the situation even
worse. Had it not been for the snow, she would have refused his offer of
the ride back to her apartment.

Outside Nuala's apartment, she slammed the car door leaving
him unsure if she had agreed, or declined, to have lunch with him the
following day, before he would leave for Belfast. Peter let two snow
plows pass before pulling away from the curb. He had not eaten since
breakfast and he felt ravenous. Dealing with Nuala's feelings and frustra-
tions would have to wait until after his meeting with Lagan.

It was almost 7:00PM by the time he had finished his burger and
parked in a rented garage, a half mile from his apartment. There was a

parking ban in effect because of the snow, so he was not able to leave his vehicle in the street. Cautiously, he placed the electronic components into a sports bag to protect them from the weather, and then zipped up his jacket. Although the plows had done a good job keeping the roads clear, sidewalks presented a challenge to the few pedestrians who were forced to use them. As he approached his apartment, Captain Lagan exited the passenger side of an *Oldsmobile Cutlass* that was parked with its engine running. The vehicle weaved slightly on the slushy surface as it moved away after Lagan shut its passenger door.

"How are you?" Lagan asked without making the effort to shake hands. The introduction was an improvement on his previous one.

"Good, Joe." Reid replied, unsure whether or not to ask more questions. He rooted around in his pocket to find the key to his front door. Every second his hands stayed shielded from the cold was a blessing.

It took barely seconds for Lagan to walk from the *Oldsmobile* into the hallway of Peter's building, but it was all she needed to see from across the street. Nuala Mallon had been hiding in the doorway of a rare book shop. Heightened paranoia, fueled by a cocaine habit, and her assignment from Clive Noakes in MI6, had driven her into the storm to investigate her boyfriend. Lagan was most certainly not the person she expected to see. While relieved to discover it was not another woman, she was, however, intrigued to see Reid in the company of a *Patriot* patron and friend of Paddy Lynch. Secretly, she had hoped Peter's engineering career would drive his life in another direction offering her an escape from the existence she had come to loathe. Sadly, she concluded he was going to be nothing more than a revenue source for cocaine, thanks to payments she would receive from Noakes and MI6 for her undercover intelligence reports.

Meanwhile Reid's kitchen table had been transformed into

an electronic laboratory test bench. Lagan was in awe of what he saw sprawled out before him. He was especially impressed when the mercury tilt switches activated the buzzer the very instant he lifted the device to inspect it.

"I should've warned you," Peter laughed, "but I thought you'd have a better appreciation for my work if you experienced it first hand."

"We've got to put a plan in place to get this technology from your kitchen table into the hands of our volunteers on the front line."

Reid, however, expressed concern about procuring electronic parts for bombs. He informed his guest that their acquisition, left to inexperienced personnel, would compromise active INRA cells because British security forces could link components to them.

"You'll have to do some research and target suppliers in Northern Ireland so we can steal what's needed. We can also hide our tracks by setting off incendiary devices that'll make it difficult to audit inventory after the fact," Lagan suggested.

"That should work. I'll look into it during my trip. We can't use items purchased with a credit card or in a store that has security cameras. We can remove mercury tilt switches from residential thermostats or cars that have been scrapped. They're often used to operate courtesy lights and are rarely properly disposed of. We can't allow our guys to get sloppy or lazy. When the Brits figure out what's happening, they're going to be relentless."

"There's no need for you to meet any of our men on this trip, Peter. I want you to concentrate on identifying safe and reliable sources for components. Also, it's not appropriate for you to have the rank of Volunteer, even though you've only just joined us. Because of what I've seen so far, I've decided to promote you to Sergeant. Given the nature of our organization, these things aren't carried out with a lot of pomp and ceremony. Our senior command has been notified of your expertise and eventually will want you in an advisory or training role. Don't worry about not seeing action. That'll happen in due course. We feel your time would be better spent training operatives."

"I'm comfortable with that."

"While you're back home, try and spend some time in Dublin. If we steal components for detonators from retailers down there, they'll be more difficult to trace by the authorities in Northern Ireland. Besides, it would be better to set you up with a lab in the Republic where you can assemble the remote detonators and teach our boys."

"Is that not a bit like putting all our eggs in one basket?" Peter challenged. "You can see everything we need to make one remote detonator can be packed into two shoe boxes. There's not a lot to it. I recommend we don't stay locked into any one location and select random venues for our meetings to train the men."

"You're probably right," Lagan conceded. "Let's begin by sourcing components. When you have your list, put it in an envelope concealed in a copy of the *Irish News*. One of our men will meet you in *White's Tavern* the Saturday after next at 2:20PM. He'll ask you if you've finished with the paper. You'll reply that you're doing the crossword and can't get 7 DOWN. He'll reply, 'Heaven'. That'll be the cue to give him your newspaper with the list of components and retailers that stock them, both North and South of the border."

When Lagan left, Reid took meticulous care as he gathered the various components and electronic devices. He wondered about calling Nuala to see if she had calmed down. Exhausted and suspecting she might need more time before hearing from him, he decided to leave that problem for the following day.

8:55AM – Wednesday December 6th 1978
Boston, Massachusetts, USA

Since the City of Boston was still trying to clean up after the winter storm, Peter elected to run five miles on a treadmill in his local gym. It was safer than dodging snow plows in icy conditions. The monotonous activity provided a perfect opportunity to think about placating the sulking Ms. Mallon. The last thing he expected to find, when he returned to his apartment, was a friendly message from her on his answering machine. From the moment she had seen him with Joseph Lagan, her plans for Reid had changed dramatically. She realized Paddy Lynch and his INRA cell had homed in on the young electrical engineer. Although she had only two shots left in the lipstick camera Clive Noakes had given her, she was determined to get a photograph of Reid before he left for Northern Ireland.

Peter returned her call, relieved the message had candidly conveyed she regretted parting on disagreeable terms.

"I want to make it up to you, love. I don't want you to go back home without me making amends. Can you come over?" she asked sheepishly when he returned the call.

"I'm on my way," he replied.

*****

After several hours of erotic sexual activity, Nuala suddenly sat up in bed and announced, "We need to get ready or you're going to miss your plane. I'll go first, then you can shower while I put on some makeup."

Later, while Peter retraced his steps to recover various items of clothing, she sat at her kitchen table applying mascara. It amused him to watch her facial contortions as she slowly and deliberately brushed her eyelashes with the thick black substance.

"Do you like this color?" she asked holding up her lipstick. He leaned back against the wall and smiled at the sight of her pouting lips. He had no idea he was the actual focus of her attention. With two perfect images recorded on the microfilm, she finished her acting performance and put the camera safely into her pink cosmetic bag. Reid never suspected he had just been photographed by an informant for Britain's MI6. Mallon had done an excellent job taking him into her confidence.

10:05AM – Saturday December 16th 1978
Boston, Massachusetts, USA

Clive Noakes was going to be very pleased with the valuable intelligence contained on Nuala Mallon's lipstick camera. He sat in the cafeteria of the Museum of Fine Arts, waiting patiently for his confidential informant. He reviewed a list of family and friends and was horrified by the number of Christmas gifts he still had to buy before returning to London.

Nuala was late leaving her apartment. It seemed the more she rushed the longer it took to get things done. Finally, flustered and frustrated, she slammed the door behind her and dashed out into the street. As she hurried along Huntington Avenue, her wrist watch confirmed she was fifteen minutes late. Growing up in Northern Ireland, she had been exposed to public service campaigns which stressed, "Look right, left, then right again before crossing the road." It would be impossible to quantify how many lives had been saved as a result of this subconscious safety ritual. Unfortunately, these instructions are wrong in a country where vehicles travel on the right side of the street.

Clive's coffee cup hit his saucer at the exact instant Mallon's head hit the icy pavement. She rolled and tumbled several times before becoming a motionless heap on top of a catch basin grate. Vehicles swerved and screeched as drivers pumped brake pedals and wrestled steering wheels to avoid each other, and the unfortunate girl. The only positive aspect of the tragic situation was the fact she had been struck by an out of service ambulance. Everything that happened to Nuala, from the point of impact to when her head hit the ground, was a chaotic spinning kaleidoscope of images and sound. Suddenly, there was nothing but silence and darkness. She neither saw nor heard the EMT who was by her side within seconds. Initially, the driver remained in his cab and radioed his dispatcher to report what had just happened but then, he too, rushed to her aid.

Inside the museum, Noakes stopped checking his Christmas list to take another look at his watch. Mallon was never late and he immediately imagined the worst. "Had Paddy Lynch or his crew discovered her camera and realized she was an informant?" he wondered anxiously. At that instant, he overheard two visitors talking about the accident outside. He decided to investigate. When he exited the building, police officers were already directing traffic and a second ambulance was at the scene. He pushed his way through the crowd in time to see Mallon strapped onto a stretcher. Suddenly, he spotted the lipstick with the concealed camera in the gutter, along with a pink cosmetic case and other items that had tumbled out of her black shoulder bag. Before he could react, a policeman scooped everything up and handed it to the EMT.

"Fuck, Fuck, Fuck!" he muttered to himself. "My Christmas plans just disappeared into the back of that ambulance!"

He waited until the police had finished taking statements not only from the driver involved, but also from the many witnesses who saw the accident. As soon as the crew had been cleared he casually approached them.

"Hey guys, I think I may know the victim. What hospital was she taken to?"

"*Boston Mercy,*" the still shaken and shocked driver replied.

Noakes could not determine the extent of her injuries, but regardless, he needed to retrieve the camera. If Paddy Lynch or his cohorts were to get their hands on her belongings and discover it, she would be as good as dead. He went back inside the museum and used a pay phone

in the lobby to call the British Consulate General. Despite the stress of
the situation, Noakes calmly explained to his boss why he needed a fake
Massachusetts driving license and other documentation with the last
name, "Mallon."

"I need them within the hour so I can convince the hospital I'm
her relative," he asserted.

Ninety minutes later, he was at *Boston Mercy's* ER asking about
his sister, Nuala Mallon. The nurse took a cursory glance at the fake
driving license and directed him to an area where a doctor could give
him an update.

"Your sister is unconscious, Mr. Mallon. She's on life support
because she's unable to breathe properly for herself," Dr. North reported
after a brief self introduction. Noakes tried to convey an air of distress
and concern but, in reality, he was intent on getting his hands on the
missing makeup bag. "It's not unusual for trauma victims to experience
a temporary coma. It's the body's own way of coping with the stress
of such an ordeal. Hopefully, she'll be back with us very soon. At the
moment, Nuala is in Radiology so we can ascertain the extent of her
internal injuries and check for broken bones."

"I know she's in great hands," Noakes acknowledged. "But
before you go Dr. North, I need to ask about my sister's belongings.
She was going to the pharmacy for me when she was ..." he paused for
effect, "run over by the ambulance."

"One of the nurses will help you with that, Mr. Mallon."

"Thank you, Doctor. I've no way of knowing if she still has the
prescription or if she already picked up my heart medication."

Shortly afterward, a nurse entered the room with a large plastic
bag and clipboard with a receipt for Noakes to sign.

"Since your sister is in a coma, it's better if you take her possessions," she explained. "I need to record your contact information and have you sign this. It'll be a while before we'll have more information," she added compassionately. He took the clipboard and completed the form as quickly as possible. She gave him a comforting smile and handed over the bag emblazoned with the letters 'PATIENT'S PROPERTY.' It had been securely closed. "Why don't you get a coffee in the cafeteria and come back in an hour."

"Thank you, Nurse. I'll put these things in my car first, and then I'll take your advice," he lied as he clutched the plastic bag.

Noakes went straight out the door and continued walking, ecstatic it had been so easy to retrieve Nuala's belongings. As soon as he was clear of the hospital, he ripped open the fasteners to recover the lipstick camera. To his dismay, the bag only contained: one black shoulder bag; one pair of gloves; a cassette walkman; a key-ring with keys; a book of matches from the *Cocoa Bean* nightclub; and a membership card for *BlockBuster Video*.

"What the fuck!" He exclaimed. He had seen the police officer hand her belongings to the EMT right before the ambulance left the accident scene. He turned immediately and hurried back to the hospital. As soon as he exited the elevator and stepped onto the floor, he saw the young nurse who had just taken his information. He quickly approached the reception area.

"Neither my medication, nor prescription were in the bag," he reported with an urgent and agitated tone. "Nuala must've had more items on her when she was transported."

"All her belongings were put into that bag, Mr. Mallon, after her clothing was cut off." The English agent was perplexed and his expression failed to hide it. "Would you like me to call your doctor so we can arrange to get you another prescription?"

"No. No thank you, Nurse. I've a couple of days left so that won't be necessary."

When he walked outside the frigid fresh air was invigorating but he was unsure what he should do next. He tried to decipher possible scenarios. "Had Lynch been following her? Had any of his associates followed her to the hospital?" he wondered.

Noakes knew he could not stay any longer and risk Lynch showing up, especially if a member of staff were to identify him as Nuala's brother. If only he had thought to look for the makeup bag in the last place he had seen it. It was, in fact, neatly wedged between the front seats of the ambulance which, due to a shift change, was being driven by another crew. It remained there until the vehicle returned to the garage at the rear of the hospital.

"Don't forget your bag, Jill," the driver warned as he closed his door.

"That's not mine. It's probably from the morning shift," his colleague responded. Together the EMTs opened the cosmetic bag and rummaged through the contents which included several lipsticks, a tube of mascara and a pay stub from *The Patriot*.

"I'll hand it in," Jill volunteered.

*****

The hospital failed to get an answer from the phone number Clive Noakes had given when he pretended to be Nuala's brother. A resourceful nurse decided to call *The Patriot* to see if anyone knew their patient.

As soon as Paddy Lynch got the call he jumped into action and rushed to the hospital. It was now apparent why Nuala had neither turned up for work nor answered his phone calls. For the second time that day, the medical staff had to explain Nuala's condition.

"I don't understand. What do you mean?" he responded to the nurse's question.

"We need another phone number for Ms. Mallon's brother. That's why we called you because we couldn't get an answer at the number he gave us."

"Nuala doesn't have a brother."

"I don't know what to say, Mr. Lynch. The file says her property was given to her brother. Fortunately, her cosmetic case was left in the ambulance and we found a pay stub."

Lynch was both intrigued and disturbed about the individual who had claimed to be his 'niece's brother'. Initially, he thought she had been the random victim of a thief who targeted ER patients, but when he considered the situation further, he could not disregard the possibility it was someone who had his INRA cell under surveillance. Nuala was not part of the cell, a fact the person who claimed her belongings may not have known. He pondered the possibility that it was not an accident. He realized the "mystery man" was looking for something she possessed, otherwise he would not have gone to the hospital, with a fake ID, and claimed her personal property.

He immediately emptied the contents of the cosmetic bag to see if there was anything of interest. Everything looked normal, just the usual contents of a young woman's cosmetic bag; mascara, a couple of lipsticks and a pay stub from his bar.

5:25PM – Friday December 22nd 1978
Belfast, NORTHERN IRELAND

R eid was pleased with his reconnaissance efforts. During the previous week he had been able to find retailers, in both Northern Ireland and the Irish Republic, where the INRA could steal components for wireless detonators. As good as things were going on that front, he was bothered he had not spoken to Nuala since he left Boston. She had neither answered his calls nor returned messages left on her answering machine.

"I didn't miss this when I was in Boston," he remarked to his little sister Catherine as their car slowed down at a British Army check point. He was annoyed by the inconvenience of random military patrols and soldiers armed with Sterling submachine guns. A voice on the car radio reported the latest developments in the authority's efforts to put an end to the sectarian murder campaign of the "Shankhill Butchers." The horrific details of the news story repulsed him. It explained how authorities believed the gang was responsible for using butchers knives to torture and murder at least twenty Roman Catholic victims.

The routine security check should have taken only a few minutes but it lasted almost thirty. It concerned the Army personnel that Reid did not own the car and rental documents showed the use of a United States credit card. To make matters worse, his Northern Ireland driving license still showed his former address in Dundonald, even though he was staying at his family's new home in West Belfast.

"Get your Northern Ireland license updated sir, if you're no longer living there," the British soldier scolded sternly. Fortunately, Reid's Massachusetts license supported his version of events. Eventually, confirmation came back that their car had been cleared to proceed.

"So how've you been since you got back from Boston?" he asked Catherine as they were waved on their way.

"My doctors are glad I went to America."

"You're a lucky wee girl," Peter agreed with a smile.

"Are you going to live here soon?"

"In a few months. I'm goin' back to Boston to make that happen."

4:30PM – Friday December 29th 1978
Boston, Massachusetts, USA

R eid dropped his luggage on the living room floor and went straight to his answering machine. He re-buttoned his jacket and turned up the thermostat on the wall beside his phone as the messages played. The fact Nuala had not called bothered him, but he was more concerned by the urgent tone of the message from Paddy Lynch. "Peter. It's me, Paddy. Give me a ring when you get back in town. It's very important." He called *The Patriot* immediately.

"Is Paddy Lynch there?"

"No, he's not here."

"Is Nuala Mallon working?"

"No. Who's this?"

"Peter Reid. I'm a friend of Paddy and Nuala's.

"You didn't hear then."

"Hear what?"

"Paddy's at the hospital with Nuala. She was in an accident and has been in a coma ever since."

"Is she okay?" he asked nervously, afraid what the response might be.

"It's probably better you talk to Paddy."

"What hospital is she in?"

"The *Mercy.*"

Peter rushed to the hospital where he found Paddy Lynch standing at the young woman's bedside.

"She hasn't moved a muscle since it happened," he lamented. "It's not lookin' good."

11:59PM – Sunday December 31st 1978
Falls Church, Virginia, USA

❝Happy New Year," Scott Hamilton toasted aloud as he and his guests welcomed 1979.

"Wouldn't it be nice if this were all it took?" Maria asked George. "And all we had to do was raise our glasses so everything would be okay?"

"If only," Mulligan agreed. Hamilton had a loyal team who not only enjoyed working with one another, but also socializing together. His wife, however, felt the atmosphere had more tension than previous events.

"Something's bothering you? Don't deny it," Angela continued before her husband of twenty years could respond. "I can tell." He squeezed her hand and kissed her affectionately on the cheek.

"Happy New Year, my love, Happy New Year."

Angela Hamilton did not expect her husband to tell her what was preoccupying him. Her intention was merely to let him know she was there to support him as much as she could. The irony of the situation was not lost on her as she studied the expressions on their guests. It was obvious which member of each couple worked with her husband at the CIA, and which one knew nothing of the stress and secrets that came with the job. In reality, her husband was contemplating several potentially volatile international problems. The situation in Nicaragua was a mess with the Sandinistas growing stronger and stronger. He doubted the Somoza administration could hold power for much longer which meant a Russian backed ultra left wing government would soon take control of the country. Meanwhile in Iran, he estimated the Shah was weeks, perhaps days away from being overthrown by supporters of the exiled Islamic cleric, Ayatollah Khomeini. 1978 had been a successful year for enemies of the United States and Scott Hamilton's predictions for the immediate future were extremely bleak, especially since he was not certain the Carter administration shared his evaluation of how critical these problems were for America.

At approximately one o'clock the last of their guests drove out of the secluded driveway, so Scott closed his front door and put aside his private projections for 1979.

11:50AM – Monday February 26th 1979
Boston Mercy Hospital **- Boston, Massachusetts, USA**

Nuala Mallon's condition had not changed since her accident. In another wing of the building, a panel of doctors, and other professionals, was about to conclude its review of their problematic cases. These issues required decisions at executive level. The hospital's general counsel advised on pertinent legal considerations while its accounting consultants addressed financial and health insurance matters.

"Let's try and wrap this up so we can break for lunch. We've only one more case to discuss," the Committee's chairman, Dr. Abrams announced. "This twenty year old woman was admitted three months ago, the victim of a road traffic accident. Scans and x-rays show no evidence of internal injury or broken bones, but due to brain trauma she remains unresponsive."

After lengthy but stoic deliberations the team narrowed down their options to two, neither of which had an upside. Since Mallon had been struck by the hospital's own ambulance, the incurred medical costs were being covered by a combination of their automobile and general liability insurance policies. Unfortunately, those policies could not cover her medical expenses indefinitely. Accounting reports distributed at the meeting predicted coverage would run out after another three months of treatment.

"At the end of the next quarter, the policy will have paid out approximately six hundred thousand dollars, at which point, if she remains comatose, we'll be in the same situation as we're in today. Our actuarial analysis shows the patient has no dependents, no siblings and her mother is the only living parent. If life ends now, we can negotiate a settlement with the mother and save an estimated two hundred thousand dollars."

Nobody interrupted as the various Heads of Department meticulously recorded the figures, mentally considering how they would impact their individual budgets and projections. The comptroller was acutely aware of the implications of his numbers. After what he considered to be an appropriate pause, he resumed his presentation.

"The CPA's report indicates costs could top in excess of one million dollars," he warned. "However there is a way to limit this. The mother lives in Ireland, so it should be easier to negotiate a lower settlement. Also, if we can persuade her to donate her daughter's organs, there's a potential for the hospital to recuperate sixty thousand dollars."

"Well it's not a decision any of us ever likes making," Dr. Abrams eventually interjected, "but there's no indication this young woman's condition will ever change. I'll see who would be best suited to convey the news to her family. I understand there's also an uncle who lives in Boston." The doctor closed Mallon's medical file and adjourned the meeting.

3.30PM – Thursday March 22nd 1979
Boston, Massachusetts, USA

Peter took a taxi directly from the airport to the hospital. When he arrived he found Paddy Lynch more agitated than he had ever known him to be. Paddy guided him out of Nuala's room, afraid she might be able to hear what he was about to say, even though she was still in a coma.

"The hospital wants me to turn off her machines."

"What the fuck are you talking about? It was their ambulance that put her in here!"

"She doesn't have health insurance and the hospital is telling me their general liability policy coverage won't provide for endless care."

"That's insane! When are they planning to do this?"

"I'm not exactly sure, but apparently the decision has been made. We're talking days, maybe weeks at best. They haven't detected any improvement in her condition and have no reason to believe the situation is going to change."

Ironically, the hospital's proposal would have solved a potentially lethal problem for both unsuspecting men because each passing day increased the risk she could regain consciousness. As an informant for MI6, she would be able to identify Reid as a probable member of Lynch's INRA cell. Blissfully unaware of their precarious situation they continued to take turns to read to her, more determined than ever not to let her life slip away.

After Peter left the hospital, he contacted Maria Quintero, carefully following security protocol.

"Can the people who helped my sister do anything for Nuala?"

"I don't know, Peter. I did warn you about getting emotionally involved in your work."

"It would really ingratiate me with Paddy Lynch, if I helped his niece. We could contrive a story that *National Semiconductor* is working with a medical team developing scanning equipment that's not FDA approved, so it's restricted to patients who doctors have given up on."

There was a long silence on Maria's end of the line.

"Let me talk to George and the team. Maybe it could work in our favor. Leave it with me, but on no account," she warned, "do you give Lynch false hope until we know what we can or cannot do."

He agreed to her conditions and then briefed her about his recent trip to Belfast. It was clear he was making progress with his inroads into the INRA.

"You know I'll do what I can for her, but things are really hectic in D.C. Everyone's focused on events in Iran since the Shah fled to Egypt last month. Good work Peter. At least you seem to have everything under control!"

4:05PM – Wednesday April 4th 1979
Norwood, Massachusetts, USA

Since he was undercover in the INRA, Maria Quintero and her team had several surreptitious ways for meeting with their agent. Sometimes they used a dental office, but the main contact location was a car dealership. Reid responded to the fictitious recall notice he had received for his *Ford Mustang* and brought the car to the facility on Route 1 in Norwood. He knew the notice was a cover used to schedule meetings because it eliminated the risk of intercepted communications due to compromised phone lines. As soon as he entered the waiting area, Maria stood up and walked in his direction, signaling with her eyes for him to follow. Once outside, he followed her to a commercial van parked in the forecourt. As they approached, its sliding door opened to reveal George Mulligan sitting inside. It was standard operating procedure for the van to be on site before the scheduled appointment. This enabled Mulligan, and his team, to confirm Reid had not been followed. If he had been, the meeting would have been aborted.

"Good morning, George," Peter greeted as he climbed in.

The seemingly innocuous and inconspicuous vehicle merged with traffic on Route 1 so discussions could take place in complete privacy.

"We're going to arrange for Nuala Mallon's care to continue for at least another year," Mulligan confirmed. "She'll be able to stay where she is. The cover story will be that her case has drawn interest from a pharmaceutical company looking for patients to participate in a drug trial."

Peter breathed a sigh of relief but, before he could say anything,

Mulligan launched into a discussion about his Belfast operation. They went over various details then planned what he needed for support in Northern Ireland. His relationships with INRA operatives were developing and the Agency wanted to make sure he had a network in place to assist his covert program.

"Remember," George chided, "the objective is to impress the INRA top brass so they'll sub-contract you to provide training for FARC guerrillas in Colombia. Let's start pointing them in that direction. Play up your Spanish proficiency and make sure they know you can use your employment at *National Semiconductor* to source detonator components throughout the world."

7.15PM – Thursday April 19th 1979
Boston, Massachusetts, USA

Paddy Lynch was ecstatic when he heard Peter's news, even when he learned the hospital would require him to sign legal papers absolving it from liability with respect to Nuala's future treatment.

"*National Semiconductor* has a contract to supply components for a company that manufactures brain scanning equipment. It requires the patient to have a radioactive dye injected into the blood stream. Apparently the scan equipment can produce images of brain activity."

"That's brilliant, Peter. If she comes out of the coma, we'll be able to tell her you're the one who made it happen."

"Let's not get ahead of ourselves. These scanners and drugs are in their early stages of development. But at least we know they're going to keep doing their best for her, while the drug company that makes the radioactive dye pays for all her medical expenses."

11:59AM – Sunday December 31st 1980
Falls Church, Virginia, USA

Once again, Scott Hamilton found himself hosting a New Year's Eve party while preoccupied with events that were clearly at odds with the evening's theme.

Fifty-two of his fellow country men and women were still held hostage in the American Embassy in Tehran, however, he was cautiously optimistic about a deal that was being negotiated behind the scenes. If successful, it would secure their release on the day Ronald Reagan would be sworn in as America's 40th President. The failed rescue mission, in April 1980, meant Iran was adamant the hostages would not be released until after President Carter left office. Problems in the Middle East were not only limited to Iran. Conditions in Libya also remained tense following the December 1979 ransacking of the American Embassy in Tripoli by rioters proclaiming support for the Islamic regime which had taken power in Iran. Muammar Gaddafi continued to rule the North African state since orchestrating a successful coup d'état in 1969, at which time one of his first official duties was to close the U.S. Air Force Base. The Libyan leader was a constant image on Scott Hamilton's radar, due to his support of terrorist groups throughout the world. Not all Gaddafi victories, however, involved arms and explosives. He had managed to embarrass the Carter regime by engaging the services of the President's brother in a fiasco the press dubbed, "Billygate." The disastrous performance of the United States economy during President Carter's tenure doomed any chance of a second term in the White House. His brother's Libyan connection further exacerbated the situation. Scott grinned to himself and considered the irony of a country which banned alcohol engaging the services of a spokesman for an eponymous brand of beer.

In South and Central America, interests of the United States were also heavily under siege. Cuba and Russia continued to supply weapons and support to revolutionary groups who emulated the late Che Guevara. During Carter's four year term, Bolivia had been ruled by six different presidents. Nicaragua's former President, Anastasio Somoza Debayale lost power to left wing Sandinista guerrillas, in July 1979, and was subsequently assassinated on September 17th, in Paraguay.

Everyone at the New Year's Eve party was looking forward to Reagan's inauguration in three weeks. It had been a long time since they felt any real good would come from raising their glasses and wishing for a Happy New Year.

6:00PM – Friday January 29th 1982
Belfast, NORTHERN IRELAND

The people of Northern Ireland were accustomed to hearing bad news on the radio and television but, in 1982, they were shocked to hear about the closure of the *DeLorean* plant. The Securities and Exchange Commission had put a halt to the public stock offering. The *DeLorean* dream had come to an end.

John Z. DeLorean had transformed a green field, in the middle of a sectarian war zone, into a factory which produced an iconic sports car recognized throughout the world. Unfortunately, its stainless steel body was not able to save it from the perfect storm into which it had been launched. A downward turn in the American economy was magnified by the US dollar to British Pound exchange rate. Creative accounting strategies involving export credits, and other financial tricks, failed to compensate for these conditions. The relationship between the American car builder and the company's largest investor, the British government, had once looked like a match made in heaven. In 1982, however, it resembled a dysfunctional and broken family with each parent publicly blaming the other for its problems.

The British government, sensing there was no way to recover its eighty million dollar investment, decided to strike back like a scorned lover. Word came down from the highest offices in Whitehall, "Destroy John DeLorean and make sure he can never engage in another business venture." A plot was hatched to entrap him in a sting operation involving the smuggling of cocaine into the United States, under the guise of raising money to salvage the motor company. For this to happen the British Secret Service was charged with the task of approaching its counterpart in the United States to ask for assistance with the mission.

1:00PM – Tuesday February 2nd 1982
Cambridge, Massachusetts, USA

Neither George Mulligan nor Maria Quintero could believe their ears when Clive Noakes finished pitching the plan to them. Noakes had no idea why the CIA had specifically selected the pair to meet with him, in response to MI6's request for assistance to entrap John DeLorean. The British Secret Service did not know the Agency already had an INRA agent embedded in the *DeLorean* factory in Northern Ireland.

"Maggie's going to owe Ronnie big time if we can pull this off." Mulligan responded with a mocking reference to Prime Minister, Margaret Thatcher, and President, Ronald Reagan.

"We have the people and product to make sure this happens," Maria assured her MI6 counterpart.

After they left the British Consulate, George and Maria discussed the urgent need to find another company in Northern Ireland for Peter Reid since the *DeLorean* operation was no longer an option. The irony of the situation was not lost on them. British Secret Service was solicitng assistance at the very same time when the CIA had an operative embedded with one of Britain's most tenacious enemies.

DeLorean's destiny was doomed when Thatcher decided to close his factory. She knew she had a friend in Reagan. From the President's perspective, shutting down an automobile company that manufactured its vehicles outside the United States had absolutely no downside. Also, targeting a high profile individual in a cocaine sting served the interests of both his anti-drug campaign and law enforcement agencies. The ensuing positive media coverage would increase the administration's approval ratings in the polls, and ultimately pay dividends at the ballot box.

10:30AM – Wednesday April 17th 1982
Managua, NICARAGUA

Eduardo Santos and his wife had spent three days in Managua inspecting their various premises and meeting with their Nicaraguan associates. Prior to the Sandinistas taking power in July 1979, the country had been a key hub in their cocaine distribution network. The former regime had established trading routes with the United States which Santos exploited to conceal much of his narcotic smuggling. Historically, beef had been a major export for the Central American country and most of it was processed in meat plants in Florida. Bribes paid to customs officers and other key individuals enabled vast quantities of cocaine to enter the United States, concealed in refrigerated containers.

Of course Santos also shipped directly from Colombia to the United States. His home country was ideally situated with trade routes to both the east and west coasts. Learning from his own experience, he realized it was easier to conceal drugs in containers shipped by sea. The volume of freight, and the need to keep commerce operating, made it a better option than the airlines.

"I don't see things getting any better here for us," Klaudia lamented. "The U.S. is putting too much economic pressure on the San- dinista regime."

"We can't just close up shop," Eduardo countered. "We need to stay diversified and continue to establish bases throughout the region. Governments change hands frequently in Central and South America but one thing remains constant: if we bribe the right people, we'll get our cocaine into the United States. It looks like we'll have to route more of our product through Panama until things settle down here. The U.S. just transferred the Canal Zone back to the Panamanians. Their influence is waning there so we should be able to exploit that situation."

Chapter 6

NEW YORK, NY - 1982

CAR TROUBLE

2:15PM – Wednesday May 5th 1982
CIA Headquarters - Langley, Virginia, USA

Mulligan and Quintero were tempted to use Reid in a scheme to entrap John DeLorean but felt doing so risked exposing their operative. They knew the British were intent on the American's destruction and suspected they probably had him, and his factory, under surveillance. Accordingly, they decided to terminate Peter's involvement in the motor car company as soon as possible.

Great care would be necessary in the selection of another employer. Although they needed to provide a plausible cover, they did not want to expose him to unnecessary danger. The sectarian troubles caused strangers to be doubted and distrusted. Patrons of city bars had retreated to the security of private drinking clubs in local neighborhoods where access was restricted only to those known to the doorman. Steel railings and grilles surrounded these structures to help minimize the risk of bombings and shootings in the occupied premises. Precautions were often no different in the work environment. Fortunately, there were already several American companies with offices and factories located in Northern Ireland. With assistance from their contacts at *National Semiconductor* and the *Ford Motor Company*, Mulligan and Quintero managed to secure a position for Reid in *Autolite*, an electronics assembly division of *Ford*. It was no more than a ten minute drive from his new family home in West Belfast, and its workforce drew significantly from the Catholic community. It was a perfect choice.

As soon as they had dealt with the employment issue they turned their attention to the John Z. DeLorean situation.

"I know it's going to work, George," Maria confidently assured him. "Everyone talks when they're stuck on a transatlantic flight."

They had tapped into airline databases and were able to arrange for an undercover agent to fly, first class, on one of DeLorean's trips between London and New York. Both were in agreement about the qualities and attributes required of the candidate for the mission. Beauty was a requisite but she also needed to have a strong banking and business background. Their plan was to have their agent represent she had access to private European capital. In order for her cover to be convincing, she needed to exude an air of confidence and maturity that would come with such power. Whereas a twenty-three year old supermodel would certainly have attracted their target's attention, it was unlikely the rest of the back-story would have been plausible. Their choice was an attractive forty-one year old woman who had spent ten years of her federal employment with the Securities and Exchange Commission (SEC). She was also fluent in German and French. Alanna Miller was given the legend and documentation to support her new role as 'Monique St. Michael.' Nothing was left to chance and no detail overlooked. Temporary offices and luxury apartments were established in New York and Zurich, Switzerland, so business cards and other aspects of her background would check out.

*****

When Alanna walked into the *British Airways* executive lounge at London's Heathrow airport as 'Monique St. Michael', she had already completed the first leg of her transatlantic trip. Her first class ticket, Swiss passport, and half eaten gourmet chocolate bar were subtleties that spoke volumes. Alanna knew she would be sitting beside DeLorean on the flight to New York so she chose to ignore him for the brief time they spent together in the executive lounge, prior to boarding their flight.

"Delighted to meet you," Monique replied as the captain announced it was safe for passengers to unfasten their seat belts. *Concorde* was traveling at Mach 2 and would arrive in New York within three hours and thirty minutes.

For someone in her business not to have recognized the automobile executive would have made any other response to his introduction foolish and implausible. Their conversation on the flight was cordial but bland, given the nature of his problems as well as Miller's agenda. She decided to distract him the best way she knew. Her slim tight skirt caressed shapely, toned thighs. The neckline of her blouse plunged lower than she would have liked, but she endured the discomfort because of the obvious pleasure it gave her target as well as other male passengers in the cabin.

As *Concorde* began its descent into Kennedy Airport she discreetly gave her fellow passenger a business card.

"I'm planning to be in New York for the next two weeks, John, and I'm well aware of your problems with the SEC. When one door closes, another one opens. I may be able to help you work through this."

The American understood the importance of branding and image. While he knew time was running out for his motor company, he was conscious of the need to conceal that fact from the rest of the world. He nonchalantly accepted the card but, in reality, he was a drowning man reaching for a lifeline.

John DeLorean cleared customs without an issue. Monique was deliberately delayed by one of the immigration officers for at least fifteen minutes. When she finally exited into the airport concourse she saw a limousine driver holding a large sign with her name on it. She briefly surveyed her surroundings and immediately located the lean, suntanned figure of her target. He was alone but appeared distracted and in a hurry

●

since he kept looking down at his watch.

"Is everything alright, John?" she asked as she gave her luggage cart to the driver.

"My Town Car isn't here yet," he replied in a manner that displayed both displeasure and dismay.

"Why don't you ride with me? I can either drop you off in the city, or you can take mine once I've been dropped at my apartment." Exhausted and jet lagged from his trip and intrigued by her offer to resolve his SEC problems, he gratefully accepted Monique's invitation.

Meanwhile, two miles outside the airport, DeLorean's driver had already spent forty-five minutes hand-cuffed in the rear of an unmarked cruiser. Apparently, the number plate on his car was a match for a vehicle that had been reported stolen. Protestations of innocence were ignored, as was his request to contact his dispatcher to request a second limousine. Neither the officer nor the driver knew the traffic stop had been coordinated by George Mulligan to make sure his agent and her target, would end up in the same vehicle.

"I source North American investment opportunities for European clients," St. Michael explained, en route into the city. "I have access to substantial capital, both private and institutional. You've a nice product. The *DMC* brand is exciting and current. It wouldn't be a match for all my clients but there are a few who understand the risks and challenges involved with such an aggressive and forward thinking venture."

When the car stopped outside her apartment building on Park Avenue, DeLorean indicated he would be interested in meeting again. She took out another business card and began to write on the reverse side.

"Here's my attorney's contact information. Why don't we get a confidentiality agreement executed so my accountants can review your financials? We can arrange to meet after I've had an opportunity to look up your skirt." The Executive was caught short by the brash characterization of the accounting procedure. He was tempted to ask if he would be extended the same courtesy, but chose not to derail, what appeared to be, an extremely fortuitous encounter. Instead, he stepped out of the car so he could assist her. As Monique St. Michael alighted, she deliberately stepped forward so the dark shaded cuff of her silk stocking peeped from below her skirt.

4:05PM – Tuesday June 1st 1982
New York, New York, USA

It was the third meeting between St. Michael and DeLorean and each hoped they could finalize details of the complicated financing package that would save the motor company. The venue was the Law Office of Monique's attorney. George and Maria had chosen the firm for several reasons. It was well established with a prestigious reputation equivalent to that of *DMC*'s legal team. The partners in the firm, and their associates, had all signed affidavits which barred them from disclosing any aspect of the government's business, and its dealings with John DeLorean. Engaging the services of prominent legal counsel gave even more credibility to the story. Neither DeLorean, nor any of his executives, suspected they were the target of an elaborate sting. Another reason for selecting the high powered law firm was its address. Their offices occupied floors thirty-five through thirty-eight of the *Chrysler Building*. Since their target had been, for a brief time, an employee of *Chrysler*, George Mulligan thought the venue would introduce a sense of irony into DeLorean's predicament.

By no means had the meeting gone smoothly. It had lasted almost five hours. Sandwiches had been delivered to the conference room so negotiations could continue through lunch. Monique, her attorneys, and accountants all realized if their offer seemed 'too good to be true' DeLorean would suspect something was not right.

"I need some fresh air," Monique announced and stood up from the table. "Why don't we take a break? Come on John, let's stretch our legs."

DeLorean was not comfortable going for a private walk since he was paying tens of thousands of dollars for legal representation.

Nevertheless, the sight of her arching her back and shaking her blonde hair convinced him to abandon his legal team.

Despite the fact they had been alone together in the elevator, Monique waited until they had stepped out onto Lexington Avenue before she abruptly announced.

"*DMC* is fucked."

"Excuse me," he retorted.

"You heard me, John. I'm not telling you anything you don't already know. It's only you and me out here and what I'm about to say can't be said in a room full of lawyers." In his heart, he knew there was little probability of finding a financial lifeline for his company. Six hours on the thirty-eighth floor of the *Chrysler Building* told him St. Michael was looking less and less like a source of funding. Nevertheless, he wanted to hear what she had to say.

"If you decide not to accept the terms I'm about to offer, I'll deny ever having this conversation. Do you understand?" Monique continued after the automobile executive nodded in the affirmative. "The current market can't provide an adequate return on investment for the *DMC-12*'s production costs, however, my people will commit to investing seventy five million dollars over the next three years. We will subrogate our loans to all your creditors and we'll require an interest rate equal to prime minus one half point. No payments will be due until January 31, 1986." DeLorean was stunned. The offer was contrary to everything that had been discussed during the previous six hours.

"In return, *DMC* will create a shell corporation to import automobile components into the United States from one of our holding companies. None of this will interfere with your manufacturing operations. I'm not going to sugar coat this for you, John. We'll be shipping radiators and exhaust components, packed with cocaine, to your New Jersey warehouse. Once our people have removed the drugs, the components can be reassembled and sold for the 'after market.' This legitimate commercial enterprise will provide a perfect cover. We'll launder proceeds through a phantom set of *DMC* accounts using banks and invoices that no one in the parent company, except you, will be privy to. For this service, we'll compensate you personally, two hundred thousand dollars a month."

DeLorean knew he had two options. He could either accept St. Michael's terms or be forced to tell Johnny Carson, Sammy Davis Jr., and a host of other high profile investors, that the company was finished.

"You have what my people need and I think you'll agree they're willing to compensate you generously. It's in their interests to keep your company operating. Its international connections make it the perfect vehicle for moving product and laundering our income. All I'll need from you, John, is your assistance in setting up the shell corporation to import the auto parts from South America. This division will lease warehouse space from your parent company and we'll take care of hiring employees to oversee the business. You won't have to do anything other than provide me with details of a bank account where you want your monthly payment deposited."

"I'm guessing this all has to be a verbal agreement between us?"

"Correct. None of this can be in writing. The loan agreement my attorneys have drafted is merely a cover for the real source of capital. When we go back inside, you need to sign that contract so we can start saving your company."

Chapter 7

BOSTON, MASSACHUSETTS - 1982

ACTIVE DUTY

4:25PM – Friday June 4th 1982
Boston, Massachusetts, USA

To make sure Reid had not been followed, George Mulligan and Maria Quintero arrived at the dental office one hour ahead of schedule. It was another secure facility they liked to utilize when they needed to communicate with their young Irishman.

"I told you we had excellent medical and dental benefits," she joked.

"Well at least you didn't pick a proctologist's office."

"We need to get you transferred out of *DeLorean*," Mulligan announced, ignoring Peter's juvenile attempt at humor. He casually dropped a folder into the younger man's lap. "We could get you a research position at Queen's University but a manufacturing job would provide a better back-story for your cover. Take a look at these and tell me what you think. Maria and I like *Ford's Autolite* factory as the best option."

Reid opened the folder and thumbed through the pages containing information about companies which were either American owned or had significant trade connections with the United States.

"This one's perfect. Short Brothers, the aircraft manufacturer. It's got a heavy manufacturing element and would suit my electrical engineering background."

"They're based in East Belfast. Will that be a problem for you, Peter?" Maria asked.

"It's not far from where I used to live. I would've had a nice commute if you guys hadn't petrol bombed our home," he retorted.

"You know that was necessary to give you and your family credibility when we moved you to West Belfast. Besides, they're happy and settled in their new house, so let's just move on," she continued. "The workforce is predominantly Protestant. Not really ideal for a good Catholic boy like you!"

"*Shorts* will be perfect," Reid countered, giving Maria a flirtatious wink. "If you guys can get me a position in their quality control department, I won't need to be on the factory floor too often. I'll be able to keep to myself. There shouldn't be a problem." Reid knew better than to inquire as to who at *National Semiconductor* was assisting with his employment search in Northern Ireland. He was more concerned his new position would withstand the rigors of an INRA background verification check.

"*Shorts* has defense contracts which might also make me more appealing to both the INRA and FARC," he added.

They discussed the pros and cons of *Short Brothers* as a potential employer, then concentrated on his most recent trip to Northern Ireland. Debriefings took place on a regular monthly schedule, either in Boston, Belfast or Dublin. They always took place face to face.

"You can rinse your mouth," Maria joked, as she tilted the dentist chair forward using the pedal beside her left foot.

After Peter had left, Mulligan studied the sheet on *Short Brothers* again.

"You know, this factory may be a better fit for him than any of us realized."

"What've you got in mind?"

"They don't just manufacture planes, they also make a neat little surface to air missile system called a *Blowpipe*. One guy can take out a helicopter or low flying aircraft with this baby. The operator rests the rocket launcher on his shoulder. Its small television screen focuses on the target from when the missile is launched until its homing signal locks on."

"This sounds just like something Oli and his friends in Nicaragua would love to get their hands on."

"I was thinking the same thing. Reid working at Shorts will be perfect. It'll give credibility to his back-story for the INRA and also provide us with excellent intelligence to maybe get some of these *Blowpipe* rocket launchers for the Contras."

Providing support for the Contra rebels in Nicaragua was an extremely delicate operation. Every move was scrutinized by zealous reporters as well as Senators and Congressmen who were opposed to any type of military intervention in the Central American country. Nicaragua's Sandinista government was an ultra left-wing regime which was virulently opposed to United States' interests. Despite fears Russia would establish a second "Cuba" in the region, politicians who controlled Capitol Hill ignored President Reagan's request and restricted funding to only humanitarian operations. Meanwhile, remnants of the overthrown Somoza regime exiled and regrouped in El Salvador and Costa Rica; and with clandestine CIA support, gathered under a counter revolutionary umbrella known as the Contras. George Mulligan and his colleagues were well aware economic sanctions, and grass roots political efforts, would not be enough to overthrow the Sandinista government. Accordingly, they had contrived a scheme to raise capital by brokering surreptitious arms sales with Iran under the radar of Washington's media and government watch-dogs. The proceeds were then used by the Contras as seed capital to develop a cocaine smuggling network. It not only provided capital to support their guerrilla war against the Sandinista government in Nicaragua, but it also raised the personal net worth of everyone involved.

"Those bleeding heart liberals on Capitol Hill think we can defeat the Sandinistas by sitting around a camp fire singing 'Kumbaya',"

Mulligan lamented. "They want to hand out welfare checks to everyone, without considering where the taxes are coming from to support such programs."

"I hear you, George," Maria agreed.

She had been instrumental in coordinating the arms deal with the Iranians due to contacts she had developed when she had been posted to Tehran. Furthermore, her South American heritage, and fluent Spanish, were an enormous advantage when it came to working with the Contras.

"Don't be too harsh on welfare programs," she chastised cynically. "A lot of this money goes to buying crack cocaine, so thanks to our President's extolled 'trickle down economics' policy, our Contras get the money they need to make life miserable for the Sandinistas!"

"I guess the end justifies the means," George agreed.

7:50PM – Friday June 4th 1982
Dorchester, Massachusetts, USA

❛❛Did you hear the news?" Paddy Lynch shouted as soon as Reid
walked into *The Patriot*. "Nuala is awake!"

"Fantastic! When did all this happen?"

"Last night her eyes opened. The doctors can't believe it. They
were able to take away some of the tubes."

"That's terrific news, Paddy."

"It's going to take a lot of physical therapy before she's back
on her feet, but this is a huge first step. Typical woman though, the first
thing she asked for was her makeup." Peter laughed blissfully unaware
of the significance of her request.

"I should go over to the *Mercy* and see her right now."

"Do me a favor, Peter? Her cosmetic bag is in my office. The
hospital gave it to me when she was admitted. Would you take it in for
her?"

Peter tossed the small pink bag onto the passenger seat of his
Ford Mustang and turned the ignition key. He was oblivious to the fact
it contained the modified lipstick with undeveloped photographs of him,
which Nuala had taken for MI6. Instead, he was preoccupied with plans
for his upcoming return visit to Belfast. The INRA had planned a bombing mission using one of his remote control detonators, but they wanted
him to accompany the active unit to ensure there would be no problems.
George Mulligan and Maria Quintero were reluctant to authorize his
involvement. He had managed to convince them, however, that any per-
ceived reluctance on his part would call into question his commitment
to the INRA. Nevertheless, all three unanimously agreed they needed to

limit loss of life while they proved Peter's talent worthy of sharing with other paramilitary organizations.

"Look at you," Peter greeted through a wide smile as he walked into Nuala's room. He leaned over and kissed her on the side of the cheek, not knowing how she would react to seeing him after three years.

"We'll get a nurse to find a vase for these," he suggested and set a small bunch of flowers on the bed.

"Thanks." The young woman uttered in a hushed, raspy voice.

"How are you feeling? Your uncle Paddy asked me to bring your makeup bag." It was too much effort for her to reply. Instead, she used all her strength to tightly hold the bag against her chest. Peter could see speaking was exhausting her, so he took control of the conversation to bring her up to date with his work assignments in Belfast. He explained how *National Semiconductor* had transferred him to *Short Brothers* after the *DeLorean* assignment had been phased out. Even though he made no mention of his other activity with the INRA, he was unwittingly conveying more information than he realized. As he was chatting, she manipulated the contents of the bag so, without opening it, she could feel two lipsticks between the forefinger and thumb of her right hand. She knew if there were two of them, one had to be the camera. As he quietly explained he would soon be returning to Belfast, her mind focused on how long it would be before she could get the pictures to Clive Noakes.

"I think you need your rest." Peter remarked as he stood up. He remembered Maria Quintero's advice about avoiding emotional involvement in a relationship and this one had definitely served its purpose. "I'll be back in Boston at the end of next month," he added, landing a soft kiss on her forehead. "It's wonderful to see you're on the road to recovery."

6:05AM – Monday June 14th 1982
Lisburn, NORTHERN IRELAND

R eid and the other two members of the INRA active service unit squinted out through boarded up windows of a derelict house. His remote control detonators were reliable up to a distance of four hundred yards. Since they were safely situated three hundred yards away, the vehicle was well within range of his signal. It would be a key test of his credibility inside the active cell. From their vantage point, and using binoculars, they could see the *Ford Transit* van they had stolen a week earlier and then packed with explosives. The location had been chosen not only because it was remote, but also because it provided an uninterrupted view, in either direction, from where the van was parked. The road was regularly traveled by British Army convoys transporting men and equipment between Lisburn Army Barracks and Aldergrove International Airport. At an earlier briefing they agreed not to detonate the bomb if members of the public were at risk. The INRA was hopeful the technology Reid was bringing into service would help reduce collateral damage.

Unbeknown to his INRA companions, their electronics guru had also been working with Mulligan and Quintero to ensure the mission would be a success, without causing injury or loss of life. The CIA was well aware of the political backlash that would ensue if its mission were to cause British Army casualties.

"What the fuck!" Tommy Geraghty complained as he peered through his binoculars.

"What's up?" Peter asked, without disclosing he knew Mulligan's team was at work. Geraghty remained focused on a tour bus that, for some inexplicable reason, had stopped beside the transit van, totally obscuring his view of the booby trapped vehicle. Reid asked a second time.

"I think we're all right," Tommy muttered as he watched the driver walk to the side of the bus and struggle to lock the luggage doors which, apparently, had not been properly closed. Geraghty had been unable to see that a second man had exited the vehicle and planted another explosive device, on the far side of the transit van. The tinted windows in the bus concealed his actions and when it proceeded on its way, there was no evidence anything had happened.

Fifteen minutes later two British Army *Land Rovers* approached the *Ford* which had been packed with five hundred pounds of explosives.

"Wait for my command," Geraghty ordered. Peter opened the hinged cover of his remote control and primed the bomb by flipping the first toggle switch.

"Fucking now!" Geraghty ordered. "Kill the bastards!" Reid flipped the second switch which only detonated the device that had just been attached to the far side of the van. The small explosion rocked the vehicle, safely deflecting a minor blast away from the convoy which immediately sped away.

*****

The mission debriefing was an ugly event. Peter's remote detonation equipment had apparently functioned correctly but his commanders were puzzled and frustrated that only a small fraction of the explosives had detonated. They had hoped the newspapers would have been filled with photographs of dead and mutilated British soldiers, but instead they featured a bomb disposal team dismantling the failed booby trap. The British were also studying the electronic components which alerted them to a new level of sophisticated danger. Reid did not mention the tour bus which had stopped briefly beside the *Transit* van, since none of his companions suspected it had anything to do with the failed mission.

11:05AM – Friday June 18th 1982
Boston, Massachusetts, USA

Nuala did not notice the doctor enter her room because she was engrossed in a copy of *People* magazine, trying to catch up on her celebrity gossip. He was hovering around her bed and studying a medical clipboard when she eventually looked up from her reading.

"How are you feeling?" Clive Noakes asked the startled patient. "I would have brought you flowers but it would've looked odd for me to have a stethoscope in one hand and a bouquet in the other."

"Jesus, Clive. You're going to get me killed, coming in here like this."

"Rubbish, I've been here every week since you were admitted. This is the first time I decided you're well enough to chat."

"I have your camera." She pointed to the drawer in the bedside table. "The last two shots are of a guy called Peter Reid. He's an electronics expert employed by a company in Boston, but he works for them at *Shorts* in Belfast."

"Excellent work," Noakes acknowledged. "You've done well, Nuala. When you get back on your feet, I'll fix you up with your backpay. I've got quite a pile of envelopes at my office with your name on them. It's good to have you back in the game."

3:15PM – Sunday June 20th 1982
Palace Barracks, Holywood, NORTHERN IRELAND

L ocated midway between Belfast and Bangor, the predominantly Protestant suburb of Holywood is only fifteen minutes from Belfast city center. The political ethnicity of a neighborhood in Northern Ireland can be determined by studying its utility poles and lamp posts because, unlike the United States, political posters are rarely removed after an election. Loyalist neighborhoods, such as Holywood, are constantly decorated with Democratic Unionist Party (DUP) posters, Ulster Unionist Party (UUP) posters, as well as those extolling the virtues of splinter political organizations with similar doctrines. Any stationary surface is regarded as a legitimate location for a campaign handbill: corrugated metal fences around construction sites; boarded windows on derelict buildings; and utility poles are examples of prime real estate. In predominantly Catholic, Nationalist areas, the posters belong to either the left of center Social Democratic Labor Party (SDLP), or the more extreme Sinn Féin. Less polarized areas exhibited a blend of posters from across the political divide including those belonging to the moderate Alliance Party.

Holywood was also home to Palace Barracks, the British Army's Intelligence Headquarters in Northern Ireland. Special anti-terrorist legislation gave the British Army access to every suspect held by Northern Ireland's police force, the Royal Ulster Constabulary (RUC). A cell in Palace Barracks was not a place Republican or Nationalist sympathizers would ever want to find themselves. It took less than twenty-four hours for intelligence gathered at Nuala Mallon's bedside to find its way to Palace Barracks. Reid's electrical engineering studies at Queen's University elevated his threat level. Ironically his education was paid in full with British government grants. Noakes' counterparts in MI5, working closely with British Army intelligence officers in Palace Barracks, reacted quickly. Their suspect was employed at Short Brothers, a major cog in Britain's defense industry. It did not take long before a link was made to the recent bombing outside Lisburn. Colonel Rodney Buttersworth elected not to involve the RUC in his plans to arrest 'the terrorist'. He did not want to compromise the intelligence they had just received. Without hesitation, he asked his sergeant to make a phone call to Major Evans requesting him to come immediately to Palace Barracks. Reid was oblivious to how his life had been jeopardized by the very person he had helped save.

Within the hour, Welsh Guardsman, Major David Evans arrived at Palace Barracks. He was the Commanding Officer of the unit targeted by the INRA's unsuccessful bomb attack, one week earlier. He had no idea one of the culprits had been tracked down, or that Col. Buttersworth wanted his team to lead the raid on their suspect's family home. The INRA had specifically targeted the Guards because they had recently been posted to Northern Ireland. The plan was to launch a lethal attack on the regiment in order to demoralize its men for the duration of their tour. As soon as the Colonel returned his salute, David Evans was given the news about Peter Reid.

"I've decided not to involve the RUC," Buttersworth continued, "it only increases the risk he'll get tipped off. Your boys can pick him up at his house tomorrow morning at zero two hundred hours."

"It won't be difficult to get volunteers for this mission," the Major acknowledged. "It's just what the men need."

"He's only one piece of the puzzle, but once we get him in here, we'll get the names of his accomplices. It's a sophisticated detonator we need to counter ASAP." Buttersworth stressed.

"Thank you, Sir," the younger officer replied with a large grin on his face as he saluted. "We'll have Reid here by zero three hundred hours for your boys to start working on him."

1:55AM – Monday June 21st 1982
Belfast, NORTHERN IRELAND

R eid had lost track of time playing poker with friends from his student days at Queen's University. It was almost 2:00AM when he spotted the blue lights in his rear view mirror. He had been driving fifteen miles per hour over the limit when he was stopped for speeding on Stockman's Lane. He waited impatiently for the RUC officer to run a radio check on his license, angry and frustrated he was only minutes from his house.

"Have you been drinking this evening, sir?" the policeman asked. Not convinced by the denial, he ordered Reid out of the vehicle so he could be observed walking a straight line. The officer then conducted a breathalyzer test.

While the sobriety test was being administered, less than a mile away six British Army *Land Rovers*, full of Welsh Guards, had blocked access to Fruithill Park and surrounded the Reid family home. Hysterical protestations from his mother were ignored as soldiers systematically ransacked each room, in an effort to find her son. Col. Buttersworth had not coordinated with his RUC counterparts so the two policemen, con- temporaneously scrutinizing the results of his sobriety test, did not know they had the INRA's top bomb technician in their grasp. The patrol had unwittingly delayed Reid and caused him to continue home at a slower speed than he would normally have driven. He had just turned onto the Andersonstown Road, from the rotary junction with Kennedy Way, when he noticed the Army Land Rovers blocking the entrance to his street. Instinctively he stopped, reversed quickly, and then drove away in the opposite direction towards the Falls Road. The headlights on one of the

Land Rovers turned on as soon as he made the U-turn which reinforced his decision not to continue home. He had been involved in the bombing of a British Army patrol one week earlier and feared the military presence was not merely a coincidence. His vehicle opened up a considerable distance as the soldiers gave chase. Taking a left onto the Glen Road he disappeared for several seconds, just long enough to confuse his pursuers. After weaving through a maze of dark side streets, he abandoned his car and then scaled a fence into Milltown Cemetery where he would hide until daybreak.

Concealed by the shadow of a Guardian Angel statue, Reid calmed himself and took stock of his situation. He decided to telephone his parents in the morning to ascertain if he was, in fact, the focus of the British Army activity in his street. He composed himself and considered the possibility paranoia may have caused him to panic unnecessarily. He concluded, correctly, that the RUC was unaware of his involvement with the INRA since he had not been arrested when its officers stopped him for speeding. If the British Army was indeed looking for him, he would need to get in contact with George or Maria as quickly as possible.

It was 6:30AM when he made his way onto the Falls Road where he caught a bus to the city center, found a public telephone, and anxiously dialed the number. His father answered but he could hear his mother in the background screaming hysterically, "Is that our Peter? Where is he? What's going on?" Sensing their line was probably tapped, he chose not to speak. Using his cuff, he wiped any fingerprints off the receiver and immediately replaced it. He was unhappy about having to remain silent, but realized there was nothing he could have said that would have made the situation any better. He knew the only viable course of action was to get out of Northern Ireland as soon as possible.

He decided not to go to the American Consulate on Queen's

Street. Not only was it located opposite a police station, but it also required a physical search to access Belfast's secured pedestrian precinct zone. Since he had evaded capture by the Welsh Guards, he knew the RUC would have been instructed to apprehend him on sight. Consequently, he made his way to Donegal Square East and boarded a bus to the Malone Road. He sat for several minutes pondering his predicament watching the pay phone from where he had called home. As his bus pulled away from the curb, two unmarked police cars screeched to a halt right beside the phone box. Four plain clothed RUC officers jumped out and proceeded to scour the area. They were too late. He had managed to stay one step ahead of them. Commuter traffic was heavy so it took almost twenty minutes before he got off the bus at Derryvolgie Avenue. His plan was to go to the home of Andrew Johnson, the American Consul General. He knew the house because he had attended a 'St. Patrick's Day' cocktail party there with Maria Quintero.

The private home was heavily secured. He pushed the buzzer at the gate, gave his name and stated he was an associate of George Mulligan with urgent business for Andrew Johnson. The information appeared to have little impact on the person monitoring the closed circuit television screen. Inside, however, the Consul General had not yet left for work. When he was told about the unexpected visitor, he immediately gave instructions to unlock the door. Peter heard a click then a voice instructed him to enter where he was searched by a tall, swarthy and muscular man who looked capable of snapping Reid's neck. After their brief but confidential meeting, Johnson informed his wife their guest would be staying for the foreseeable future.

"Can we put Peter in the guest room, dear?" the American diplomat asked. "He didn't get much sleep last night and he needs a shower."

"Yes, of course! You two look about the same size, so I'll get some of your sweats while I throw his clothes in the wash," Mrs. Johnson offered graciously.

"You get some rest, young man, and we'll work on a plan when I get back from the office this evening."

*****

By 7:00PM, when Johnson arrived home, Peter was rested, showered, shaved and fed.

"Well, you certainly kicked a hornets nest," the Consul General observed as he tossed a copy of the *Belfast Telegraph* onto the coffee table. There, on its front page, was a picture of Reid below a headline linking him to recent terrorist attacks.

"Maria Quintero will be here in the morning," he continued. "You've to keep a low profile for the present time. No phone calls and absolutely no stepping outside this house."

Peter studied the photograph and tried to identify when, and where, it had been taken. The background was somewhat blurred and grainy, but he was able to identify an American style electrical outlet on the wall behind his head. On further scrutiny, he realized the photograph had been taken in Nuala Mallon's apartment. It made no sense, however, because he had consciously avoided situations that involved photography. For the remainder of the night he contemplated the problem but his mind kept returning to the same question. Could Nuala Mallon have given his picture to the RUC or British Army? Was there a correlation between her recovery and the perilous predicament in which he found himself?

10:05AM – Wednesday of June 23rd, 1982
Belfast, NORTHERN IRELAND

Since she had flown into Dublin and taken a bus to Belfast, Maria Quintero had been able to meet with Peter Reid without leaving documented evidence that she had entered Northern Ireland. She took a taxi from the center of Belfast to Queen's University, and then a brisk ten minute walk through its campus. She wanted to be absolutely certain she was not followed to the Consul General's residence.

"We don't plan on moving you for at least another two weeks," she explained. "I've brought some clothes and toiletries because this'll be your home until we firm up a plan."

Peter shared his concerns about Nuala Mallon and asked that Maria not say, "I told you so."

"Now's not the time to be assigning blame but since you brought it up," she shook her head as if to rebuke. "Our first step is to get you down to the Republic so you can make contact with your INRA colleagues," she continued. "They're going to know Northern Ireland isn't safe for you and this whole episode may even help us in our plan to infiltrate FARC. You'll need to suggest they lend you out to other paramilitary groups. They'll probably suggest ETA, the Basque Nationalists in Spain. We're not interested in ETA, so you'll need to object."

"OK, but what're we goin' to do about Nuala?"

"We, are not gonna do anything," Maria replied with an emphasis on the word, "We."

"I'll personally be taking care of Ms. Mallon. Can't believe we went to so much bother to save her life? Don't worry about her. I'll be back next week and we'll have a new ID for you with an appropriate legend, one you could've manufactured yourself so it won't spook your INRA friends. You won't be able to get in and out of the UK anymore as Peter Reid."

"It's not all bad," Peter joked. "At least I'll be able to drink in the Felons Club from now on."

"I thought you actually had to be convicted of a crime to be a member there?" Maria inquired as she continued the joke.

7:20AM – Friday July 2nd, 1982
Boston, Massachusetts, USA

Thanks to physiotherapy, Nuala Mallon was not only delighted with her progress but also with the prospect of discharge from the hospital. She had been submitted to a battery of neurological tests and they had all yielded positive results. The medical team also had moved her to a private room closer to the physiotherapy department. The morning's breakfast had been served earlier than usual, but that suited her. She had been awake from six o'clock reading fashion magazines.

Maria Quintero smiled smugly, delighted with the success of her plan. She was dressed as a nurse's aide. The narcotic she had just put into the orange juice would act within minutes. She pretended to review notes on the chart as if checking to confirm the patient had been given the correct meal. There was no doubt.

"This doesn't taste right," Mallon stuttered as she dropped the plastic cup onto the tray in front of her. The young Irishwoman knew something was very wrong but she could do nothing about it. Quintero lifted the remainder of the juice and flushed it down the toilet in the adjoining bathroom, then carefully rinsed any trace from the cup.

Mallon did not know Maria Quintero had already been to the apartment to inspect its décor. She wanted to see if it matched the background in Reid's photograph. Although Paddy Lynch had removed Nuala's belongings and terminated her lease, her former roommates had no problem getting another girl to share the rent. A sham call pretending the girls had won concert tickets from a local radio station was all it took to gain access to the premises. Convincing them she needed to take a picture for a publicity shot seemed plausible to the unsuspecting 'contest winners'. For the price of four tickets to a J. Geils concert, Quintero was able to confirm Peter's suspicions. The background in the photograph, did indeed match the apartment.

Maria detected a look of horror as she leaned over to tell Nuala she should never have photographed Peter Reid. She removed one of the pillows and placed it over the frightened face, taking care not to disturb the long red hair. The narcotic prevented her victim from putting up a struggle. Three minutes later, she replaced the pillow and checked to ensure there was no pulse. The vacant stare in Mallon's eyes was confirmation the mission had been successfully executed. Quintero opened the door and pushed the food cart into the corridor and continued in the direction of the elevators. The hospital would soon be serving breakfast but, by that time, Maria and her cart would be long gone.

Chapter 8

DUBLIN, REPUBLIC OF IRELAND - 1982

ON THE RUN

10:05AM – Sunday August 22nd, 1982
Dublin, REPUBLIC OF IRELAND

R eid had tried to grow a beard but it was too itchy on his skin so he settled for a moustache and cut his hair short, in an attempt to alter his appearance. Maria Quintero and her team had helped set him up in an apartment with a new identity which he had used to get a driver's license. Within the week, he also expected to receive an Irish passport, issued in the name of Martin Quinn. The original Martin Quinn had been born in Newry, but his family had emigrated from Northern Ireland to America when he was sixteen. Unfortunately, the rebellious teenager was killed in a car accident thus providing the new identity for Reid.

"I got the idea when I remembered a benefit for a girl, with no health insurance, who was injured in a car crash in Boston," he lied to his two INRA comrades. "It was ridiculously easy."

Tom Geraghty and Sean Ryan had made the trip south of the border after Reid contacted an INRA safe house in Dublin.

"My biggest problem is cash," he continued so his story would have more credibility. "I know it was risky, but I emptied my bank account the morning after my home was raided, otherwise I'd have nothin'." Geraghty and Ryan not only found his story plausible, but were also impressed by his resourcefulness.

"And to think we were worried about you," Geraghty laughed. "We thought you were nabbed by the Brits, but your family told us you hadn't come home."

"You spoke to them," Reid asked anxiously.

"We did, and got them a contractor to repair the damage after the fuckers ransacked your house."

"I don't know if they got it, but I sent a letter inside an envelope addressed to our next door neighbor. I suspected the Brits would be monitoring our mail but I wanted my parents to know I was okay. I'm hoping they got it. I'm sure the line is tapped, so I couldn't phone."

"We've no idea how they fingered you. No one else was picked up."

Reid could not share with them what he knew about Nuala Mallon. Instead, he used the situation to plant the idea about relocation to Colombia.

"Something went wrong and now I'm fucked when it comes to living in Ireland. At least for the next few years," he sighed. "I don't trust the Garda down here any more than I trust the RUC. I've no doubt they've undercover agents in the Republic! I'm lucky I've got this new identity, but I don't want to push my luck. I need to get out of the country."

"Our ETA friends in Spain could use your help for a few months," Geraghty suggested.

"My Spanish is good but I don't think Spain is an option. It's too close to Gibraltar. I'm thinking somewhere further afield."

"How about this," Ryan offered. "I met a couple of FARC guerrillas last year in Libya and I know you'd be a great asset to their program."

"I should have my new passport next week and I plan on getting away as soon as that happens. Gettin' lost in South America would work. If you can set that up, I'd be cool with it, but after what happened in Belfast they're goin' to have to pay me. I don't have a job now. I can't afford to live there without money." Reid knew if he did not make compensation an issue, he risked making Geraghty and Ryan suspicious.

"I'll try to pick up a job teaching English when I get there. I could teach electrical engineering, but that might attract attention. The Brits have embassies everywhere. It would be too risky." Ryan gave

Reid the contact information for law offices in New York and Dublin. These would function as intermediaries once he got settled in Colombia.

"Also, you can't be negotiating employment terms with these guys." Ryan continued. "When you get there, set up a bank account and we'll wire you three thousand dollars every month. I'll arrange for our FARC friends to pay us. The leadership council has been talking about diversifying by taking our mission beyond Northern Ireland, so you goin' there can only help this. Don't worry about your family. We'll look after them and make sure they know you're alright. It's too soon to arrange face time because they'll be under surveillance for the foreseeable future." He handed Peter an envelope containing two thousand Irish punts and made arrangements to meet the following week, after his passport had been issued.

"I'm in a flat with two students," Peter explained. "They think I'm trying to transfer from Leeds University. I had to come up with a story so I picked a university in England I hoped they'd no connection with. I keep to myself and they haven't quizzed me. Paying them two month's rent up front did the trick, so they're happy."

6:30AM – Tuesday October 19th, 1982
Sharon, Massachusetts, USA

Clive Noakes did the same thing he always did when he had a problem that needed quiet contemplation. A keen ornithologist, he loved to immerse himself in the tranquility of the Massachusetts Audubon Sanctuary in Sharon, Massachusetts. He spent many happy hours studying the huge variety of birds that lived there primarily during the summer months. International postings had enabled him to amass a considerable log of personal sightings. Many dated back to 1956 when, as a precocious ten year old, he hiked the English Lake District with his father. Sometimes his expertise was used as cover when MI6 sent him on reconnaissance missions. He often travelled using an Irish passport, which he held legally, because his mother had been born in Dublin but moved to England when she was a child. The passport, plus a sound knowledge and interest in birds, provided a perfect cover for traveling to foreign countries with cameras, binoculars and recording equipment. As long as the migration pattern and calendar could be substantiated for the particular bird species Noakes could assimilate with other ornithologists, while going about the business of Her Majesty's Secret Service.

His love of birds had taught him the importance of patterns and routines. Even though the official death certificate stated Nuala Mallon had died from complications following a road traffic accident, Noakes was not convinced. He had narrowed down the options to three possible scenarios: (1) The cause of the young woman's death was exactly as it had been recorded in the coroner's report; (2) Paddy Lynch, or one of his crew, had uncovered her agenda and murdered her; (3) Some unknown party was responsible. He considered each option carefully. The official report seemed vague and imprecise considering Nuala had been under constant medical attention. Furthermore, he had personally infiltrated the hospital on a regular basis to observe her progress. She had been subjected to brain scans, and all types of tests and examinations, none of which had given any cause for concern. Accordingly, he concluded his confidential informant had been murdered and the prime suspect was Paddy Lynch. He continued to be perturbed, however, by one piece of the puzzle. "Whoever killed her must've had access to the coroner's office to cover their tracks," he postulated.

A cardinal interrupted Clive's thought process as it flittered from one branch to another on a sugar maple at the edge of a clearing, about fifty feet away. The colorful collage of fall leaves enabled the bird to blend in with its surroundings. The irony of the situation was not lost on him. Whoever killed Mallon had to have been someone, or some organization, with serious resources and connections. "It had to have been an agency of the American government," he determined.

He put down the binoculars and took stock of where he was in his analysis. "Why would the Americans want her dead?" The only answer to make sense was that she had exposed one of their agents. Since her contacts were Irish, he wondered if the Americans had an operative who was somehow connected with Paddy Lynch's INRA cell. Each conclusion he came to led him further along an implausible train of thought. "Is Peter Reid an American agent?" Noakes asked himself. He did not know the answer to that question, but he knew the Irishman had been working for an American company in Northern Ireland. He wiped the lenses of his binoculars before returning them to their case. Of one thing he was certain. His CIA counterparts would never admit to anything. The more he thought about it, he suspected even his own colleagues would find it difficult to believe the Americans were complicit in a bombing campaign that targeted British soldiers. Noakes accepted the reality of the situation. He knew he needed irrefutable evidence before he could share his suspicions with anyone. Until then he had nothing but a crazy and implausible theory. Besides, he had other problems to solve. He needed to infiltrate Paddy Lynch's cell again because his informant was dead, and he was not convinced he knew why.

Later that afternoon in his Cambridge office, Noakes received a phone call from George Mulligan in Langley. The conversation was short and to the point.

"Scott Hamilton has just spoken to Rupert Huntley-Palmer in London. I don't know if you've heard already but DeLorean was arrested today. He's charged with conspiracy to obtain and distribute fifty-five pounds of cocaine, worth twenty-four million dollars. The whole thing was videotaped so you'll be able to see how it all went down."

Chapter 9

COLOMBIA - 1983

FINDING FARC

4:55PM – Tuesday March 22nd 1983
Bogotá, COLOMBIA

It had been more than four months since Peter Reid moved to Colombia, nevertheless, his INRA colleagues had been unable to set up a meeting with their FARC counterparts. Maria Quintero had warned nothing would happen until FARC had thoroughly checked him out. Accordingly, he could not be seen in the company of anyone who would give the guerrillas cause for concern.

Initially the change of pace suited the Irishman and he took advantage of the opportunity to explore the city sights. Maria had helped find an apartment and arranged for him to teach conversational English classes at a university. "Practically an unlimited budget," Reid sighed sarcastically, "and I have to live in a studio apartment with no A/C." The pseudo-bohemian neighborhood was mainly home to students and academics who were disillusioned with the government.

Care had been taken to ensure everything supported his cover as an INRA soldier on the run from British authorities. Total immersion in Colombian life elevated his proficiency in Spanish so, when he taught the students he was comfortable conversing with them. As the last one exited the classroom, Peter recognized the familiar face of Sean Ryan, peering in from the corridor.

"How's it goin' man?" Ryan asked as he pretended to shadow box his friend.

"Don't start what you can't finish," Reid warned in jest, initially squaring off against his INRA comrade.

"Where can you get a proper beer around here?"

After several hours and many drinks, Ryan and Reid were feeling relaxed and happy.

"I may as well be on another planet when it comes to gettin' news from back home," Peter lamented. "I'm reduced to listening to the fuckin' *BBC World Service!*"

"We're still fightin' the good fight and tryin' to find out how your cover was blown. Paddy Lynch thinks there's a mole in his Boston cell. I flew out here via Boston to pay my respects. His niece passed away after a car accident or something. You probably met her – Nuala Mallon? Anyway, Lynch asked me to give you that news, if I saw you. I didn't tell him I'd be seein' you. If there's a leak, we definitely don't want to disclose your location."

Peter was shocked but not entirely surprised by what he had just heard. He recalled the warm June night, at the home of the American Consul General, when he saw his face in the newspaper. He knew he had been betrayed to the British authorities and when he recognized the background in the picture, he suspected the culprit was Nuala Mallon. He had shared his suspicions with Maria Quintero but, from that point on, had not given the young Irishwoman much thought. His own situation was more serious and urgent. Despite his inebriation, he managed to continue the conversation with Ryan.

"Agreed, but I'm sure you didn't come out here for fun," he continued.

"You're right. Our friends here are interested in meeting you. They told me to stay at the Alicante Hotel and wait for contact."

"Are you sure you can trust these people? I don't need a repeat of Belfast!"

"My contact here is solid, Peter. You don't need to worry about Carlos Falcao. I've meet him twice in Libya and once in San Sebastian. He's definitely a mover and a shaker in FARC. His father was a journalist who refused to back down when he was warned to stop investigating corrupt government officials. Six *Polaroids* were later mailed to his editor showing, in graphic detail, the final horrific hours of his life. Vincente Falcao's body, however, was never found. The police investigation cited alleged gambling debts as a motive for his abduction but, just as the newspaper expected, no arrests were ever made. The photographs were taken by the police as evidence but were conveniently lost. Falcao's life mission is to overthrow the government of Colombia and avenge his father's death."

10:05AM – Thursday March 24th 1983
Bogotá, COLOMBIA

❝Jesus, Sean, you've been here two days now and nothing's happened," Peter complained.

"What can I tell you? These people are thorough and cautious."

The Irishmen sipped black coffee and looked out over the plaza. The morning sun cast a shadow of a church steeple across the tables where they were seated, outside the Alicante Hotel.

"Well, you're a better man than me. I couldn't do it. I couldn't live anywhere where I couldn't get a good cup o' tea."

"Well, it's not like I've got a choice!"

"Señores. Can I get you anything else?" the waiter asked as he hovered over them.

"No gracias. We're all set." Peter acknowledged. The waiter stooped a little lower so none of the other breakfast guests could hear.

"In thirty seconds, two motorcycles will stop at the curb. They will bring you to Carlos Falcao," he instructed.

Each motorcycle rider had an extra helmet for his passenger but safety was not the reason for the precaution. The inside surface of each dark tinted visor had been spray-painted black, which meant neither Peter nor Sean could see where they were going.

Twenty minutes into the trip, the driving conditions deteriorated. Both men correctly surmised they were no longer traveling on a paved surface. Without warning, the bikes stopped and the two passengers were ordered to dismount and remove their helmets. Then the motorcycles disappeared leaving the two Irishmen in the company of six heavily armed paramilitaries.

"Vamonos," one of the soldiers shouted with a signaling motion of his Galil assault rifle. Thanks to Maria Quintero's meticulous preparation, Reid recognized the Israeli developed weapon which was manufactured under license by Colombia's *Indumil* corporation.

The group hiked for about an hour through the jungle which expended as much energy as a four hour run through the streets of Boston. It was evident Ryan had not benefited from Quintero's coaching.

"Too much *Guinness*," he replied in response to Peter's teasing about his fitness. "but I could murder a cold beer right now."

The FARC guerrillas had no problem with the pace because they were chewing coca leaves mixed with a little lime powder. The drug which modern society had labeled, "PUBLIC ENEMY #1," has been a source of sustenance in South American culture for centuries. Neither Irishman knew what the guides were chewing and spitting. They had no idea it was the reason their escorts were able to fight the fatigue caused by the oppressive humidity and altitude. Each guerrilla carried a little pouch containing small wads of neatly folded coca leaves. Their ancestors had learned when these were chewed along with a small amount of finely ground sea shells, the effect was invigorating. The shells, or other substitutes such as burned roots, raise the saliva's pH which then acts as a catalyst for extracting cocaine from the coca leaves.

3:30PM – Thursday March 24th 1983
FARC Guerrilla Camp, COLOMBIA

The FARC encampment, into which Sean Ryan and Peter Reid had been taken, comprised of at least twenty tents. Despite being many miles deep in the jungle, the guerrillas had managed to equip themselves adequately. Radio communications, computers and other electronic devices were kept operational by the use of several small generators. Peter took note of a large antenna strapped to a tree at the perimeter of the clearing.

"Sean!" boomed a loud voice with a strong Latino accent.

If modern science had enabled Che Guevara and Fidel Castro to have a child together, Reid was sure he would have looked like the man who was marching towards them. Carlos Falcao greeted them flashing a huge smile showcasing two gold canines which glistened in the afternoon sun. The magazine cartridge belts crisscrossing his chest cut into Ryan's ribs as the two men embraced in a friendly hug. His compatriot was spared the painful ritual and received a strong handshake instead as Sean introduced him to Carlos.

"You must be hungry," their host surmised, "Let's eat."

The men feasted on a wild boar which had been slow cooked over an open fire.

"Do you like movies?" Falcao asked. Their host did not wait for an answer. "I love movies," he continued and helped himself to another slice of pork using a razor sharp ten inch Bowie knife. "Did you know we have a movie business here in Colombia? It's an important part of our economy."

He skillfully balanced the spinning blade on the tip of his middle finger as gold canines ripped into the meat. Although Reid was intrigued to hear about the movie industry, he was distracted by the glittering and sparkling mouth. With the panache of a magician waving a wand, Carlos signaled to one of his men.

"Just like in Hollywood," he proclaimed proudly, "we have found the movie business to be very profitable and today you're going to see me direct FARC's next box office hit!"

Within thirty seconds, the guerrillas had set up a video camera on a tripod and pointed it in the direction of a terrified young man and woman. The two unfortunates were then forced, at gun point, to kneel approximately twelve feet in front of the lens. They both appeared to be in their early twenties and were very distressed by their predicament. The young man, Antonio Barreto, was the sole heir to the *Barreto Trucking Corporation*. He and his wife, Katarina, had been married only six months earlier. The newlywed's marital bliss had come to a screeching halt when Falcao's gang abducted them as they left their favorite restaurant.

"Sound is so important," their Colombian host continued. "Many directors don't concentrate enough on sound. If my movies are going to make money, it's important the audience hear the fear." His gold teeth flashed again in the sunlight as he laughed heartily. "Hey, that would be a great name for our FARC movie company! *HEAR THE FEAR PRODUCTIONS.*"

The few guerrillas who understood English agreed with their leader and joined in the fun. The others just grinned. Ryan and Reid were unsure what to do. They were, however, certain about one thing. They had absolutely no desire to star in a '*HEAR THE FEAR PRODUCTION*'.

"Peter, when I give you the signal, I need you to shout, ACTION, just like in Hollywood." Reid nodded in the affirmative. "You seem a little pale. Was the pork not to your liking?"

"Everything's good, thank you Carlos. It's just my Irish complexion."

Falcao tied a bandana across his face and stood behind the terrified young woman. He gripped a fistful of her long, jet black hair with his left hand and tapped her right shoulder with the blade of his Bowie knife.

"Antonio, do you remember your lines? We have a guest assistant director on set and I want to make a good impression." Carlos explained in Spanish to his fellow actors. Reid had never worked in the movie business, but they were a natural team. On Falcao's silent signal, the Irishman uttered the instruction, "ACTION."

Instantly, Antonio started to recite his lines with the emotion and sincerity of an Oscar winning performance. Even Ryan, with his limited knowledge of Spanish, was moved. He picked out words, here and there, and was able to get the gist of what the actor was saying. He seemed to be pleading to his, 'Papa,' there were also references to: 'dinero; Jesus Christ; and Katarina.' Falcao kept a grip on the young woman's hair and when her husband had finished his soliloquy, he jerked her head back and stared down into her eyes. Antonio watched helplessly as the Bowie knife carefully lifted a tear that had started to trickle down his bride's cheek.

"I want you to taste your wife's fear and share the experience with your Papa," Falcao growled as he positioned the blade in front of the male victim's lips. Reid could tell the performance had not been rehearsed. There was an authenticity and realism emanating from the young actor that the camera was picking up. Carlos tilted the knife slightly as the young husband's tongue captured the tear which, as if by magic, reappeared in the corner of his eye.

"Ay, Madre de Dios!" Falcao exclaimed, "This is marvelous. Antonio, I need you to keep very still because I want to, as they say, kick it up a notch. Remember, this is for your Papa back home." The terrorized victim's eyes welled up. "I need you to zoom in on Antonio's left eye," the guerrilla leader instructed as he gently nicked the skin immediately below the tear drop. The depression in the skin was just enough to cause the tear to roll onto the blade and mix with a drop of blood that had appeared simultaneously. Never in their wildest dreams had Ryan and Reid envisaged participating in such a spectacle.

Antonio stared into his wife's eyes and tried to comfort her as Falcao held the weapon in front of her lips. She, in turn, attempted to communicate with her father-in-law by staring into the camera as she licked the blade clean.

"Bravo!" Carlos exclaimed as all three performers stared into the camera. "Normally we like to inject a sense of urgency into our negotiations by including a souvenir, such as a finger or perhaps an ear. Today, Antonio and Katarina have been outstanding so I think we'll reward their hard work by breaking with this tradition."

He then released his grip on the young woman's hair and steadied her head against the outside of his thigh, with the face of the knife pressed against her cheek. Methodically, he trimmed a lock of her ebony hair and used it to wipe away a tiny trail of blood that had trickled down Antonio's cheek. Turning to the camera one more time, Falcao announced he would enclose the hair with the video tape so Señor Barreto would have a memento in the event he chose not to pay the two million dollar ransom.

"You have one week to comply with the instructions which accompany this tape," the FARC guerrilla warned, "otherwise I will mail back your son and daughter-in-law to you, one piece at a time."

He motioned in Peter's direction but the Irishman was totally absorbed with the proceedings and did not pick up on the signal. Falcao repeated the gesture, staring intensely and making a slicing motion across his own throat with his left hand. Reid immediately remembered he was the assistant director for the shoot!

"CUT!" he shouted.

"It's a wrap!" Falcao announced with a grin. "You guys were great. I've no doubt Papa will have you released very soon."

The distraught newlyweds were re-shackled and taken back to one of the tents. Reid pondered their plight, convinced of the ruthlessness of the FARC guerrillas. He considered how rapidly his circumstances had changed. Only one week earlier he had been lamenting Ryan had been unable to communicate with them.

"So Peter, Sean tells me you are some sort of electronics whiz-kid." Reid decided it was not the time to be modest.

"He's correct."

"He also tells me you have talents that would be a major help to FARC."

"I'm certain I can bring major improvements to your bomb making techniques," Reid boasted.

"That wouldn't be difficult but I doubt you've seen our top secret technology," Carlos confided with a smile. "Do you want to see one of our bean detonators?"

"Bean detonators?" he responded, not certain he had heard correctly.

Carlos ordered one of his men to get the detonators and he returned with a sack of beans and one gallon paint can.

"This technique has never failed us," he explained. He filled the can with dried beans but, before pressing down the lid added water to the brim. "In three or four hours the beans will absorb enough water to swell and pop off this lid. We set a trigger switch on the lid that closes a detonator circuit when it pops off. This gives our men time to leave the scene after the bomb has been placed."

The men discussed the pros and cons of various explosives and firearms. Before he went undercover, Maria and George had arranged for Reid to undergo a three week firearms training course in Quantico, Virginia. They also told him to join a gun club in Easton, Massachusetts, so he would have a plausible story to explain his expertise. Accordingly, he used his knowledge in the conversation despite his limited active service with the INRA. It was obvious Falcao was conducting an informal interview and Reid appeared to impress the FARC leader.

Without warning, the lid suddenly popped off the can and interrupted their conversation in mid sentence.

"I thought you said it takes between three and four hours?" Reid challenged.

"Shit happens," the guerrilla chuckled, "but now that we have you on board it should happen a lot less."

Peter considered how rapidly events had unfurled, just as George Mulligan and Maria Quintero had warned. His mentors had also told him that when nothing appears to be happening, it is often not the case. He had, in fact, been under surveillance by Falcao and FARC ever since Sean Ryan made his initial approach. The Americans had insisted they avoid all communication for six months. Consequently, FARC investigators discovered nothing about his past other than what Ryan had conveyed. In order to avoid British Intelligence, Reid also avoided contact with Paddy Lynch in Boston.

"Let's get you back to town," their host suggested. "We'll get together next week and make arrangements to set you up with everything you'll need to help us."

"I'm returning to Belfast on Saturday, so I'm going to leave you two to work together from here on, but I'll be back in a few months," Ryan explained.

"Before you go, my Irish friends, there's one more thing I want to show you. As you can see from our bean detonator demonstration, our methods are basic but they are effective. Both of you have been welcomed into our FARC family and with that privilege comes responsibility. Nothing you've seen or heard today can ever be spoken about. If Pepe could speak he would tell you there are serious consequences to such behavior."

Falcao explained Pepe was one of the motorcycle riders who had transported them from the city to his camp, earlier that morning.

"We've been watching him for some time and discovered exactly why he was so interested in helping our cause."

The two Irishmen turned around to meet Pepe and saw a motorcyclist standing behind them. He was not wearing a helmet, but had placed it on the ground beside him.

"Forgive me gentlemen for the confusion," Carlos apologized. "This is Hector; he's replacing Pepe for the return trip." Hector knelt down and gently opened the visor on the helmet at his feet to reveal Pepe's motionless face.

"If only he could talk, he'd do a better job explaining how serious we are about confidentiality," the guerrilla continued. "Hector and my men will get you back to the city safely."

Without warning, Carlos stepped forward and gave both men a friendly slap on the back. Peter wanted to vomit but managed to smile and give the impression he was unfazed. He concentrated on the two gold teeth that looked like book ends on a shelf and managed to control his breathing.

"I know what you're thinking, boys. This seems like a waste of a perfectly good helmet, but it makes it easier to return Pepe's head to Police HEAD QUARTERS!" The Colombian laughed heartily at his own joke as Ryan and Reid followed their guides out of the camp.

In the following days, Pepe's colleagues would get an insight into the perils of working undercover to infiltrate FARC. The lesson was not lost on Reid who wondered if capture by the British Army might be preferable.

10:05AM – Sunday March 27th, 1983
Bogotá, COLOMBIA

P eter Reid had just taken the first sip of his morning coffee when he saw two gold teeth smiling at him.

"Muy buenos días, Carlos," he greeted, in an effort to impress the Colombian with his Spanish.

"My young Irish friend, how are you today, hombre?" Without waiting for a response, he snapped his fingers to catch the waiter's attention. "Today we're going to a football game. Not like your Irish sport of kick the ball and chase it. Proper football, the way it's supposed to be played."

"Is soccer big in Colombia?" Peter asked, innocently pretending not to know the answer.

"Are you crazy?" Carlos quickly realized from the grin on Reid's face that the Irishman had been teasing him with the question. "You're a funny guy, Peter. You're a funny guy."

*****

"Do you go to many games?" Reid asked as the two men approached the soccer stadium.

"I go to a few home games each year but that's only when I've business to discuss with the team's owner, Eduardo Santos. He's a generous benefactor of our revolutionary struggle. He's got many commercial interests and has agreed to employ you so you'll have a job and everything you'll need to help us with our bomb making." Falcao motioned for Reid to follow him toward a small door, away from where fans were entering the stadium.

"This is where you go when you don't have a ticket," the Colombian explained with a grin. He gave a surreptitious signal to the imposing gentleman standing guard which went unseen by his Irish guest. Quickly and silently the door opened so they could enter and make their way to the owner's private box.

"A word of warning for you, my friend! No jokes about soccer. Mr. Santos takes it very seriously."

The game was not scheduled to begin for twenty minutes. They entered the private lounge adjoining a block of premium seats situated immediately behind the dug-out of the home team.

"Carlos, how are you?" an attractive woman greeted as the two men entered.

"Very well, thank you, Klaudia. How are you?" he enquired politely, flashing his gold teeth before affectionately kissing her on each cheek. "Allow me to introduce my friend. Peter Reid, this is Klaudia Santos. Her husband Eduardo owns the team."

"Welcome, Peter. It's a pleasure to meet you. Please excuse my husband, he's with the coach and players in the changing room. He likes to say a few words before every game."

"How is little Xavier?" Falcao asked.

"Growing like a weed. Today he's getting spoiled by Eduardo's mother."

Reid could not believe the man who was conversing so eloquently was the same evil psychopath who had cut the head off an undercover police officer. He also had absolutely no idea that the woman, chatting so lovingly about her son, was every bit as evil.

The stadium erupted in a deafening roar as players spilled out onto the field. At the same time, Eduardo Santos returned to his wife and guests in the private lounge where he was introduced to the young Irishman.

"I've heard very good things about you, Mr. Reid. Tomorrow, I want you and Carlos to come to my office so we can set you up with everything you need, but in the meantime, let's enjoy the game!"

Santos raised his beer towards Peter who returned the gesture. As the glasses met, Carlos and Klaudia also joined in the toast. Eduardo Santos emptied his drink in one gulp. The game, unfortunately, did not live up to anyone's expectations. With only minutes remaining in the second half, events took an ominous turn for the home side. Their star forward was tackled harshly which resulted in a frightening crack as his tibia snapped. South American soccer players have been known to embellish the consequences of questionable tackles but, that afternoon, there was no need for number eleven to do so. The home crowd's reaction was to be expected. Their anger and frustration was magnified because the referee did not witness the foul. He had chosen that very moment to confer with his linesmen as to how many minutes of play remained. The official's brief encounter meant the linesman's view of the tackle was also obscured precisely when the players collided. The club's owner could not believe his eyes. It was clear neither his yelling nor that of forty thousand fans would influence the referee to make a call. Santos jumped up from his seat. As he shuffled past Falcao he tapped him on the shoulder and signaled for him to follow. Reid consciously avoided catching the attention of either man. It was obvious his host was irate and he knew he did not want to get involved in that conversation.

"I feel so sorry for Marcos," Klaudia Santos confided as the star player was carried off the field on a stretcher. "He got a call from the coach of our national team last week. This is such a shame."

"Señora Santos, would you like more wine?" a waitress asked.

"Yes thank you. It looks as if my husband will be tied up for some time."

"Would you like another beer, Señor?" Peter looked away from the action on the field to decline the offer, but when he saw the waitress was actually Maria Quintero he hesitated, took a deep breath to hide his surprise, and replied.

"Why not?" For months he had operated without communication from anyone. Seeing Maria unexpectedly, was not only a relief but also a concern. As she handed the drinks to them, Eduardo Santos was finishing his conversation with Carlos Falcao on the other side of the luxury box.

"I don't want anything to happen to the other player. He was just playing the game, but I don't want to see that man in my stadium ever again. Do I make myself clear?"

Carlos Falcao immediately left the room and made his way quickly to the changing rooms. He wanted to get a good look at the referee as the players and officials came off the field. Once he had identified his target, he quickly exited the building.

Fifteen minutes later he followed the nervous father of three to his car which was parked in a remote corner of the stadium parking lot. When it happened it was rapid, painless and silent. The lifeless body of the referee slumped sideways into the driver's seat of his *Toyota Corolla*. Falcao cleaned the blade of his knife on his victim's shirt and discreetly lifted the man's feet into the vehicle. He closed the door using his elbow to avoid leaving fingerprints.

By the time Eduardo Santos returned to the company of his wife, she had already invited Peter to dine with them that evening.

"I'm not really dressed for going out to eat," he protested, realizing Maria would probably want to meet.

"Rubbish," Klaudia countered, "Eduardo will bring us some-where appropriate."

Within minutes, Reid found himself in the back of an armor plated *Rolls-Royce Phantom VI*, sandwiched between two black *Range Rovers* carrying armed guards.

"Colombia can be a dangerous place," Santos pronounced as he noticed the Irishman scanning the security team accompanying them. Many industrialists in Colombia took similar precautions to protect themselves from FARC guerrillas. Consequently, to the authorities, Santos' security measures appeared warranted. In reality he was protect-ing himself from competing drug cartels.

As the convoy moved off, Santos instructed his driver to inves-tigate two police cars which were parked beside a red *Toyota Corolla*.

"It's the referee," a police sergeant reported through the window of the *Rolls-Royce*. "I guess some of the fans had a problem with how he officiated the game."

"That's a shame," Santos responded sarcastically. "Make sure my club gets his name and address so we can send flowers and condolences to his family." The window closed and a satisfied Santos sank back into his seat.

Eventually the convoy stopped outside a popular restaurant where the party was escorted to a private alcove. For the remainder of the evening Reid listened attentively while Santos espoused his personal idealogy.

"America and its European partners have been pushing their noses into our affairs for too long. Simon Bolivar was the first to tell them it had to stop. The coca plant has been a part of our commerce and culture in South America for thousands of years. We're certainly not going to listen to a bunch of politicians in Washington telling us what we can, and can't do, while they get fat and happy with lobbyists for arms manufacturers, alcohol distillers and pharmaceutical companies!" Santos continued. "There's a market for our commodity just like there's a market for oil or corn. But Ronald Reagan and his friends on Capital Hill have manipulated the statutes in America so coca leaves can only be imported for their *Coca-Cola Company*. Then the U.S. interferes with every country south of the Rio Grande and attempts to eliminate the cocaine cartels. That's why I support the FARC cause, Peter. They share my goal which is to get Colombia properly compensated for its resources. It doesn't matter to me whether it comes from a mine or grows on a tree. If my people sweat all day producing it, then they need to be paid properly."

"That's enough politics for one night," Klaudia interrupted. "It's time to bring our guest home."

Reid watched as the *Phantom VI* drove away from his apartment building. He was surprised by how reasonable and charming the cartel leader appeared to be. Nevertheless, he thought about the horrific last moments of the unfortunate referee's life and remembered the indelible image of the motorcycle helmet containing the severed head of an undercover policeman.

******

"Hurry up and get into bed," Quintero instructed, as the young Irishman entered his apartment.

"Jesus, Maria, I don't hear from you or George for months and suddenly, you're serving me beer and stopping by for a booty call!"

"We couldn't risk any contact until we knew Santos and his FARC friends had invited you into their lives. Believe me, Peter, these guys have been watching you since you stepped off the plane. Mulligan and I were right on target when we came up with this plan to get you undercover with this crew."

The following morning, Reid woke to a breakfast of fresh coffee and orange juice Maria had prepared before slipping under the sheets again to enjoy her own "Irish Breakfast."

10:05AM – Monday March 28th 1983
Bogotá, COLOMBIA

Peter Reid and Carlos Falcao sat in the conference room on the tenth floor of a modern office building, located in the city's financial district.

"Señor Santos will be with you presently," the attractive receptionist informed the two men as she closed the conference room door. The Colombian gently caressed his gold canines with his tongue as he surveyed out over the metropolitan vista. Reid got up from his seat and studied a large map with pins which identified affiliated offices throughout the world. The wall between the conference room and reception area was constructed completely of glass. The stylish chrome framed conference table supported a clear plate glass top and was surrounded by twelve black leather chairs. It was stark yet elegant but most of all it was secure. Santos could always see what the hands of his visitors were doing, above and below the table. When he eventually entered the room, the atmosphere changed. An important, self-confident and powerful man had arrived and wanted both of them to know it. The formalities were trite. The Colombian got straight to the point.

"I understand the British government is looking for you." Reid swallowed hard then answered slowly and deliberately.

"Yes they are, I mean, it is. The Brits are looking for me because I've perfected a sophisticated remote-control detonator. Last year, when they analyzed the remnants of my bomb they knew it was a game-changer. My design and specifications are still intact: components, suppliers, everything. The Brits got nothing when they didn't get me. I can do the same thing again, anywhere, anytime, and they know it!"

"So our mutual friend, Sean Ryan, helped you to get here?"

"Yes. The INRA provided the cash but I picked this country because I can speak Spanish and I knew I could always see a good game of football." Santos did not move a muscle in his face. The silence was disconcerting but Reid decided to continue. "They suggested ETA in the Basque region, but that's too close to Gibraltar for my liking." Careful not to divulge too much, he chose not to mention his new passport in the name of Martin Quinn which the Americans, Quintero and Mulligan, had procured for him. He had told Sean Ryan about it, but not how he got it. That was information he would never reveal. An unlikely informer had already betrayed him to the British, so he was reluctant to share more than was absolutely necessary.

Reid stopped talking. For several moments there was silence. Santos had swiveled his chair to face the window so they could only look at the top of his head. Eventually he spoke, but did not turn back into the room.

"I think I could use your expertise and I would reward you well for it. There will be money, lots of it, a nice house with cars and ..." He suddenly swung around to face the two men, "anything, anything else you would like!" Peter was so excited he was afraid Santos would read it in his expression and body language. He took a long, slow breath before answering.

"What would you want me to do, exactly?"

"Exactly what you were doing in Northern Ireland but, this time, you'll be teaching others how to do it. You'll tell me what you need and I'll get it for you. You have until noon tomorrow to let me know your answer."

"That won't be necessary, sir, I'd be delighted to be part of your team. Thank you. When do you want me to start?"

"You just did, Mr. Reid!"

6:05AM – Friday April 8th 1983
Cardiff, Wales, UNITED KINGDOM

Clive Noakes wiped a tear from his eye as he listened to his brother-in-law eulogize his son. Minutes later, a color guard of Welsh Guardsmen stepped forward to carry the coffin of their comrade, Lance Corporal Jonathan Davies.

Days earlier, the twenty-one year old had taken his own life after surrendering to an enemy he could not see. He fought his battle every second of every hour of every day. As described by those afflicted with the condition, Tinnitus is the loudest noise no one else can hear. Jonathan's condition began ten months earlier after he had survived a bomb explosion in Lisburn, Northern Ireland. The young man's suicide note begged for forgiveness and described how his sanity had been robbed by the insatiable ringing in his ears. It never stopped despite the best efforts of doctors, and his own attempts to self medicate with alcohol.

Chapter 10

NICARAGUA - 1983

REVENUE STREAMS

8:05AM – Monday September 26th 1983
Managua, NICARAGUA

Since recruiting Peter Reid in February 1978, George Mulligan and Maria Quintero were fastidious about protecting their agent's safety. Maria's fluent Spanish made her the ideal asset and contact for the mission. Mulligan normally stayed in Europe, or the States, so when he arranged to meet in Nicaragua's capital city, Peter knew something important was on the horizon. Drug cartels had agents and informers imbedded in every facet of the community so phone systems, post offices and independent courier companies could not be trusted.

"We have a problem," George began after they had caught up on small talk. "Maybe it's not a problem, more of a challenge."

"Something tells me your challenge is going to become my problem!"

"The covert nature of our operations," Mulligan continued, "makes it difficult to hide our 'fiscal needs' in bills that pass through Congress and the Senate. My mandate is to develop additional revenue sources to further the goals of the Agency. To put it bluntly, we need more money to keep our operation going and the drug cartels have lots and lots of it. So we need to find ways to take their money and use it to put them out of business."

"I had no idea there was a government program that tried not to rely solely on tax payers," Reid observed cynically. "It sucks you can't let anyone know what you're up to!"

"You've now spent six months with Eduardo and Klaudia Santos," the American continued deliberately ignoring the young man's flippant remark. "So we need you to use that influence to suggest ways for them to launder their profits. We've already got people in investment banks throughout the world who will assist us. They're already laundering money for your INRA friends as well as other European paramilitary groups, so there won't be a problem if Santos carrys out background checks."

Mulligan revealed a plan to gain control of the Santos family's assets and employee pension funds. Reid agreed the Santos mining operations, as well as the farm laborer cooperatives, were ideal vehicles for laundering drug profits. Each had a need for legitimate bank accounts and investment holdings. The bank accounts, however, could reflect numbers that were inflated in order to justify weekly deductions from thousands of phantom union members. These pension funds would be obligated to diversify their investments which could include stock and bond portfolios managed by CIA agents who worked for legitimate financial institutions.

"If we start off slowly we can systematically show how our investment funds repeatedly out-perform the competition. Eventually, Santos will be inclined to trust us with more and more of his money."

6:05PM – Friday December 30th 1983
CIA Headquarters - Langley, Virginia, USA

S cott Hamilton sighed heavily as he finished reading his final security brief of 1983. It was not unusual for him to visit his office on a Saturday, but he planned to make an exception for New Years Eve. He could not remember ever feeling so exhausted and hoped both he and his wife would benefit from the two day break from his work.

Three years earlier, as soon as President Reagan took office, the hostages were released from the US Embassy in Iran. Hamilton remembered he had naively hoped that positive beginning would set a trend for the new administration but, unfortunately, things did not turn out that way. Threats to American interests throughout the world continued. Iran was at war with Iraq and the US had found itself bolstering Iraqi efforts with both satellite intelligence and military equipment. In Central America, the Contras were having little success in their efforts to topple the Sandinista government in Nicaragua. The most harrowing development, however, had occurred two months earlier in Beirut when 220 Marines, 18 sailors and 3 soldiers lost their lives in a terrorist bombing of their barracks. From Scott Hamilton's perspective, that tragic event, more than any other, underscored the importance of his work at the Agency. He switched off the light and closed his office door before heading home to spend a quiet evening with his wife.

2:20PM – Wednesday August 8th 1984
MI6 Headquarters - London, ENGLAND

C live Noakes shuffled through the twelve black and white photographs before sitting back to listen to his boss, Rupert Huntley-Palmer. Noakes had been in London for more than a year since his return from Boston, but had made no real progress tracking down Peter Reid.

"I think if we squeeze Sean Ryan, he'll lead us to Reid," Huntley-Palmer suggested, tapping one of the photographs on the desk. "The Metropolitan police got this photograph of Ryan by accident. They were actually following the chap he was meeting. They've had a tail on every Libyan diplomat since Constable Fletcher was shot and killed during that demonstration outside their embassy in April."

"Ryan has to be the key. He's been running an INRA cell in Belfast since 1982, when Reid was working at *DeLorean* and *Shorts*," Noakes interjected. Huntley-Palmer gently slid a file across his desk toward him.

"In the past two years, Ryan has visited: Libya; Spain; Italy; The United States; Colombia; and Nicaragua. My guess is Reid is laying low in one of these countries."

"Do you have any advice, other than suggesting a good sunscreen?" Noakes asked, frustrated by his lack of success in finding the man he blamed for his nephew's death.

"The Americans say they've got no record of him being back there since he left Boston. Not that they're on top of things when it comes to undocumented aliens but they know we're looking, and I'm sure they'll tip us off if they locate him."

"I wouldn't be so sure," Noakes countered. "Some of their

government and law enforcement agencies have people with a nostalgic sympathy for the Irish Republican cause."

"I agree, Clive, but photographs like these are sobering and Ronald Reagan has Gaddafi in his cross-hairs. If we can link the INRA to Libyan acts of terrorism, Reid will not be able to hide in America. Besides," he continued, grinning as he aimed and fired an imaginary gun at the photograph of Ryan, "we're not asking them to give him up. All they need to do is look the other way while we eliminate the problem."

"Don't discount other possibilities, either. The INRA have alliances with the Red Brigade in Italy, Basque separatists in Spain and FARC guerrillas in Colombia. Reid could be in any one of those countries and living under a new identity. Plus the Sandinista administration has made Managua a safe haven for every fucking terrorist on the planet."

"I think the best course of action is to pick up Ryan and show him we've got evidence implicating him in Libyan terrorism, including Officer Fletcher's murder. He can choose to either give up Reid or spend the rest of his life getting bum fucked in Holloway Prison."

3:30PM – Saturday April 20th 1985
Lago Titicaca, BOLIVIA

Steffen Bremner and Klaudia Santos lead the audience in its applause after the inaugural concert in the newly constructed auditorium. It seated two thousand people who were also guests of the recently renovated and expanded hotel and conference center. The evening's music program had featured compositions by Adolf Hitler's favorite composers and his birthday had been specifically chosen for the special event. Over the years, the orchestra had received several grants from a foundation created by the Bremner family, in memory of Klaus, to promote German culture. Its members, however, were oblivious to the political aspirations of their benefactors.

"We need to be careful," Steffen whispered softly in his sister's ear. "The war may have ended forty years ago, but it's not over for the likes of Simon Wiesenthal. We don't want to end up like Klaus Barbie."

"Remember what we promised Father before he died. The war will not be over for us until we make the United States pay for its interference in Europe's affairs. Besides, Klaus Barbie was careless and relied solely on his Bolivian contacts to protect him. Thanks to my marriage, we have expanded our base into Colombia which has also provided us with assets in Nicaragua and Panama."

"This is not the venue for such discussions," Steffen cautioned as the applause subsided and the house lights brightened. "I'm just saying we need to be careful. That's all."

Klaudia turned and hugged her brother. She was confident her husband would be able to cement relationships with officials close to Mañuel Noriega in Panama thus guaranteeing another safe passage for their cocaine into the United States. It would have been difficult to convince Eduardo Santos that CIA sanctioned flights were transporting Noriega's narcotics from Panama to the United States, had he not gone to Panama himself to see the operation with his own eyes. From what he could ascertain, profits from these shipments were being used to bankroll the Contra guerrilla war against the Sandinista government in Nicaragua. Intelligence about CIA support for the Contras, gleaned from his visits to Panama, was then passed along to the Sandinistas via Carlos Falcao and his FARC comrades.

The Sandinista administration had turned Nicaragua's capital, Managua, into a safe haven for all left wing terrorists. Revolutionaries from around the world were able to relax, network and help one another. Arms dealers were welcomed and able to operate freely as well as anyone else whose business was at odds with that of the United States of America and its Western allies.

Chapter 11

LONDON, ENGLAND - 1985

BRITISH INTELLIGENCE

5:00PM – Monday December 23rd 1985
Heathrow Airport – London, ENGLAND

S ean Ryan had used the alias, Stewart Girvan, for previous visits
to and from Libya. Everything about it checked out, including an
address at a rooming house in Dumfries, Scotland. The second leg of his
itinerary was a connecting flight from Heathrow to Glasgow. It supported
the back-story of his employment as an oil worker in Libya, an industry with which the Scottish were familiar because of the North Sea oil
boom. In reality, all Ryan's visits had been as a guest of its ruler, Colonel
Muammar Gaddafi. While there, he trained at some of the many terrorist
camps hosted by the dictator. A convincing Scottish accent and flawless
documentation, which included a British passport and driving license,
always earned him a courteous warm greeting from immigration officers.

Ryan's previous trips, however, had all been made before Metropolitan Woman Police Constable, Yvonne Fletcher, had been killed on
17th April, 1984 by a shot fired from Libya's London Embassy. While
he slept through the four and a half hour flight from Tripoli, a Police and
Secret Service joint task force was scrutinizing passport photographs of
all passengers on board the *British Airways* flight. Even before the Irish
terrorist stepped off the plane, his picture had already been matched to
photographs taken only days after the WPC's murder. On that occassion,
he had been in London to meet with a Libyan diplomat and receive a
large cash donation in recognition of the INRA's terror campaign against
the inhabitants of mainland Britain and Northern Ireland.

Clive Noakes could barely control his emotions when he received
the fax. As soon as he recognized Ryan's photograph, he knew his holiday
plans would have to be scrapped. The only thing he regretted was not

being able to tell his sister why he was going to be late for Christmas dinner on Wednesday.

The initial greeting from the immigration officer disarmed Ryan. Confidence tinged with arrogance allowed him to relax because, as Stewart Girvan, he had successfully negotiated the security check on many occasions. Consequently, he disregarded three individuals who were standing beyond the line of Customs and Immigration booths. Clive Noakes smiled smugly as he approached with his two colleagues. Sean Ryan immediately realized all was not well.

Four hours later, the INRA terrorist lay on the floor of a concrete cell, somewhere in London. Blood was still trickling from both nostrils but a clot had congealed and stopped the bleeding from his left ear. The discomfort from three broken ribs made it difficult to breathe, however, it was nothing compared to the excruciating pain in his groin. Through the loudest ringing in his ears he had ever heard, he struggled to hear what his interrogator was saying to him.

"When I saw your photograph earlier today, Sean, I was both delighted and sad," Noakes sneered at the motionless heap at his feet. "Delighted we were finally going to meet after a search that's lasted two and a half years, yet disappointed I'm going to miss my Christmas dinner so I can spend the day with you!"

Ryan had neither the physical ability nor strength to yell out in pain as Clive's black leather shoe kicked him in the back of his rib cage.

"Fuck you, you filthy Irish fuck!" he yelled. "I'm not going to miss my Christmas dinner because of you – you sick fuck. Why don't you enjoy your Christmas here and I'll see you on Boxing Day! Fuck you and fuck the Anglo Irish Agreement!"

The noise of the cell door slamming was merely a soft distant thud as Sean Ryan finally lost consciousness.

08:10AM – Thursday December 26th 1985
MI6 Headquarters - London, ENGLAND

C live Noakes could not remember the last time he felt so enthusiastic about going to work. The day before had been surreal. He had to sit opposite his sister at the Christmas dinner table, but not tell her he had captured one of the men responsible for the death of her son.

As he locked the door of his *Ford Granada*, he was intrigued to see Rupert Huntley-Palmer's *Jaguar* already parked in the adjacent space. He pushed the button to summon the elevator for the underground parking garage. Simultaneously, he retrieved his pager from its clip on his belt. The message was brief yet ominous.

"Call office. RHP."

He emptied all the metal objects from his pockets before passing through a full body scanner at the security check. The pager chirped a second time.

"Call office now. RHP." Sixty seconds later he walked into Huntley-Palmer's office.

"Ryan is dead."

"No fucking way!"

"You fucked up, Clive, and now I've got to clean this up. He never regained consciousness."

Noakes slumped into one of the two seats in front of the large mahogany desk. It did not bother him Sean Ryan was dead; he had always planned to kill him, but not until the INRA operative had led him to Peter Reid.

"I need to get you out of London while I handle this," Huntley-Palmer ordered. "I'm sending you back to Boston for a few months. You can come back here in the summer when things have died down. Maybe you can pick up a fresh scent on Reid through Paddy Lynch. Also, see if you can find out what the Americans have planned for Charles Taylor. He was supposed to be extradited to Liberia but somehow managed to escape from a maximum security prison in Massachusetts. Hardly the sort of skills they teach you at Bentley College. Maybe somebody on campus can enlighten you."

"Christ, I hate New England winters," Noakes protested.

"Would you rather clean up the vomit and blood in Ryan's cell, then stash his body in some abandoned building in the docks to make it look like he's been there for days?

"I'll pack my thermal underwear!"

*****

Clive Noakes returned to his office where an evidence box had been left containing Sean Ryan's personal belongings including the Stewart Girvan passport. After his untimely and unfortunate death, MI5 had obligingly provided a wallet with a driver's license and credit cards for a false identity. Everything had been placed on the Irishman's corpse before it was dumped in a derelict and abandoned area of London docks. A female agent had already reported her brother missing, explaining to Police he had been in and out of psychiatric hospitals since surviving an attack on HMS Sheffield, during the Falklands War with Argentina, in 1982. MI5 was able to falsify Royal Navy records to substantiate their fictitious version of events. Noakes chuckled when he realized Sean Ryan would not get his paramilitary funeral back in Belfast but would, instead, be given the burial of a British Seaman who had put his life on the line serving Queen and Country.

The Stewart Girvan passport Sean Ryan had been using contained immigration control stamps from multiple countries. USA stamps
showed recent visits to Boston where Noakes suspected he had visited
Paddy Lynch. The MI6 agent clenched his fist, frustrated and furious he
had not been able to get information from the Irishman. Killing him had
been a costly mistake. Hopefully, some time with Lynch in Boston would
rectify the situation. He was determined not to let Ryan's inconvenient
death obstruct his goal. He would begin again, armed with seven years
documentation about the dead man's movements.

Noakes swiveled his chair and bent over to open a drawer in a
credenza from where he retrieved a neat cardboard file box. Its flap was
secured by a long brown ribbon, wrapped around a metal button. He
emptied its contents onto his desk. There was a small, black shoulder
bag; a pair of gloves; a cassette walkman; a key-ring with keys; a book
of matches from the *Cocoa Bean* nightclub; and a membership card for
BlockBuster Video. They were Nuala Mallon's belongings which he had
recovered from the hospital on the day of her accident. None of the items
had yielded any leads when he investigated her death, but the Colombian
stamp on Ryan's false passport reminded him that he had, in fact, spoken
with the owner of the *Cocoa Bean*, Eduardo Santos.

Another visit to the credenza produced a file containing field
notes he had taken at the time. Noakes wondered if there could be a
connection between Ryan's trips to Boston and Eduardo Santos. His
hypothesis was correct. He had, unwittingly, identified the country to
which Peter Reid had escaped, as well as the individual who was funding
his FARC bomb factory.

Chapter 12

LANGLEY, VIRGINIA, USA - 1985

BUILDING RELATIONSHIPS

10:15AM – Tuesday December 31st 1985
CIA Headquarters - Langley, Virginia, USA

S cott Hamilton summoned George Mulligan and Maria Quintero to his office to discuss Peter Reid's expanding role in their operations. A recent field report citing his visits to Nicaragua and Libya, with Carlos Falcao, demonstrated just how proficient the Irishman had become at infiltrating the FARC organization.

"We've got serious problems with our Contra operations," Hamilton began, stating the obvious. "Kerry and Harkin are doing everything in their power to impede the President in his quest to remove the Sandinistas from power. Ortega has turned Nicaragua into a country club open to every damn left wing terrorist in the world."

"God forbid we'd be left alone to do our job and protect the country," Maria quipped caustically.

"Twenty years with the Agency and I've come to learn, no good deed goes unpunished," Mulligan lamented. "Even if you're killed in the line of duty, there's no recognition except for an anonymous star on the wall in the lobby."

"Well I don't want Reid getting a star for his efforts," their boss interrupted. "Every month I get a call from Clive Noakes at MI6, asking if he's showed up on our radar. We've got to sort things out with London."

"What's up with that Noakes guy?" Quintero asked. "We made sure no one got killed or injured in the Lisburn bombing, but he's just relentless about tracking Reid down."

"Leave that with me," Hamilton suggested. "I think I can get them to back off. We're working with the British on a plan to send a message to Gaddafi. That's why I had you two facilitate Charles Taylor's escape from that Massachusetts prison. We need as much intelligence on those Libyan terrorist camps as we can get. Taylor understands we didn't pay his way through Bentley College just so he could embellish his resume. The British have had enough of Gaddafi arming and training Irish Republican militants. The President wants accurate intelligence about potential targets for an air strike. It looks like the Brits are going to play a role in this mission, so if Reid is going in and out of Libya, I think I can get MI6 to get off his case."

"Are you sure you can trust Taylor to give us good information?" Maria asked with concern.

"The short answer is, 'No,' but we've got to get as many agents into Libya as we can. Anyone who breaks out of an American prison will be a hero in Gaddafi's eyes. Taylor knows if we'd extradited him to Liberia to stand trial, his Presidential aspirations would have crashed and burned. If he works for us and gives us good intelligence on Gaddafi, then it won't be long before he's in the Presidential Palace in Monrovia."

"Well you're certainly, a Man with a Plan," she joked.

"Just trying to push along our foreign policy agenda!" Hamilton mocked cynically. "We're going to have Sandinista rebels in Disney World unless we shut them down in Nicaragua. We're getting practically no money from Congress which leaves us brokering arms deals with the Iranians, peddling cocaine and this new crack derivative. We need other revenue streams and Liberia seems promising. If we get Taylor propped up in power, we can get control of their diamond mines."

1:30PM – Tuesday April 15th 1986
MI6, London, ENGLAND

R upert Huntley-Palmer, Clive Noakes and a dozen other MI6 officers
huddled around the mahogany desk to review satellite images, following the US air raid on Libya. Initial reports were unable to confirm
if Colonel Gaddafi had been killed, but five terrorist training camps had
been hit along with several other strategic targets. British relations with
Washington were at an all time high. Margaret Thatcher was Ronald
Reagan's most supportive European ally for the raid since she assented
to the use of United States Air Force Bases in the United Kingdom for
the mission. Photographs were projected for scrutiny on a large screen.
There was consensus that even if Muammar Gaddafi survived the attack,
he would know he had been sent a lethal message.

Huntley-Palmer adjourned the meeting but asked Clive Noakes
to remain. Once they were alone in his office, he dropped a bombshell
of his own.

"Are you fucking serious?" Noakes retorted. "I've been tracking
this Irish fuck for years and he's been working for the Americans, the
whole time!"

"I'm no happier about this than you are, Clive, but there's nothing I can do."

"As far as I'm concerned nothing's changed. My nephew is dead
and fucking Reid is the culprit."

"I got a phone call this morning from Scott Hamilton at Langley,
and he assures me that's not the case."

"Try telling Nuala Mallon that! Reid is the reason she's dead and
he's the reason my nephew is dead. No bullshit from some CIA spook is

going to change my mind."

"Reid is deep undercover with both the INRA and FARC. Intelligence Uncle Sam used for the Libyan bombing mission is from time he spent in Gaddafi's training camps. I know it's not what you want or need to hear, but their version of events is that he deliberately scuttled the attack on your nephew's unit."

"Well, I'm not prepared to shake his hand just because you got a call from Langley."

"Maybe you should take some time off, Clive. This job takes a toll and you can't let emotions cloud your judgement. They want additional staff at our embassy in Mexico for the World Cup. I've signed you up for that assignment. You need to step back from chasing Reid, watch some football and drink as much tequila as you can."

Noakes stared at his boss without uttering a response. The image on the projector screen of a bombed out terrorist camp accurately depicted how he felt.

1:55PM – Sunday June 29th 1986
Mexico City, MEXICO

I n Mexico City's 'Estadio Azteca,' the referee blew the final whistle
heralding Argentina's 3-2 victory over West Germany in front of
114,000 spectators. It was the culmination of a four week visit to Mexico
for the Santos family. Eleven year old Xavier had no idea that most of
the people his parents had been meeting with were criminal business
associates, responsible for safe passage of cocaine into the United States.
Eduardo and Klaudia had used the Federation Internationale de Football
Association (FIFA) World Cup tournament as a cover for the real purpose
of their visit.

Klaudia had piloted the *Aryan Air Grumman Gulfstream III*,
twin-engine jet, into Mexico City International Airport at the beginning of the tournament. She then used the plane to fly Eduardo, Xavier,
Carlos Falcao and Peter Reid around the country. Their Irish passenger
made sure none of the group overlooked the fact Northern Ireland, with
a population of less than one million, had managed to qualify for the
tournament's final stages in Mexico. Unfortunately, a tie against Algeria
in their first game was followed by losses to Spain and Brazil ending the
World Cup Dream of the Northern Irish squad.

"You guys need another George Best," Falcao teased, referring
to the legendary soccer ace who charmed the soccer world in the 1960s
and 1970s. Many independent pundits of the game regarded him to be
on par with, if not better than, Pelé. Sadly, the soccer star's alcohol abuse
and fast paced lifestyle were regularly chronicled in tabloid newspapers
and gossip magazines. In addition to his skill the soccer legend would
also be remembered for witty quotes such as, "I spent 90% of my money

on women, fast cars and alcohol, and the rest I wasted!"

Meanwhile Clive Noakes had spent two weeks supporting the English soccer team. The MI6 agent had mixed business with pleasure by also attending the Northern Ireland games, where he hoped he might find Peter Reid. He believed his terrorist was hiding in South America and thought the tournament would be a temptation for him. Noakes had no idea the young Irishman was flying around the country in a private jet, watching games from the comfort of luxury boxes, while he scrutinized faces in the cheaper seats where he was sitting.

9:00PM – Tuesday November 13th 1985
Newton, Massachusetts, USA

E duardo had just finished helping Xavier with the final arithmetic question on the young boy's homework assignment when Klaudia called him. She was watching the President's television address to the nation regarding alleged arms dealings with Iran. The broadcast was transmitted throughout the country, but few viewers understood the ramifications better than they did. In their quest to flood the United States with illegal drugs they never expected to have the assistance of the Central Intelligence Agency, but despite the President's claims to the contrary, that was the case. The Reagan administration could not secure adequate funding from Congress to aid the Contras in their fight against the Sandinista regime in Nicaragua. Consequently, it resorted to ferrying cocaine and marijuana into the United States so profits could be used for arms and equipment. Most of the President's statement denied the revenue source, but Eduardo and Klaudia knew the problem was more pervasive. For several years, they had flown tons of cocaine into Contra controlled airfields in Honduras where pilots, employed by the CIA, ferried the contraband into the United States.

The rise in addiction to 'crack cocaine' heightened demand to levels no one had anticipated. Regular cocaine (hydrochloride) powder could not be smoked. The introduction of a derivative which could, however, led to the proliferation of 'Crack'. By the mid 80s it caused more havoc than Klaus and Gabriele Bremner could ever have imagined in 1945. American cities were plagued by the drug. Smoking crack enhanced the high but the sensation was very short lived. Accordingly, addicts craved another 'hit' and would stop at nothing to achieve it. More efficient smuggling routes into the country made the drug economically more accessible. Cocaine transitioned from a lavish indulgence of the wealthy to its crack form which invaded, and pervaded, lower income neighborhoods. Rampant crime and excessive demands on the healthcare industry, such as the care of addicted infants born to destitute parents, gave Klaudia and Steffen a great sense of pride. They felt they were succeeding in their goal to accomplish their parents' mission to punish the United States. The feeling was even more satisfying when they considered the key role the CIA was apparently playing in the demise of its own country.

"This is why it's so important to diversify, Klaudia. We can never allow ourselves to become complacent and rely on any one route into the U.S."

"It won't be long before the CIA will close down its cocaine operation. We'll just have to re-route our product and avoid Central America."

"It doesn't matter how much money they invest in anti-drug campaigns," Eduardo observed, "Once a person is hooked on crack, it's game over!"

"We shouldn't panic," Klaudia countered, "I doubt Reagan will want to shut down operations over night. He's half way through his second term. He'll probably run interference for the CIA so his Vice President can deny any knowledge and avoid jeopardizing his own Presidential campaign. He could not have selected a better Vice President than George Bush for dealing with a situation like this. Bush previously served as Ambassador to the United Nations and then as Director of the CIA. For the moment, I think we should get Carlos Falcao and Peter Reid to make more trips to Central America so they can keep an eye on things."

8:35AM – Monday May 17th 1987
CIA Headquarters - Langley, Virginia, USA

❝The Iraqis are saying it was a mistake. Some fucking mistake!"

George Mulligan scowled and tossed the copy of the *Washington Post* onto his boss' desk. "Thirty-seven American sailors lost their lives and 'sorry' is all they can say."

Scott Hamilton was also angry the USS Stark had taken fire from an Iraqi plane in the Persian Gulf, however, it was not the only reason he had summoned Mulligan to his office.

"I got a call from London last night. Huntley-Palmer at MI6 is insisting we sit down with him and one of his agents, Clive Noakes. His nephew was just days into his first Northern Ireland tour when his patrol was attacked by the blast Reid set off."

"No one was killed … and that's thanks to Peter," Mulligan interrupted.

"Well, that may be so, but Noakes' nephew got his hearing fucked up in the explosion. He couldn't live with the Tinnitus that developed, so he blew his brains out with his service revolver. Noakes is convinced our guy is to blame."

"So it's a personal crusade for this guy?

"Who knows what the fuck it is, but we need to give him proof Reid is more use to them alive than dead. Have him cozy up to some of his terrorist buddies in Managua and get some intelligence that would help MI6."

"Jesus, Scott, the world's falling apart and we've got to take Peter off point to placate some whining Brit?"

"As long as Ronnie and Maggie have each other's ear, this sort of thing will have to be done. It's not 1776. Britain is our biggest ally in Europe. We're running out of friends over there. Gaddafi is still alive and most likely it's because the Italians warned him about our bombing mission last year. How long do you think it's going to be before Gaddafi strikes back? We need to give the Brits something!"

11:40AM – Monday November 9th 1987
Key West, Florida, USA

Peter Reid relished the thought of a three week vacation in the United States. It would also involve a little work since Eduardo and Klaudia Santos had invited him to Boston for Thanksgiving, later in the month. Prior to that, they had given him full access to their yacht which was docked in Key West, Florida.

Maria Quintero did not look out of place as she claimed an empty bar stool adjacent to Reid in the popular sports bar.

"Are you going to buy a girl a drink?" asked a familiar voice. Reid was lost in the "World News" section of the local newspaper. He was reading an article about a bomb at a British Legion ceremony in Enniskillen, Northern Ireland, which had killed eleven people.

He tried to keep emotions out of his job but the ensuing conversation with Maria made it very difficult. For the first time, his CIA handlers were asking him to gather intelligence which would assist the British in their military campaign in his homeland. Atrocities such as the 'Shankill Butchers', and the 'Miami Showband' murders that were perpetrated by Loyalist paramilitaries against Roman Catholics, salved his conscience when it came to assisting the INRA. He reminded himself himself that his contributions were aimed at minimizing collateral damage. Nevertheless, explosions like the one in Enniskillen left him nauseous and numb. Maria could see he was not comfortable with the discussion so she decided to lighten the mood and change the subject.

"Let's take a walk," she suggested and stood up from the bar leaving a twenty dollar bill beneath a half empty bottle of *Corona*.

Outside, Peter proceeded to update her on his latest visit to

Nicaragua with Eduardo Santos.

"I've managed to get friendly with some ETA members in Managua who made a passing reference to their collaboration with the Provisional IRA on a mission in Gibraltar."

"Do you have any details?"

"No, it was a casual remark. I didn't want to appear too interested. I could probably get some information if I spend more time with these guys. They have quite a presence masquerading as an auto repair business."

"Any particular reason they've set up an auto repair shop?"

"I'm not sure, but I suspect there's more going on in there than repairing mufflers!"

"Why don't we give you something to ingratiate yourself with these people," Maria suggested. "How about a dozen blank Irish passports?"

"Six would probably be better. I don't wanna look too pushy."

"In the meantime, I'll let MI6 know they need to pay attention to security at the border between Spain and Gibraltar."

9:30PM – Thanksgiving evening, 1987
Newton, Massachusetts, USA

Despite promising himself he would not do so, Reid ate and drank too much. Thanksgiving dinner at Eduardo and Klaudia Santos' home had morphed into a global strategy session in the drug cartel leader's private study. Neither Eduardo nor his wife had any idea their Irish guest had the benefit of CIA intelligence briefings to back up his statements. They were very impressed by his insightful advice.

"We're entering the final year of Reagan's Presidency. From what I can see the Democrats aren't going to be able to defeat George Bush. Reagan's economic policies have undone much of the damage Carter's regime caused, while his foreign policies are promoted as necessary reaction to attacks on American interests in Central America and the Middle East."

"You should be teaching at Harvard," Klaudia joked.

"Voters aren't going to go against Bush because Reagan attempted to resolve the hostage situation in Lebanon with some shady arms dealings with Iran. The price of gasoline is more important to the American public. Reagan will take the heat on the Contras fiasco so Bush can focus on campaigning. We all know he had to have been involved. How could he not have been? The guy used to be the CIA Director!"

"You're right!" Eduardo interjected. "And this is why we need to diversify and maintain redundancy in our drug routes into the United States. We must be prepared to react whenever one of them gets closed down. How long do you think we have before things go bad in Panama?"

"Probably one year, two at most," their young guest predicted. "Noriega is becoming too cocky. Reagan has had other issues to deal with, but George Bush isn't going to be so forgiving, and besides, the canal is too important to U.S. interests."

Chapter 13

COLOMBIA - 1988

INTERNATIONAL CONFLICT

6:15PM – Sunday March 20th 1988
Medellín, COLOMBIA

R eid's stature in Eduardo Santos' drug operation meant he was very
well compensated. Threats from competing cartels, however, forced
him to take necessary precautions. In order to avoid predictable schedules, he had several residences. Each had security features, including a
secret tunnel exit.

The *BBC World Service* news presenter faded away as Peter
slowly turned off the radio. More than ever, the news from Northern
Ireland seemed to be an endless litany of tragic events. Two weeks earlier,
on March 6th, three Provisional IRA operatives had been shot dead in
Gibraltar by an elite British Army unit. Subsequent news reports of the
shootings questioned whether any of the three victims had been armed.
It took over a week before funerals could be organized. The Irish government would not allow its national airline, Aer Lingus, to transport the
bodies, so a private jet had to be chartered.

Funerals for Republican volunteers were always tense occasions
but on March 16th the sectarian conflict plummeted to a new depth. Three
Catholic mourners were murdered in Belfast's Milltown Cemetery by a
Loyalist paramilitary who attacked the grave-side ceremony with hand
grenades.

Three days later, the funeral for one of the cemetery victims was
itself the scene of more murders. Two undercover British soldiers were
challenged by a mob who surrounded their car. Surveillance helicopters
were unable to intervene as the two men were dragged from the vehicle,
stripped naked and then shot with their own guns.

Reid stared at the radio. When it came to generating depressing news, Northern Ireland was in a league of its own, but things seemed to have deteriorated even more. He made no effort to chase the cap of the Tequila bottle as it danced across the kitchen floor after slipping from his hand. He remained pinned to his seat and poured another glass.

6:05PM – Sunday May 1st 1988
Newton, Massachusetts, USA

Young Xavier Santos was delighted his father had managed to call him before his bedtime. When he was younger, his parents did not worry about taking him out of school if their work required travel. They thought traveling as a young family would be less likely to attract the attention of custom officials. Since Xavier's enrollment at a private middle school, however, the family rarely travelled together during the academic term.

"I'll be in to say goodnight when Papa and I have finished talking," Klaudia whispered, as she took the phone from her son.

She chatted to her husband for some time about normal, mundane matters. Eduardo's mining and shipping business interests had been established primarily to provide a legitimate cover for his extensive international travel. His itinerary that evening had taken him to Panama. The political situation there continued to deteriorate which was unfortunate for him, considering the volume of cocaine he had been able to route through the Central American nation. Several weeks earlier, President Reagan had imposed stiffer sanctions on the Panamanian regime. His action followed the unsealing of a federal indictment in Florida against its military leader, Mañuel Noriega, for bribery and drug trafficking.

Eduardo did not have to tell his wife how dire things were. The Sunday newspaper on the couch in their family room had a photograph of Noriega waving a machete during a political rally. It was his response to efforts by the United States to oust him from power and it was not the kind of media attention Santos needed. Panama was effectively finished as a significant transportation hub for drug shipments which was extremely disappointing, considering how good things had once been.

10:45PM – Wednesday December 21st 1988
Washington, D.C., USA

Despite his demanding work schedule, Scott Hamilton always made a point of joining his wife at the fundraiser for a homeless shelter in D.C., since she was on the charity's board of directors. As the car radio delivered the sobering news, Angela's eyes welled up as she and her husband listened to the heartbreaking report.

"All 259 passengers and crew are feared dead following the downing of *Pan Am* Flight 103, along with an undisclosed number of victims in the town of Lockerbie, Scotland. Early reports from the scene indicate a wide field of debris in addition to extensive carnage at the primary crash site."

Hamilton processed the information using his twenty-five years of experience with the CIA. The large debris field told him something catastrophic had happened mid-flight causing the plane to fall in pieces to the ground. It was either mechanical or criminal. He hoped and prayed it would be the former.

11:35AM – Friday January 20th 1989
CIA Headquarters - Langley, Virginia, USA

In the corner office on the third floor, Scott Hamilton and George Mulligan finished their meeting early so they could watch George W. Bush deliver his inauguration speech on the television.

"Does it seem like eight years since Ronnie took the Oath of Office?" Mulligan asked.

"I remember like it was yesterday. It was also the day the Iranians announced they'd release the hostages. We may've gotten our people out of the embassy, but not much else has improved."

"Well, at least we have another friend in the Oval Office."

"True. Plus we won't have to spend a lot of time bringing him up to speed."

9:30AM – Thursday April 20th 1989
Berlin, GERMANY

" Die Narbe der Stadt" was the title of the feature article in the *Berliner Morgenpost* newspaper. "The Scar of the City" headline reminded readers about the events that had taken place during the tragic era of 'the Berlin Wall.' It was a story most people would read. Only a select few would turn to the page with a small, innocuous advertisement that read:

WANTED: good homes for six Rottweiler puppies.

The only information was a telephone number interested parties were invited to call. Steffen Bremner anxiously dialed the number.

7:35AM – Thursday December 21st 1989
Newton, Massachusetts, USA

The wealthy Colombian gulped his coffee and quickly scanned the front page of the *Boston Globe*. Operation 'Just Cause' had been launched and initial reports indicated Panamanian opposition to the invasion was no match for US forces.

"Xavier is going to be late unless you two get on the road," Klaudia warned.

"Life goes on!" Eduardo joked, as he kissed his wife and scooped his car keys off the counter.

Xavier followed his father out of the house, oblivious to the fact that one of the most important shipping hubs in his parent's cocaine import business had just been shut down.

2:50PM – Saturday June 30th 1990
Rome, ITALY

The Santos family and their guests stood motionless in the luxury suite at Stadio Olimpico as ten thousand Irish soccer supporters sang their national anthem. This would be the only time the other sixty thousand supporters attending the World Cup quarter final would remain silent. They were there to cheer for the host nation, Italy. From the moment the military band began playing, "Il Canto degli Italiani," the noise never stopped. It bothered the Colombian that his national team had lost to Cameroon in the previous round of the tournament, while small countries like the Republic of Ireland were still playing soccer in front of a world-wide audience. Eduardo privately resolved to do everything in his power to assist his national soccer federation in its quest to win the next World Cup. In 1994, the competition was scheduled to be held in the United States which meant Xavier, his son, would get another chance to see Colombia provided, of course, they qualified. He had also brought him to see Team USA, as it was making its first appearance since 1950. Unfortunately, 1990 was not a good year for the Americans who were defeated by all three opponents in the initial round-robin phase.

Carlos Falcao shared Eduardo's pain, however, other aspects of the Italian trip were more successful. He and Reid had been introduced to the Red Brigade in Nicaragua and these contacts continued to provide an excellent distribution network for the Colombian's drug business. In addition, The World Cup had attracted a quarter million tourists to Italy which had increased demand for cocaine even more than Santos had expected.

Klaudia was looking forward to Germany's match-up against

Czechoslovakia, the following day, and was thrilled for Reid who was realistic about his nation's chances of advancing to the semifinals. The Republic of Ireland had never qualified for a World Cup tournament, yet had managed to get into a position where they could eliminate the host nation in one of the four quarterfinal fixtures.

Robert Grey and his wife, Linda, had no interest in soccer. They did not appreciate Team USA's achievement of qualifying to play in Italy. Although Linda was happy to be on vacation in Rome, she was annoyed her schedule was being dictated by Eduardo and Klaudia Santos. The more she thought about it, the more it bothered her that so much of her life was influenced by her husband's South American clients. The contrast between the fortunes of Xavier Santos and those of her son only fueled her disdain. She stared at the fifteen year old Xavier and considered his privileged upbringing. His life was akin to that of royalty. His home in Newton, Massachusetts, was one of many his parents owned throughout the world. The trip to Italy was nothing out of the ordinary for the young man who had just finished his freshman year at a prestigious Boston preparatory school. Conversely, her son, George, had attended public school and had, in her opinion, graduated far short of his potential. Thirteen years earlier, a high school knee injury not only robbed him of a scholarship to Notre Dame, but also sent him spiraling into a deep depression. Consequently, young Grey lost all interest in academics. After a year, spent mostly on a couch in their basement, he took a job as a corrections officer with the Suffolk County Sherriff's Department. Unlike Xavier Santos, however, who was destined for an elite college experience, George eventually obtained a criminal justice degree after five years of night classes at community college. A further two years of part time study resulted in a Juris Doctor degree from Suffolk Law School.

As Robert Grey squeezed his wife's hand, she surveyed the eclectic group of guests assembled in the luxury box. Her husband never discussed his clients' business, so it was left for her to wonder why an individual like Carlos Falcao would be invited to such a gathering. While she did not expect anyone to attend a soccer game in business attire, the Colombian's ostentatious gold canines led her to surmise he probably did not even own a tie.

7:10AM – Thursday January 17th 1991
Newton, Massachusetts, USA

E duardo Santos dusted toast crumbs off the front page of the *Boston Globe* and took another sip of coffee.

"I can't believe America has time to mess around and screw up our operations in Central and South America, with everything else it has going on."

"They were never going to let Saddam Hussein invade Kuwait and do nothing. Certainly not when Capital Hill is crawling with lobbyists for oil companies and arms manufacturers. It's a win-win for everyone in Washington and an opportunity for the U.S. military to test its toys," Klaudia mused.

Meanwhile, Xavier shoveled cereal into his mouth while the earphones on his portable CD player isolated him from his parents' Desert Storm discussions.

10:10AM – Wednesday November 4th 1992
CIA Headquarters - Langley, Virginia, USA

❝If only we were allowed to put as much effort into influencing elections here at home, then maybe our former boss would've won a second term," Scott Hamilton lamented.

"I think we can thank Ross Perot for screwing things up. We've had it good for the past twelve years. Somehow I can't see Clinton being as good a friend to us as Reagan and Bush have been. Our job isn't easy but having a sympathetic ear in the Oval Office has definitely helped," George Mulligan replied.

He finished briefing his boss on issues related to Central America. The political climate in Panama was a lot calmer. Noriega's conviction, and forty year prison sentence, sent a loud message to the region about Washington's intolerance of blatant nefarious activities. Similarly, in Nicaragua, conditions were less volatile since Violeta Chamorro had defeated Daniel Ortega in the 1990 presidential election. Nevertheless, reports from Peter Reid, and other CIA field agents, confirmed the country was still a safe haven for Sandinista backed left wing terrorist groups.

"What's the story with that MI6 agent with a bug up his ass for Reid?" Hamilton asked.

"Clive Noakes?"

"Yes."

"I don't think we need worry about him anymore. Ever since we gave him a heads-up on that Gibraltar mission, he seems to have backed off. Plus, I gave him some shares in the mining concern we set up in Liberia. Charles Taylor appears to be making steady progress with his National Patriotic Front of Liberia (NPFL). It's only a matter of time before he controls the whole country. The diamond deposits are much better than we expected and he's going to need the revenue to bolster up his government."

"Well, once we've established Taylor as president, he'll need to settle down and do what he's told. We don't need another Saddam Hussein or Mañuel Noriega on our hands. Let's keep our eye on the prize and concentrate on getting those diamonds."

Chapter 14

NICARAGUA - 1993

DANGEROUS LIAISONS

2:40PM – Sunday February 28th 1993
Managua, NICARAGUA

Violeta Chamorro was three years into her six year term as President of Nicaragua. Not the most perfect of regimes from Washington's perspective, nevertheless, it was a vast improvement on the Sandinistas' left wing policies of the previous eleven years. The United States acknowledged her election victory in 1990 by lifting its trade embargo with the Central American nation. President Clinton, however, was well aware Sandinistas still had considerable influence and control throughout the Nicaraguan government.

Eduardo Santos had capitalized on the thawing relationship by utilizing the newly reopened trade links to expand his cocaine shipping routes through the country. For many months, Peter Reid had been working with Santos to oversee the venture which also included the establishment of smuggling routes into Europe. As far as Scott Hamilton was concerned, expansion of Santos' drug operations provided an excellent cover for Reid who was also developing relationships with numerous European terrorist organizations. His status in both FARC and the INRA allowed him to gain the confidence of key operatives in Germany's Baader-Meinhof, Italy's Red Brigade, and Spain's Basque ETA.

Reid had been spending more and more time in Managua, working for Santos. While there, he resided in a secure compound on the outskirts of the city. Although the decade long embargo had been lifted, the aftermath was evident on Nicaraguan roads. The *Lada* was the most common car in the country. The Russian auto maker filled the vacuum created when Washington prevented *Ford* and *General Motors* from doing business amid the sanctions. Peter had acquired a

Lada Samara 2108 hatchback, not that he wished to drive around in the style the Kremlin decreed appropriate for the proletariat, but because it served an important purpose. He utilized his interest in cars to modify the *Samara* much like moonshiners did during prohibition in America. The Irishman engaged the services of the auto repair shop in Managua which was owned and operated by Basque ETA members. Grinding down the head of the engine block; installing twin carburetors; and upgrading the brakes, were just some of the many improvements he asked the mechanics to make. By putting a small additive into the fuel, the *Lada*, which had taken fifteen seconds to reach 60 mph when it left the Russian factory, was rendered capable of reaching that in less than eight. Operating the vehicle at such an aggressive pace was not without cost. Tires required regular replacement as did brake pads and rotors. While most owners cringe when their car needs a service, Reid's reaction was the opposite because he used these opportunities as an excuse to ingratiate himself with the ETA commanders. CIA technicians had concealed microphones in and around his vehicle so activity in the shop could be monitored even when he was not present. The unreliable nature of the Russian automobile meant his frequent unannounced visits were not a cause for suspicion.

Reid kept his communications with Langley to a minimum, but even he did not need prompting by Scott Hamilton to be vigilant following the attack. Two days earlier, a car bomb had exploded in an underground car park of the World Trade Center in New York. Six people were killed and more than a thousand injured. The terrorists hoped the 1,300 pound bomb would have caused catastrophic harm to the North and South 'Twin Towers'. Upon hearing this news, he hastily devised another reason to visit the repair shop in Santa Rosa to gather as much intelligence as he could. Peter deliberately clogged the air filter with fine dust and advanced the ignition timing by slightly adjusting the distributor cap housing. The 1.5 Liter engine reacted exactly as he intended, laboring to propel the vehicle and giving every indication it was about to shut down at any minute.

Reid brought the *Lada* to a stuttering halt halfway through one of the doorways into the premises, and had already lifted its hood by the time one of the mechanics reached him.

"I don't have a strobe light and tried to adjust the timing myself," he explained. "I've really fucked it up." He then stretched himself over the front quarter-panel and attempted to remove the clips on the air filter manifold. This allowed him to eavesdrop on two men engaged in conversation with an individual he recognized to be an ETA terrorist. He tossed the clogged air filter to the mechanic and headed towards the huddled group in the corner of the shop.

"Paco!" he hailed. "Does anyone want to buy a *Lada*?" He barged right into the middle of their discussion without regard for the confidential nature of the meeting. His presence clearly concerned the two Middle Eastern visitors who immediately made their excuses to leave.

"Relax! What's your rush?" Reid asked as he put his arms around their shoulders to prevent them from leaving. "I'll leave my car here, but I'll swing by tomorrow to see if you've been able to reset the timing." He had seen and heard enough. Paco was holding a briefcase that looked very out of place in its surroundings. The slick Egyptian leather finish suggested it had been exchanged for the oversized manila envelope one of the men was holding. The little piece of conversation he had overheard told him the group had just concluded a negotiation. As he exited the building he spotted Libyan diplomatic plates on a large black sedan parked across the street. He kept walking and made his way to a café where he claimed a seat with a clear view of the repair shop.

On reflection, it did not surprise him agents from the Libyan

Embassy were meeting with ETA terrorists. Their embassy in Managua was several times larger than that of the United States. When the Berlin wall collapsed in November 1989, vibrations were felt throughout the world. Regimes that depended on the Soviet Union for support realized "The Bear" could no longer be relied upon for military protection, as well as economic support. This fact was confirmed, on December 26th 1991, with Declaration No. 142-H of the Soviet of the Republics of the Supreme Soviet of the Soviet Union. The proclamation heralded the independence of twelve soviet republics creating the Commonwealth of Independent States (CIS). The previous day, Soviet President Mikhail Gorbachev had resigned as the final leader of the Soviet Union when he handed over control of the Soviet nuclear arsenal to Russian President Boris Yeltsin. The iconic hammer and sickle flag was lowered from the Kremlin for the last time and replaced with the Russian tricolor. Satellite bastions of leftist ideology, such as Cuba and Nicaragua, were forced to cultivate relationships with other countries. Nicaragua's proclivity for supporting terrorist groups struck a chord with Libya's Colonel Gaddafi. Atrocities such as the bombing of *Pan Am* Flight 103 over Lockerbie, Scotland on December 21st 1988, underscored the horrifying consequences of Libya's investment in global terrorism.

2:40PM – Wednesday March 31st 1993
CIA Headquarters - Langley, Virginia, USA

The news not only concerned Maria Quintero and George Mulligan, but it also instilled a sense of pride.

"Your boy Reid has certainly stumbled upon a hornets nest," Scott Hamilton observed as he clicked through satellite photographs on the projector screen. "The arrests in New York have confirmed the connection between this ETA auto repair shop in Nicaragua and the group behind the bombing of the World Trade Center."

"Yes, but the last thing we need is for his cover to get blown," Maria added.

"We haven't figured out a plan yet, but when we do, I'm going to want you to go down there and help implement it."

Hamilton went on to explain how additional CIA operatives had been sent to Managua to increase surveillance of all known ETA terrorists and Libyan diplomats in the City. There would also be constant electronic interception of phone communications. Finally, and most importantly, a stationary satellite had been positioned over the auto repair shop in Managua to monitor everything and everyone.

"Don't worry about your boy," Hamilton assured Quintero and Mulligan. "I've ordered him to stay away from the target for now. We've enough operatives in the field watching it, so there's no need to compromise his cover."

7:35PM – Thursday April 29th 1993
San Jose, COSTA RICA

❝I had to change my plans at the last minute," Maria explained as they each scanned the menu. "I didn't want you to leave Nicaragua, but we got an alert that my cover has been compromised. I couldn't risk continuing to Managua."

"No big deal. It wasn't a problem for me to come down here."

"I wish that were all," Quintero continued in a quieter tone.

"What's the big panic?" Reid quizzed.

"The information you gave us in February from the ETA auto shop turned out to be major. We ordered you to keep away from it because we didn't want your cover blown while we investigated further. Arrests we made last month following the World Trade Center bombing have links to terrorist groups in Nicaragua. Your ETA friends are not just repairing cars. They have a secure bunker concealed at the rear of the premises. We believe it contains a considerable arms cache as well as blank passports and other forged documents. We want to send in explosive experts and we're also going to augment the number of agents in Managua."

"I'll take care of it," he responded nonchalantly. "It's been a while since I got involved in any excitement, Maria. Leave it with me."

"It's not as simple as that and you know it!"

"You've been hanging out in Washington for too long. By the time everyone in D.C. has checked their calendars and coordinated their meetings, I'll have taken care of it. I'm assuming you want the site …" He hesitated momentarily, not only to take a sip of wine, but also to introduce an element of tension. Maria finished his sentence.

"… neutralized?"

"We're turning into an old married couple," the Irishman joked, "finishing each other's sentences."

7:10PM – Sunday May 23rd 1993
Managua, NICARAGUA

After analyzing intelligence reports Maria had shared with him, it was obvious breaking into ETA's vault would not be an option. Nicaragua was a sovereign nation with which the United States did not enjoy a cordial relationship. Reid needed his scheme to be 100% successful. There would be absolutely no chance for a second attempt.

The plan was to detonate an explosion inside the repair shop when he knew the vault would be open. He convinced Quintero to let him work alone which reduced the risk of his plot being discovered. Several weeks had past since his last visit but Langley decided it was safe to resume contact. His first step was to observe customers when they collected their repaired vehicles. After careful consideration, he chose a 1989 *Lada*. He followed the car until the unsuspecting owner parked it outside her downtown apartment. One week later, he returned a little after 2:00AM, having spent the intervening days practicing how to break into his own *Lada*. Within thirty seconds of sliding a jimmy past the rubber window seal he was able to drive away in the stolen vehicle. By 2:30AM, the car was safely concealed in the garage of his compound outside Managua.

The following day was spent carefully hiding seventy-five pounds of Semtex inside the upholstery of the rear seat. Reid constructed a detonator using two solenoids from an automatic door mechanism. They were selected because they could be easily wired into the vehicle's twelve volt electric supply. Each solenoid had its own remote car door opener to operate it. One would be used to arm the bomb and the other to detonate it.

Once everything had been tested and the car's interior returned to its original condition, he dented and scratched some of the vehicle's bodywork. For his plan to work, he needed its owner to return the car to ETA's shop. He also wanted the repair process to require more labor than materials. He needed the vehicle to be parked inside the building for at least twenty-four hours. Accordingly, he made sure the damage would require infilling dents with epoxy filler, followed by sanding, priming and finally repainting.

01:36AM - Wednesday May 26th 1993
Managua, NICARAGUA

R eid had followed the hapless *Lada*'s progress since its return to the repair shop. A casual visit earlier that afternoon, under the guise of a service for his own car, confirmed the vehicle was in the midst of its new paint job. He also used that earlier visit as an opportunity to prime the bomb using one of the automatic door openers.

The neon digital clock on his dashboard indicated 01:36am, signaling exactly six minutes since he had tripped the intrusion alarm by hurling a brick through the auto-shop's window. Then, safely back in his car, he waited until an ETA operative responded to the alarm. He was parked at a safe distance but close enough for the second automatic door opener to detonate the bomb. He remained absolutely motionless as an approaching motorcycle came to a screeching halt. The rider kept his helmet on but lifted his visor. After having retrieved a revolver from a shoulder holster, he then unlocked the door and cautiously entered the premises. Reid knew the search would include checking the security vault. During the previous week he used a stop-watch to rehearse what the search might entail. He was able to make an educated estimate as to when the vault door would be opened. The instant the ETA motorcyclist entered the building Reid depressed the button on the watch. As each second ticked by, a different terrorist atrocity flashed into his mind: the World Trade Center bombing; *Pan Am* Flight 103; the USS Stark. At exactly one minute and thirty-five seconds, seventy-five pounds of Semtex exploded. The deafening and violent blast shook the entire Santa Rosa neighborhood. As Reid started his engine, multiple secondary detonations confirmed the hydraulic vault door had indeed been opened.

6:10PM – Friday September 24th 1993
CIA Headquarters - Langley, Virginia, USA

❝Your Irishman certainly came through for us," Scott Hamilton acknowledged."

"We got lucky when we arrested Ibrahim Elgabrowny, otherwise we'd never have discovered the connection between the ETA cell in Nicaragua and the World Trade Center bombing. There's no doubt Reid's been a great asset. We're gonna need more like him in Central and South America, especially now we've uncovered this link with Mid East terrorist groups."

"I've read your report, George, and I agree with you. We can use next year's World Cup as a platform for this operation. It looks like you've enough time to work on the details so, if everything goes according to plan, we'll have Eduardo Santos in our pocket. He'll provide us with excellent intelligence about FARC's terrorist operations as well as affiliated organizations."

"Gone are the days when their collaboration was limited by geographical boundaries," Mulligan sighed. "Networking between South American, Central American, European and Middle Eastern terrorist groups has been facilitated by agitators like Gaddafi. My fear is the World Trade Center attack was a wake up call and harbinger of worse things to come. We need to step up our game. I hope this new administration is going to get on board and help us."

"Clinton has only been in office a few months, so the jury's still out, but I agree with you. There's definitely cause for concern. It's not like when we had Reagan or our former boss in the White House," Hamilton reflected.

"We know from Reid's reports how fanatical Santos is about soccer. He's ecstatic his national team is coming to the U.S. next year. I've got another Irish agent in Boston ready to assist with the next phase of this plan."

"Well George, if he's even half as good as Reid, he'll be a worthy asset.

Chapter 15

BOSTON, MASSACHUSETTS, USA - 1994

WHAT ARE THE ODDS?

8:05AM – Monday March 14th 1994
East Boston, Massachusetts, USA

Paul Jennings opened his post office box and retrieved several items. He immediately discarded advertising and grocery flyers into a trash can. It amused him that a receptacle had been thoughtfully provided by the U. S. Postal Service for junk mail it had been paid to deliver. He slipped two utility bills into the back pocket of his jeans before tearing open an innocuous envelope with a Washington D.C. postage stamp. Like his utility bills, it also arrived every month. The contents always included twenty, clean, one hundred dollar bills. Occasionally, there would also be a simple type written note with a date and name of either a horse or college sports team. That morning, however, there was an extra two thousand dollars so he knew additional services would soon be required of him.

The monthly missive from Washington was a retainer fee for helping George Mulligan. His assignments dated back to 1986 when an Irish Trade Mission came to Las Vegas for Barry McGuigan's World Title fight. On that occasion, Jenning's job was to make sure his compatriots had discreet access to bookies who gave unbelievably high odds on their Irish hero. McGuigan's unexpected loss left the Irish visitors vulnerable to Mulligan's approaches since none of them realized the outcome of the fight had been influenced by CIA operatives.

Jennings paid the fifty cents bail to free a newspaper from incarceration in a dispenser, outside the post office, and made his way to the coffee shop across the street. He liked to start Mondays slowly. Saturday was the busiest day at the race track so his weekend routine was out of sync with the rest of New England by one day. Monday was his Sunday. The waitress smiled as he entered the diner. She picked up cutlery, a mug and a paper place mat while motioning him to meet her at an empty booth near the back of the restaurant.

"When are we going to run away together?" he asked jokingly.

"Always with the Blarney," replied the woman who was old enough to be his mother.

He grinned and the waitress made her way back to the kitchen without having to ask what he wanted for breakfast. Jennings opened his copy of the *Boston Globe* and went straight to the sports section. As usual, most of the coverage focused on the Red Sox, Bruins, Celtics and Patriots. He was pleasantly surprised, however, to see a soccer story headline and photographs of two sports personalities, both of whom had flamboyant hair styles. One was Alexi Lalas of the United States national soccer team, and the other was Colombian hero, Carlos Valderrama. The article explained that, internationally, football is completely different from the game played by the New England Patriots, and that the World Cup, hosted by the United States, was only three months away. The tournament takes place once every four years and is organized by FIFA which, some would argue, has more influence on world events than many governments. As defending champion, West Germany was guaranteed a place as was host country, the United States. Thirty other national teams had qualified in regional heats that began two years earlier.

Not only was Jennings delighted USA would host the elite soccer competition, but he was also thrilled the Republic of Ireland had qualified to play in the final stages. Ironically, Northern Ireland had been placed in the same preliminary play-off group as the Republic but failed to make the cut. Whereas sports like boxing and rugby draw their national teams from all thirty-two counties, soccer does not. The Republic of Ireland selects players from twenty-six counties, while Northern Ireland must play with a team drawn from the remaining six.

To Reid's delight, the *Globe* reported that the Northern Ireland team had been invited to play in pre-tournament practice games, including one against Colombia at Foxboro Stadium in Foxborough, Massachusetts.

Engrossed in the sports article, the young Irishman did not notice George Mulligan as he entered the restaurant, arriving at the table at the same time as the breakfast order.

"Good morning, Mr. Jennings."

"George! Good morning," he responded with surprise. "Have you had your breakfast yet?"

"Just coffee please," Paul tidied the newspaper off the table to make room for the dapper American who sat down opposite him.

"Are you backing any winners?"

"Yes, thanks to the tips you send me every month. I just picked up today's mail with your latest selection."

"There oughta be a law against that sort of behavior," Mulligan smirked.

"I'm guessing you've got another assignment for me."

"That's right. It involves your friend Fr. Foley. He's got to be impressed by your ability to feed him quality tips."

"He is, and he's got quite the gambling habit. If it weren't for my ... your tips, I think he'd be stripping lead off the church roof."

"The actual target is one of his parishioners, a guy called Eduardo Santos. Our plan is to use the priest to get to this guy."

"I've heard of him, but I've never met him. Isn't he involved in the nightclub scene?"

"Yes, Paul. That's him but he's the real reason I've been telling you to coach the priest to make bigger bets."

"I've done that. Last week I convinced him to put twenty-five thousand dollars on a horse. It's been tough, but recently he's been getting more adventurous."

"That's because he's been using money from the new community center building fund that Santos has been contributing to."

Mulligan went on to explain how his colleagues in Langley suspected Santos had plans to use the parish's building fund to launder profits from his drug business. Fr. Foley had managed to secure a verbal agreement with the Cardinal that the Colombian would be involved in the selection of a general contractor, once his donations surpassed a mutually agreed sum. Initially two bank accounts had been set up to hold his donations to St.Theresa's. Fr. Foley was the primary signatory and statements were sent to the parochial house. Ostensibly parish accounts, they were subject to audit by the Archdiocese which was also a signatory on each of them.

Despite these precautions, Fr. Foley managed the bank accounts while concealing his illicit gambling from the Chancellery. One was a money market which had a generous interest rate as long as money was not withdrawn frequently. The second was a checking account in which he kept a sufficient balance to cover soft cost expenses for preconstruction planning tasks. As his benefactor continued to make larger donations, Fr. Foley became more adventurous with his management of the money. He instructed the bank to invest half of the money market account in bonds that yielded more interest. He then opened a third account by skimming from the parish's weekly collections. No one was aware of his third account, nor was anyone aware he negotiated a fifty thousand dollar line of credit using the money market balance and bonds as collateral. All bank statements and loan agreements for the third account were kept concealed from both the Archdiocese and Santos. As his confidence in

Jennings' ability to pick winners grew, he used the line of credit to cover bets on horses and college sports teams. As a fortunate consequence of the young man's tips, the parish priest's winnings slightly offset losses from his own selections.

A gambling addiction is a compulsive obsession like alcohol and other drug dependencies. Unlike chemical afflictions, gamblers rarely have physical symptoms. They do not necessarily show up late for work on a regular basis or call in sick on a Monday. There is no sniffing or paranoia to indicate a dependency on cocaine. No aroma of marijuana or needle tracks to suggest other drug problems. In their parlance, the odds are against discovering someone is a gambling addict, especially if there is access to sufficient sources of cash to support the habit. Thanks to Eduardo Santos, an accommodating bank manager, and winning tips from Paul Jennings, Fr. Michael Foley had access to an unending supply of cash. He, of course, thought no one knew about the extra bank account but his assumption was wrong. As a consequence of their surveillance of Santos, George Mulligan and his colleagues uncovered Fr. Foley's expensive habit and the creative banking arrangements he had set up to fund it. Accordingly, Mulligan was able to tell Jennings how to coach the priest about the bets he needed to place.

"You're going to have to start prepping him for a major tip involving the World Cup tournament. Tell him your sources are sound and when the bet comes along, it will be an absolute certainty with a major pay off."

"What's your ultimate plan?"

"We need Fr. Foley to introduce you to Santos and then you're going to convince the two of them to bet the entire building fund on a single soccer game in the tournament."

"Holy fuck! Do you have a particular game in mind?"

"We want them to bet three million dollars on Colombia to beat USA. The bookmaker's odds are going to be so low it will require a huge bet to get a decent pay-out. It's your job to insist they allow you to place the bet fourteen days before the game in order to get more favorable odds. The game is scheduled to be played on June 22nd, so the money can be taken out of the church's accounts and returned in full, with the profits, before the Archdiocese sees this activity on the monthly bank statement."

"We've got two problems," Jennings responded. "First, I'm not sure I can get a man to place a multi-million dollar bet, especially since he's never met me before; second, even if I could, where would I find someone to take such a large wager?"

"The Colombians are fanatical about their team and you'll have Fr. Foley on your side. You've never let him down and we're going to make sure you get the right result. Leave that part to us. We'll set you up with an account at a major casino in Las Vegas. You'll explain that by putting your name on the account, it will help provide the church with a degree of anonymity. You'll get a check from Fr. Foley which you'll deposit in another bank. Once the funds clear, you'll make the bet with the casino."

Mulligan could see Jennings was far from convinced the plan could be implemented. "Relax, Paul. Have I ever let you down? All our tips have been solid. We only allow you to bet on certainties. Fr. Foley thinks you're a saint."

He then gave Jennings the name and address of the bank for the new account and also the name of an attorney who would set up a real estate trust. If ever there were to be an audit, nothing would look amiss since no checks would be made payable to him personally.

"The envelope you picked up at the post office box this morning should have had an additional two thousand dollars in it. Use it for the trip to Vegas to set up the account and pay the lawyer."

"Do you guys need more coffee over here?" the waitress interrupted.

"No thanks," Mulligan replied as he stood up from the table. "Breakfast is on me this morning." He discreetly handed her a neatly folded fifty dollar bill and politely excused himself.

7:40AM – Thursday March 17th 1994
Boston, Massachusetts, USA

It was the first Mass he had been to in several years. Apart from weddings or funerals, Paul Jennings no longer attended church on a regular basis. It was not how he had been brought up in Northern Ireland where he went more out of obligation than from spirituality. His parish church and school were vandalized routinely. On one dreadful day, several of his fellow high school students were shot while playing Gaelic Football. Fortunately, they all survived their physical wounds. There was another incident when he witnessed the murder of two senior citizens who were shot to death as they left church one Sunday morning. Atrocities such as these prevented Jennings from turning his back on the Roman Catholic religion while he lived in Northern Ireland, however, they were also the impetus for his emigration to the United States. It did not take long for him to realize people in America did not care if you were Protestant or Catholic. In Massachusetts, where New Englanders prayed in the hallowed surroundings of Fenway Park, Boston Garden and Foxboro Stadium, religious affiliation was even less important.

On March 17th, St. Patrick's Day, St. Theresa's Irish community was well represented at the seven o'clock service. Jennings remained in the Church while parishioners, predominantly dressed in green, filed out past their parish priest. Fr. Foley acknowledged the last of the worshipers before releasing the main door which had been held open with an ornate hinged doorstop. When he turned, he immediately spotted Jennings waiting at the end of a pew.

"Happy St. Patrick's Day, Father."

"Well this is a surprise," the priest remarked with a grin.

"I wanted to talk to you about the building fund and how we can reach your goal in three months." Like everyone else who visited the church, it was impossible for Jennings to miss the large thermometer shaped poster which tracked donations for the new parish center, and school addition.

"We're a million dollars short of our goal, Paul. How on earth could we close that gap in such a short time?"

"I've never let you down Father and now I've got a tip that's an absolute certainty. Unfortunately the odds aren't good, so it'll take a considerable wager to earn that million dollar return."

"How much would we need to bet?"

"Everything in your building fund."

Paul could tell from his facial expression that the priest was shocked by such a suggestion. The nervous cleric quickly grabbed the young Irishman's arm and herded him towards an alcove enclosing a small altar. He was determined their conversation would not be overheard by any stragglers who were still inside the church.

"Let me finish before you say anything, Father," Jennings continued. He began to speak in a hushed voice in response to Foley's signal of placing his finger on his lips. "This is a sure thing! We can get one to four odds on Colombia to beat USA when they play in the World Cup in June. Colombia is heavily fancied to win the whole tournament. It will be their second game of the round robin stage in their group, which means the result will be important to them. The only reason the U.S. has a team in the tournament is because it's the host country."

"I'm surprised you can get one to four odds," the cleric conceded.

"In America, people will be influenced by their heart. Patriotic pride will cause them to bet on the home team which will make the odds on Colombia higher than they really should be." Paul had all the right answers for the priest who was beginning to see the wisdom of making such a bet.

"How certain is your source?"

"Rock solid. They've never been more certain. I'm assuming what's been collected so far is in an account under your control," he continued, confident George Mulligan had provided him with accurate intelligence. "Since the game is scheduled for June 22nd, you can withdraw the money earlier in the month, and wash it through a bank account in Las Vegas that I'll use to place the bet. It will be repaid, with the additional million dollars, before June's statements are released."

"Let's not get ahead of ourselves. Nothing's going to happen unless you're able to convince our benefactor that it's something we should do."

"Who is he?" Paul asked, knowing Foley would never reveal his identity.

"He's a very private individual who doesn't want public recognition for the good work he's doing for St.Theresa's Church and the community. If he agrees to meet you, I'm sure he won't want you to make his identity known."

"Absolutely, Father, I understand."

"He's out of the country at the present time, but I'll try to set up a meeting for next week. That's if he's willing to meet with you at all."

12.20PM – Thursday March 24th 1994
Boston, Massachusetts, USA

❛❛I love this city," Fr. Foley proclaimed.

"If only you had a decent baseball team," Jennings teased as he peered in the direction of Fenway Park. It was more appropriate for the clergyman not to meet Eduardo Santos at his nightclub, so they had agreed to meet on the observation deck of the Prudential Tower.

"Boston loves its history," he sighed, "Even if the Red Sox have caused us more pain than we'd care to admit."

"Can you believe they ran marathons wearing shoes like those?" Jennings commented as he pointed to old photographs of the Boston Marathon decorating the walls in the observation deck.

"At least they had shoes!" The remark startled both men since neither had seen Eduardo Santos approach. "Where I come from, many of our children still run around barefoot," he continued. There was an awkward silence amongst the trio until Fr. Foley initiated the perfunctory greetings. Until that moment, Jennings had given no thought as to what his first meeting with Santos would be like. He had certainly not anticipated a discussion on world poverty.

"Not only is Eduardo helping St. Theresa's with its parish center and school addition in East Boston, but he also built a school for under privileged children in Colombia where I did missionary work in the seventies," the cleric gushed.

Jennings was unprepared for this topic of conversation. The focus of George Mulligan's preparation had been the Santos cocaine business. He had not expected Foley to pontificate about a veritable modern day saint. His initial impression of Santos changed, however, when the

Colombian began to quiz him about the plan to use the building fund to
bet on the soccer game.

"How come you're so certain about the outcome of this game?"
he probed.

"As Fr. Foley will tell you, my sources have been rock solid.
I've never let him down. Granted, we've never made a bet this big, but
I'd never jeopardize the building fund unless I was certain we could get
it more money."

Santos was as confident as every other Colombian about the success of his national team in the World Cup. The more he thought about
the Irishman's proposition, the more he liked the idea. He would not be
betting Colombia would win the whole tournament, only that they would
beat the USA. His only problem was his lack of knowledge about Fr.
Foley's prodigy. Jennings read the situation accurately and embarked on
a strategy to strengthen and fortify his situation.

"I'm sure you're cautious about people, but don't let my hand-
some Irish looks and charm deceive you. I've been places and seen
things and I know how to play this game." Santos and the priest were
both intrigued by Jenning's confidence. "Well," he continued, "there was
once a horse owner who did not want his horse to win a particular race.
Instead, he wanted it to be held back so bookmakers would underestimate
its potential and increase the odds the next time it competed. Immediately
before the race he met with the jockey and instructed him not to let the
horse win but to bring it home in third place. As it approached the finish
line, the horse was tight against the inside rail and leading the runners by
half a length. Remembering the owner's instructions, the jockey eased
off and allowed himself to be overtaken. Then, right at the line, he was
passed by another horse, causing him to finish in third place. So, later
in the unsaddling enclosure, the owner tried to look dejected as he sur-

reptitiously asked the jockey if his horse could have beaten the two that finished in front of it. 'Without a doubt ... but I don't know about the ones that finished behind me!' he added with wry smile."

The Colombian was silent for a moment, then threw his head back and laughed heartily, appreciating the subtlety of the tale.

"Good job, Fr. Michael. I like this young man, but I have news," he announced, changing the subject. "I just discovered something about the land where we're going to build."

He explained how a 21E environmental survey had uncovered asbestos in buildings scheduled for demolition. In addition, a former manufacturing plant on the property had apparently allowed other contaminants to leach into soils and groundwater. The term 21E is familiar to everyone involved in the conveyance of real estate or construction in Massachusetts. State regulations require these reports be authored by registered industrial chemists who quantify all environmentally harmful elements uncovered in the components of buildings, or soils. The most common hazards include lead paint and asbestos, however, some manufacturing operations, especially those carried out when regulations were less stringent, cause even more hazardous and expensive pollution. When these chemicals leach into the ground and its water table, the impact can reach far beyond the property limits with horrifying and, sometimes, fatal consequences for people in the community. Despite the best efforts of environmentalists to punish culprits, United States bankruptcy statutes often allow offending corporations to wind down operations, in a legal manner, in order to avoid penalties. Consequently, these entities and their shareholders are shielded from the cost of cleaning up their pollution.

"We could take legal action against former tenants and owners but if they settled their business affairs in the bankruptcy courts, it would be pointless," Santos concluded.

"Didn't these companies have insurance?" Fr. Foley inquired in a frustrated tone.

"I had my attorneys check the insurance policies that were in place and they proved to be useless. Various riders limited pollution clean up to no more than twenty-five thousand dollars. It would cost more in attorney fees to prove one of their policy holders was responsible. One of the tenants was involved in applying chrome to automobile trim at a time in history when car bumpers needed to be shiny. By-products from that process mean we've got a lot of expensive clean up."

The parish priest looked stunned and dejected. It was exactly the reaction Santos had intended.

"Don't worry my friend. I'm not going to let any of this get in our way. I want St. Theresa's to have its community center and it looks like our friend, Paul, has a way to make this happen, and a lot sooner than we'd expected."

Jennings was shocked and surprised by the positive and receptive response to the use of the building fund as a conduit for the bet. The Colombian stressed he did not want parishioners to know how much he was donating to the fund. Rarely a month went by without an announcement from the pulpit that there had been a large contribution from an anonymous donor. Fr. Foley regularly asked the congregation to pray for their benefactor who, privately, was greatly amused to know people were actually praying for a drug dealer.

"Over the next two months, I'm going to arrange for another million dollars to be deposited into the building account. This will bring the total to four million. Once Paul here delivers on his promise, we'll be able to break ground in July," Santos continued.

Jennings was speechless. His apprehension about the plan had disappeared. "This is even better than Mulligan could have expected," he thought to himself. He did not know Santos was, in fact, behind the 'contamination' reports on the proposed construction site. He needed to launder his drug proceeds and because Fr. Foley trusted him, he had managed to keep control of the process. None of the environmental reports concerned him because he had altered them to misrepresent the extent of the contamination. Licensed professionals had overseen the actual recovery of soil samples and materials from abandoned buildings at the location. Prior to the testing process, however, Santos had befriended a technician from the environmental laboratory and supplied him with cocaine at the *Cocoa Bean* nightclub. He then arranged for the technician to tamper with samples recovered from the proposed job site. Consequently, even though most of them actually came back with clean test results, the technician complied with the request and represented that the site was heavily polluted. The erroneous environmental report cost the Colombian less than one thousand dollars worth of cocaine. Morally, the technician had no problem falsifying the results because Santos owned the real estate, and was not trying to pass off contaminated soils as being clean. Reports of the fake contamination were created so he could justify exorbitant environmental clean-up costs. By using the church funds he had previously donated, he would be able to filter back his money through his construction company. Thanks to Attorney Grey's corporate filings, no one would be able to find out that Santos was the primary stockholder of Marshall Builders.

The discussion ended with an understanding that over the next two months, Eduardo Santos would deposit an additional million dollars into the building fund in small cash amounts that would not create an issue with the bank. On June 10th, Fr. Foley would transfer four million dollars into a real estate trust account which had been opened by Paul Jennings. The Irishman would then use the money to bet on Colombia beating USA when the teams played on June 22nd.

9:15PM – Friday June 3rd 1994
Foxborough, Massachusetts, USA

If Northern Ireland had played any other country, Paul Jennings would have been disappointed with the 2-0 loss but, on this occasion, he was relieved. Although his national team had not qualified to play in the World Cup, it had been invited to the United States to play 'friendly' warm-up games against several national teams that had qualified to play in the tournament. As luck would have it, one of these games was against Colombia and the venue was Foxboro Stadium, in Foxborough Massachusetts. Both he and Fr. Foley were guests of Eduardo Santos who had rented a luxury box for the game.

"I think your Northern Ireland team is very similar to the US," Santos remarked as the referee blew the final whistle.

"Valderrama looked good out there," Jennings acknowledged. "He certainly controlled the midfield."

Many of the twenty thousand Colombian supporters wore blonde curly wigs in tribute to Valderrama who had played a strong game for his country. The noise of drums and horns was deafening as the South American fans celebrated the victory over Northern Ireland.

"I want you and Fr. Michael to come back to the *Cocoa Bean*. We're having a private party and many of the Colombian players will be there," Santos invited.

The *Cocoa Bean* nightclub was not a place Fr. Foley would have chosen to go of his own accord. He was relieved he had not worn his liturgical collar which would have been very inappropriate for the sur-roundings. Colombia's performance, however, in its first soccer game in the United States, gave the priest reason to feel good about its upcoming game with the host country.

*****

Within minutes of their arrival at the nightclub, both Foley and Jennings were comfortably situated in the 'VIP' section. Eduardo's son, Xavier, was sitting with them and it was not long before several of the Colombian soccer stars arrived to celebrate as special guests of the owner.

"Having the World Cup tournament take place in the United States is a dream come true for my father," Xavier observed. "He has tickets for all Colombia's games."

"I hope that includes watching them play against the Republic of Ireland in the final," Jennings replied wishfully.

"What is it with Ireland?" Xavier asked, "You have less than four million people on your little island and yet there are two separate international soccer teams.

Jennings tried to explain how politics and sectarian undercurrents caused the problem, but the noisy surroundings were not conducive for such a lesson. At that moment, Eduardo approached the table accompanied by one of the Colombian players.

"I'd like you to meet my son and two of my friends. This is my favorite player, Andrés Escobar," he gushed.

"Hey dad, if Andrés doesn't mind, why don't I take a photograph of the two of you?" Xavier suggested. The elder Santos translated for Escobar who placed his arm around Eduardo and smiled while the young man focused his camera.

As the evening progressed, agitated members of the coaching squad looked on with trepidation as Escobar and his teammates appeared to be enjoying themselves a little too much. The FIFA tournament was scheduled to begin in twelve days so partying in nightclubs was not really appropriate. The comfortable win over Northern Ireland had placed Eduardo Santos in a very positive frame of mind. Despite his overtures to the coaching staff, it was clear they did not share his desire to let the players relax and celebrate their victory. Eventually, the athletes complied with their coaches' instructions and left the *Cocoa Bean*, but not before taking more photographs with both Santos men.

On the drive back to East Boston, Fr. Foley confided in Jennings that he would like to have seen the Colombians score more goals against Northern Ireland.

"Relax Father, there's no way the United States is going to beat this Colombian team."

"Even so, I don't feel good about this, Paul. Placing a four million dollar bet is just insane."

"It would be insane if you were betting on USA to win. The people I get my tips from are infallible. Just like the Pope!"

"I don't think I can go through with it. It's all gotten out of hand."

"Santos donated the money with the understanding it would be bet on Colombia to beat USA. There's no turning back now, Father."

Jennings pulled up outside the rectory.

"I've already explained we're going to get the best odds because people in Vegas will be betting with their heart instead of their head, so more money will be put on USA to win. This will drive down their odds and give us slightly better ones for Colombia," Jennings assured the doubting priest.

"You're not the one who's supposed to be looking after this money for the Parish," Foley protested.

"The money will only be missing from the account for two weeks and by the time it's returned there'll be an additional million dollars. No one at the Archdiocese is going to question anything after that."

"Things have gotten way out of control," Foley lamented. "I should never have let you talk Eduardo and me into this. What was I thinking?"

"You saw the Colombian team play this evening, plus, I've never given you a bad tip. Not one of my tips has failed to come through for you. I can't believe I'm telling a priest to have a little faith."

Fr. Foley gave Jennings a little grin as he stepped out of the car. The young Irishman had no doubt his betting tips were sound but he could not divulge the source. As he drove off he watched as the silhouette in the rear view mirror faded into the distance. It concerned him Foley had chosen to stand motionless at the curb and not go into the rectory. It was obvious the parish priest was a troubled man.

9:25PM – Saturday June 11th 1994
Logan Airport - Boston, Massachusetts, USA

Jennings crammed his carry-on luggage into the storage bin before settling into window seat 4A and discreetly adjusting the money-belt under his shirt. He was cognizant it concealed the four million dollar check representing the entire building fund for St. Theresa's community center and school addition. To add to his anxiety, there was an additional check for two million dollars which Eduardo Santos had entrusted him to bet on Colombia.

As the plane was towed away from the jet bridge its captain welcomed passengers on the flight to Las Vegas, Nevada. The Irishman's day had started at 5:00AM. His stable had horses in three races that afternoon and he had to rush to get everything organized so he could get to the airport after work in time for his flight. His focus was to get six million dollars deposited at the casino as soon as possible. He reclined his seat, put on the in-flight head phones and gently rested his folded hands on top of the concealed money-belt.

"Sir… Sir," the flight attendant repeated. "I need you to return your seat to its upright position." He had slept for several hours and, instinctively, checked to make sure his money belt was safe. "Sir… I need you …" He nodded and sat forward before the attendant had finished her request. While the cockpit crew conversed with air traffic controllers, Jennings shuffled through paperwork in the envelope he had retrieved earlier from his post office box. Two thousand dollars were wrapped in a printed itinerary. George Mulligan was always generous when it came to per diem allowances. The itinerary confirmed a room at the Excalibur had been booked for two nights, as well as a seat on the 3:05PM flight

back to Boston on Monday. He had to wait until then to allow his check
to clear before he could place the wager.

As the cab approached the iconic illuminated strip, he thought
about his last Vegas visit during Barry McGuigan's 1986 World Title
Boxing fight with Steve Cruz. A cold chill traveled down his spine,
however, when he remembered he was there to place a multi-million
dollar bet on a single soccer game.

He entered through the revolving doors of the hotel and considered the contrast between the gambling industry in Nevada and the
bookmakers in Northern Ireland. In Belfast, he recalled, customer service in betting shops was limited to brushing the floor at the end of the
day. Even though there were televisions on the premises, most patrons
opted to watch the sporting events from the comfort of a bar stool in an
adjacent pub. Both establishments catered to the same demographic but
while one offered hope, the other offered consolation.

"Thank you for choosing the Excalibur Hotel, Mr. Jennings,"
the hotel receptionist acknowledged as she handed him his room card.
He thanked the young woman and, with his left hand, reached down to
lift his bag. Suddenly, he felt a tight tug on shoulder.

"Mr. Jennings, welcome to Las Vegas!" He turned immediately
to see a smiling George Mulligan.

"Put your things in the room and come back down. I'll be over
there in the bar."

*****

"So you couldn't trust me here by myself?"

"Not at all," George replied, setting down his empty glass.
"There's been a slight change of plan."

"How could there be a change at this stage? I've talked Foley and Santos into giving me six million dollars! If they don't get a return on their investment, my life won't be worth living. Santos will kill me and the priest will bury me!"

"Don't worry. Nothing's going to happen to you but this is what you're going to do. You're going to bet the whole lot on USA beating Colombia and not on Colombia beating the USA."

"That's fuckin' ludicrous! You're going to get me killed, George. They're expecting me to bet on Colombia and there's no way USA will beat them."

"You're going to bet everything on USA winning. Neither Santos nor the priest is to know what you've done until the final whistle blows."

"This is insane, it's fuckin' crazy. This can't be happening!" Jennings pleaded, pressing the palms of his hands against his temples. Santos is not someone you fuck with."

"Relax! The bookies are paying 3-1 odds against the USA. You're going to walk away with a twenty-four million dollar payout."

"I'm beginning to wish Fr. Foley had pulled the plug on all of this. How sure are you Colombia is going to lose?"

"Have I ever let you down? Trust me." Jennings shook his head in disbelief and dismay.

"I need another fuckin' drink, George. I hope you know what you're doing."

11:10PM – Thursday June 16th 1994
East Boston, Massachusetts, USA

Since returning from Las Vegas, Paul Jennings had managed to avoid meeting either Eduardo Santos or Fr. Michael Foley. He knew they both planned to fly to California for Colombia's first game against Romania, scheduled for Sunday at the Rose Bowl in Pasadena. He blamed a heavy workload and a sick stomach for his inability to meet with them. Paul was afraid if they were to meet, face to face, he would have been unable to convince either the drug dealer or the priest everything had gone as planned in Las Vegas.

His phone had rung many times before he went to bed at 11:00PM, but not once did he pick up the receiver. On each occasion caller ID showed the call was coming from the *Cocoa Bean* nightclub. Since Fr. Foley had previously stated he and Santos were booked on a 9:00AM flight the following day, the Irishman felt confident he had evaded both men.

The next morning he was out of his apartment by 5:30AM. Two of his horses had upcoming races and he planned to give them a good workout before breakfast. Unfortunately, he was not the only person with plans for an early start. As soon as he stepped out onto the street, Eduardo Santos opened the door of his silver Mercedes convertible which was parked immediately behind Paul's Honda.

"You're a difficult man to get in touch with."

"What do you mean?" the Irishman asked, pretending not to know anything about the numerous calls from the previous night.

"Where's the ticket for the soccer bet?" Santos inquired menacingly.

"I've got it locked in my safety deposit box. There's no way I'm walking around with that in my back pocket!" It was not the answer the drug dealer wanted to hear, however, it did make sense.

"You're going to make another trip to Vegas on Sunday evening. I want you to bet another million dollars on Colombia to beat USA." The color drained from the shocked Irishman's ashen face as Santos lifted a designer canvas luggage bag from the back seat of the Mercedes.

"What's wrong?" he quizzed. "I thought you said your tips were foolproof. Once you've placed this bet, I want you to come to Pasadena and watch the game with Fr. Michael and me. The plane tickets and everything you need are in this envelope." As Santos walked toward him, the younger man made a conscious effort to compose himself. He had no choice but to take the drug dealer's money.

"When you get to Pasadena you'll be staying in the same hotel as the Colombian team," he continued as he handed over twenty pounds of one hundred dollar bills. "I also want you to fly first class. If what Fr. Michael tells me is true, this soccer bet will be the first of many we'll be doing together. Pack a sports jacket and a pair of dress pants. I've organized a small reception for Colombian dignitaries on Tuesday evening before the USA game. Some of the players will also be there. Nothing fancy, just a way to show the guys how much we appreciate their efforts."

"I'm on my way to work, Eduardo. Where am I supposed to put a million dollars in cash? I can't leave it under the bed in my apartment."

"Relax, Paul. No one would ever believe there's anything in the trunk of that Honda other than a lug wrench and a jack."

After personally putting the money into the young man's car, Santos immediately returned to his own vehicle. He lifted his right hand off the steering wheel to wave as the silver Mercedes drove away. The Irishman struggled to conceal his feelings and somehow managed to acknowledge the gesture with a broad smile.

9:30PM - Saturday June 18th 1994
Medellín, COLOMBIA

The two men had already consumed several beers as well as a whole bottle of tequila by the time Romania scored its third goal against Colombia. Peter Reid and Carlos Falcao sat in the crowded café surrounded by two hundred drunk, dejected and demoralized Colombian fans.

In preparation for the World Cup, Eduardo Santos and his colleagues had shipped excessive amounts of cocaine into the United States. Their strategy was to make sure the demand would be met by an organized network of dealers and suppliers who would saturate clubs and bars in the host cities. Although the illegal drug industry could not match *Snickers* and *Coca-Cola* for endorsement deals with FIFA, it still used the event to increase interest in its product. Just as with any major sports competition, the World Cup was expected to attract sporting and entertainment celebrities from all over the world. Accordingly, hotels and nightclubs would be full of cocaine users with copious amounts of disposable cash and habits that needed to be satisfied. Santos and his cohorts did not have the added expense of endorsement fees, nor were their profits taxed like the *Mars* and *Coca-Cola* corporations.

Peter Reid had wanted to return to the United States to attend the Republic of Ireland's World Cup games but George Mulligan told him to leave Nicaragua and go back to Colombia. The CIA wanted information about money that had been bet on the Colombian national team by cartel leaders. To assist him in his task, Mulligan gave the Irishman a substantial bankroll to use.

"What the fuck!" Falcao exclaimed as a stunned and defeated

Colombian team left the field. It was not how anyone had expected Valderrama and his colleagues to perform in their opening game. Despite the loss, Falcao was impressed by the large wager Reid had placed on the Colombian team.

"Now they've got to win their next two games, Carlos."

"I don't know, hombre. They didn't look too good out there."

"The next game is against the USA which shouldn't be a problem. I want to bet fifty thousand on that game. Can you take care of that?"

"Madre de Dios!"

"I want to cut my losses in case Colombia doesn't win the tournament but I know they'll beat USA."

"You know, that makes a lot of sense," Falcao acknowledged. "I think I'll do the same. I can call my guy right now. He'll take the bet over the phone but we'll need to give him the money by Tuesday at the latest."

4:15PM – Wednesday June 22nd 1994
Pasadena, California, USA

❝You're here. I was worried." Santos announced as Jennings entered the luxury box the Colombian had reserved for the game. Fr. Foley also appeared relieved as he greeted the new arrival.

"Don't worry, I took care of the bets," the young Irishman assured them, "but I had a bad dose of food poisoning. I literally couldn't leave the hotel room."

"Well you're here now!" Santos acknowledged. "Xavier, get Paul a beer." The younger Colombian responded obediently while his father expressed his disappointment with their national team's debut performance in the tournament. Jennings wondered how Santos would react if he knew that, contrary to his instructions, all the money had been bet on the United States winning the upcoming game.

"I want Fr. Michael to hold the betting slips for good luck. Give them to him please!"

"They're locked in the safe in my hotel room," Jennings lied.

"You're always so very careful," laughed the Colombian as he guided him towards the private bar.

"There wouldn't be a fucking problem with these bets, would there?" he whispered threateningly in Paul's ear. He put his arm around the Irishman and squeezed, ostensibly in an affectionate manner.

"No, not at all, Eduardo. I'm just not comfortable walking around with seven million dollars in betting slips."

Santos smiled but said nothing. Instead he walked towards two burly men who were standing by the door. Suddenly the roar of ninety thousand screaming soccer fans saturated the room as Team USA and

Colombia took to the field. Jennings was unable to hear what Santos was saying to his guards. From glances they made in his direction, however, he appeared to be the subject of their conversation.

"Is everything alright, Paul?" Fr. Foley inquired discreetly.

"Sure, Father. Everything's good. We've a lot of money riding on this game and Eduardo doesn't have the benefit of your experience with my betting tips."

"You're lucky you missed last night's party at the hotel. A few of the players came along but not as many as my father had expected," Xavier added.

"I'm surprised the coach let any of the team attend. This has become a must-win game after their defeat," the Irishman reflected. "Who'd have thought Colombia would lose to Romania, the Republic of Ireland would beat Italy and USA would tie with Switzerland? It's just one surprise after another."

"Eduardo was stunned after Sunday's game," the cleric recounted. "We really need to win today. I didn't sleep a wink last night."

A hush descended over the stadium as both teams lined up for their national anthems. Once the game started, it was clear the Colombian players were suffering under the intense pressure of their country's expectations. Meanwhile, the U.S. team had already tied their opening game against Switzerland and had nothing to do but enjoy playing on the world stage. Not only were the eleven Colombians nervous, but their compatriots watching on television at home were also anxious. Eduardo Santos and Fr. Foley were even more stressed with the added tension of their multimillion dollar wager.

The priest stared stoically at the action on the field while Santos paced back and forth glancing briefly at the drama unfolding below. Thirty-four minutes into the game the stadium erupted with a level of noise never before experienced in the history of the Rose Bowl. Santos emerged from the bathroom at that precise moment and knew immediately something very bad had happened. Fr. Foley could scarcely believe what his eyes had just witnessed. Colombia's defender, Andrés Escobar, had attempted to deflect a threatening ball but his interception had dire consequences. The move caught his own goalkeeper short-footed. Both players could do nothing but watch the ball strike the back of their own net. Jennings surreptitiously manipulated the betting slips folded deep in the front pocket of his pants. Fr. Foley, the only American unhappy with what had just happened, turned and looked directly at Eduardo Santos.

"Escobar just scored an own goal," the priest reported with an air of desperation. Santos stared at Jennings and then at the two thugs by the exit who, in turn, glared at the Irishman. Until that moment, Paul had never thought of his life in terms of its monetary value. Insurance actuaries employ complicated formulae to determine such figures but, in that instant, he knew exactly how much his life was worth: seven million dollars; the exact amount he had been given by Santos and Foley. There were, however, another fifty-six minutes remaining in the game, but the Colombians had their backs to the wall. The bookmakers had given odds of three to one which meant the payout would be twenty-eight million dollars. Provided George Mulligan maintained his unblemished record, he would be safe. "Fifty-six minutes," Jennings thought to himself. "Fifty-six minutes to find out if I'm going to live or die!"

"There's still a lot of time left to play," Paul uttered in an unsuccessful attempt to reassure everyone within earshot. Santos disappeared again into the private bathroom and did not return until the half-time break. The atmosphere in the luxury box felt more like a funeral than a world class sporting event.

The second half of the game was only seven minutes old when

disaster struck again for the Colombians. Team USA's Ernie Stewart scored a goal which put the host country in a commanding 2-0 lead. Santos glared at Jennings who elected not to say anything. Every minute in the game, from that point on, seemed like an eternity.

By the time Colombia scored a consolation goal in the final minute of the game, Santos had taken up a position at the door beside his bodyguards. Ninety thousand elated and screaming fans drowned the noise of the final whistle when it was blown by the Italian referee. USA had defeated Colombia by a score of 2-1. The tension in the room was palpable.

"I have a confession, Fr. Foley," Jennings whispered.

"I don't think now's a good time to hear your confession, Paul."

"All your money was bet on USA to defeat Colombia." Despite the fact Jennings was smiling and waving both betting slips in front of him, the priest found it hard to comprehend what was going on.

"It's all good, Eduardo," he shouted, "I bet all the money on USA winning. Not Colombia. My source insisted on complete secrecy. I got odds of three to one. These two slips are worth twenty-eight million dollars!" Santos was motionless.

"Are you fucking serious? Fr. Michael told me you were good, but I never saw this coming," he finally admitted in disbelief at the shocking turn of events. Xavier was stunned also. Although he had been born in the United States, he was sad Colombia had been eliminated from the tournament. The fact his father and parish priest had won twenty-one million dollars plus their initial wager of seven, only made the experience more surreal.

Eduardo Santos took his bodyguards outside to speak with them privately. Jennings had just made the announcement but the drug dealer immediately realized the news of his good fortune would not be well received by the Colombian community.

"What you heard here today doesn't get repeated to anyone," he instructed. "Did either of you bet on Colombia?" Each of the men had gambled several thousand dollars on their national team. This second loss meant the result of their final game against Switzerland, the following Sunday, would be inconsequential. Despite being one of the favorites, Colombia's aspiration of winning the World Cup was over. The players would be returning home two weeks sooner than anyone had anticipated.

"I'm going to reimburse you for your losses and give each of you another ten thousand, but none of this goes anywhere. Neither of you is to speak of this again. Not even to one another. Do I make myself clear?"

Both men nodded and thanked their boss. Santos felt himself sweat as he visualized the consequences of anyone discovering he had profited by Colombia's demise.

8:00AM – Thursday June 23rd 1994
Lago Titicaca, BOLIVIA

While Eduardo and Xavier followed the misfortunes of Colombia's soccer team in the United States, Klaudia Santos had taken a trip to Bolivia. It had been several months since she had seen her brother and there were issues with their pharmaceutical and air-freight businesses she needed to review with him. At least, that was the story she told her husband.

"That was a crazy phone call you got from Xavier last night," Steffen Bremner remarked. Klaudia's son had called to share the news that her husband and Fr. Foley were on their way to Las Vegas, with Paul Jennings, to collect twenty-eight million dollars because of the USA victory.

"Bizarre," she agreed. "For the last three months, all I've had to listen to is how Colombia was going to win the World Cup. I don't know what his associates would think if they knew about this. They all gambled fortunes on their country winning the tournament."

"Perhaps now they'll get back to the business of shipping our cocaine," Steffen mocked.

"I've got to take a shower and get on the road or I'll miss my plane." Klaudia had planned to stay in Bolivia for a week but thought it unlikely Eduardo would stay in California for Colombia's final inconsequential game. She pulled back the sheets and scampered toward the bathroom.

"Before you leave, we need to talk about the Rottweiler advertisement. I can't believe it's been five years since I answered the ad, but you'll be happy with the way things are turning out, and so will Mother.

I just wish Father had lived to see how successful the other cells have been."

"So is it time to move to the next phase?" she shouted from the shower.

"I believe it is. It's just a question of picking the right place and the right time. We've already got the Reich people!" Steffen joked smugly.

Chapter 16

BOSTON, MASSACHUSETTS, USA - 1994

GAME OVER

5:00PM – Friday June 24th 1994
Newton, Massachusetts, USA

T he last message on the family's answering machine was from the local pharmacy reminding her husband to pick up his photographs. Klaudia had done a lot of thinking during her long trip home and the message was somewhat fortuitous. Immediately, she retrieved the ticket from under a magnet on the refrigerator where it had been placed several weeks earlier. Soon she was standing in the store thumbing through photographs of Eduardo with various Colombian soccer players. They had been taken during the party at the *Cocoa Bean* after the team had beaten Northern Ireland.

"How quickly can you make two more sets of prints from these negatives?"

"It shouldn't take more than twenty minutes," replied a young, gum chewing, assistant.

As Klaudia waited, she debated the pros and cons of what she had resolved to do. By leaking news of her husband's bet that USA would beat Colombia, and sharing photographs of him partying with the team during their time in the United States, she would essentially be signing his death warrant. It was an open secret in Colombia that drug cartels had bet heavily on their national team winning the World Cup. With Eduardo out of the way, she would control everything. Xavier was a young man and heir to the Santos estate, so she no longer had any use for her husband. For years she had shadowed his negotiations and deals. She knew all his associates, and they knew her. More importantly, they knew she and Steffen Bremner controlled the flow of cocaine from Bolivia. Eduardo's own people would take care of the situation once they saw the photographs. If she was careful, no one would ever suspect she had played a part in his betrayal.

Before leaving the premises with the extra photographs, she lifted a fresh 'drop-off' envelope from the counter. She did not want Eduardo and Xavier to know she had opened the packet and seen the prints. With care, she could repackage the original order in the new envelope and neither of them would suspect she had seen anything.

3:30PM – Tuesday June 28th 1994
Bogotá, COLOMBIA

W hen he opened the manila envelope Carlos Falcao was irate. It had only his name printed on a small white label and nothing to indicate where it had originated. A typewritten note, along with photographic proof, explained how Eduardo Santos had hosted parties for the Colombian team, prior to their World Cup games, then bet heavily on their opponents. The evidence was irrefutable. Copies of travel itineraries confirmed Santos left California after the USA game and went immediately to Las Vegas to collect twenty-eight million dollars, before returning to Boston.

Betrayal of Colombia's soccer team was unforgivable. Apart from the financial loss, the dreams and aspirations of a nation had died when the final whistle heralded USA's victory on June 22nd. Santos could never be trusted again. There was only one course of action and it could not be delegated. Although the risk would be considerable, Falcao resolved to complete the task himself.

8:30AM – Friday July 1st 1994
Washington, D.C., USA

Peter Reid was relieved to go back to the United States and to get a break from his undercover work in Central and South America. Carlos Falcao and his cohorts were a crazy bunch and since Colombia's World Cup upset, they were even more volatile. When he got the call to return to Washington to meet with George Mulligan and Maria Quintero, he used the Republic of Ireland's unexpected success in the Tournament as an excuse to make the trip. Falcao accepted it was a good reason for the Irishman to escape the gloom and despair that had descended upon Colombia.

"We're almost able to pull you out of there," Mulligan began. "Thanks to your intelligence reports, as well as our gambling sting, we'll be able to flip Santos to work for us. He can't refuse because he knows he's a dead man if the cartels find out about his Vegas bet."

"Sounds like you have him exactly where you want him. So what's next for me?"

"We've got several projects actually, but first I want you to take some time off to relax. We've already briefed our British cousins about your participation in our operations. Besides, if things don't go as planned with Santos, Colombia may not be the best place for you to be at the present time."

"So it's safe for me to go back home?"

"Well, it's more of an understanding between us and MI6. You'll need to use the Martin Quinn alias we gave you after your visit to our Consul General's home in Belfast," Mulligan explained. "Other than that, you'll be left alone. We've given the British the remote control codes you developed for the INRA. That sweetened the pill. Maria has some cash and credit cards for you with updated ID and travel documents for Martin Quinn. You'd better get over to her office ASAP. Everyone's trying to clear their desk to get an early start on the holiday."

8:00PM – Friday July 1st 1994
East Boston, Massachusetts, USA

Fr. Foley was elated. Eduardo Santos had returned eight million dollars to the parish building account. There were ample funds for construction of the parish center, an addition to the East Boston school, as well as its sister school in Colombia. There was even a substantial endowment to assist with operating costs for decades. All the anguish and stress associated with the bet was behind him and he had resolved never to do anything like it again. The priest had considered naming the parish center in honor of Santos and Jennings but realized he could never divulge how the funds were actually raised.

*****

While Fr. Foley was dining with the Cardinal at the Chancellery, Eduardo Santos was sipping tequila in the office of his Newton home. He was alone, taking time to privately reflect on the events of previous weeks. There was one thing, however, he had wanted to do ever since his premature return from the World Cup. Carefully, he placed the photograph in the frame and gently wiped away his fingerprints from the glass. He gazed at the picture of himself and Andrés Escobar which Xavier had taken at the *Cocoa Bean* nightclub. Smiles on the faces of the two men reflected hopes and dreams when they were still alive for Colombia. He did not blame Escobar for the team's demise. He would always be his favorite player. That fact would never change.

10:10AM – Saturday July 2nd 1994
Newton, Massachusetts, USA

Falcao's trademark gold canines meant it was impossible for him to legally enter the United States without triggering the attention of federal agencies including Customs, DEA and FBI. Consequently, he had ceased to use conventional channels when entering and leaving the country. The border between the Gulf of Mexico and the Pacific Coast stretches for 1,969 miles. Authorities, on the northern side, constantly try to control the passage of people and contraband between the United States and Mexico. The cartels' extensive smuggling routes, however, presented Falcao with numerous secret options.

The town of Nogales straddles the border which made it a key hub in the Santos cocaine trafficking network. Its maze of tunnels and storm drains provides numerous unregulated gateways into, and out of, Arizona. Once he had crossed from Mexico, Falcao used Greyhound buses and Amtrak rail to travel to Boston where he scanned the classified ads for a used motorcycle. He paid four thousand dollars, in cash, to a graduating medical student to equip himself with an untraceable mode of transport. The deal included a helmet with a tinted visor that would help conceal his identity.

It had been two years since he had last visited Boston. On that occasion he had partied at the *Cocoa Bean* and dined at the Santos residence in Newton. His previous trip to the nightclub enabled him to identify the venue where the photographs had been taken. Falcao reached inside his black leather motorcycle jacket and carefully slid back the safety button on the automatic pistol, tucked snugly underneath his left armpit. Only two vehicles and one jogger passed the Colombian while he waited in the secluded Newton side street, just out of sight of the Santos home. He slightly cracked open the tinted visor to give the impression he was studying a map strategically unfolded on the bike's gas tank. As Eduardo's convertible reversed out of his driveway, the map was put away and Falcao started his engine. Santos drove along the street seemingly unaware he was being followed. As they both approached Newton Corner, the traffic signal at the exit ramp to the Massachusetts Turnpike turned red. Falcao stopped beside the vehicle as its preoccupied driver changed the station on the radio. He had the advantage of a stationary target as well as the element of surprise. He did not engage his prey. Two slugs ripped through the skull causing Santos to slump forward against the steering wheel. The Mercedes, which had not been put into PARK, immediately began to inch into the intersection. Falcao fired two more shots into the rib cage of the lifeless body, before speeding off. There was no other vehicle within sight of the assassination.

At the moment of his death Eduardo Santos had been listening to his car radio. It was shocking news. "Andrés Escobar, the Colombian defender whose own goal, against the United States, helped eliminate Colombia from the World Cup, was shot dead today in his home city of Medellín. Escobar, 27, was shot multiple times by three men who, according to witnesses, fled after shouting, 'Thanks for the own goal.'"

By noon, Falcao was already south of Providence, Rhode Island, traveling further and further away from the scene of the crime.

7:50AM – Wednesday July 6th 1994
London, ENGLAND

There would be a two hour wait at London's Gatwick airport for the second leg of his itinerary. Twelve years had passed since Peter Reid had last been home and he was really looking forward to seeing his family. His new Martin Quinn passport got him through British Customs and Immigration, as well as the additional security check for passengers flying to Belfast. While he sat in the departure lounge he imagined how he would spend his four week vacation. He decided not to have breakfast until he landed on Irish soil and his mouth watered at the thought of an Ulster Fry. He joined fifteen other passengers aboard a British Midland flight. With all preflight procedures performed, he was pushed back into his seat as the plane accelerated down the runway. A passenger on the earlier outbound leg from Belfast had left a copy of the *Newsletter*. One of two morning newspapers available in Northern Ireland, the Newsletter is the oldest English printed publication in the world. Recognized for its editorial support of the union between Northern Ireland and the United Kingdom, the publication advertised an upcoming special edition, planned for the Province's July 12th celebrations. Reid, however, was more focused on an article on the front page. Apparently an INRA operative had been killed, two days earlier, when a bomb detonated prematurely. The account detailed a technical breakthrough in the British Army's battle to combat remote controlled explosive devices. It cited electronic jamming equipment developed by *National Semiconductor* of Waltham, Massachusetts, for countering the terrorist bombing threat.

The plane banked prior to making its approach to Belfast City Airport as he picked out landmarks on the skyline including *Sampson* and *Goliath*, the monstrous cranes in the *Harland & Wolff Shipyard*.

Reid had not told his family he was returning home. As the taxi traveled along Sydenham Bypass he scanned freshly painted red, white and blue curbstones, and the flags and bunting commemorating the upcoming July 12th holiday. Murals and ceremonial arches in Protestant neighborhoods paid tribute to the victory of William of Orange over James I, at the Battle of the Boyne, in 1690. This adherence to sectarian tradition and history was an indication little had changed during Peter's absence.

Wendy Austin had just begun to read the news on *Radio Ulster* as his taxi turned into Fruithill Park. He mistakenly produced a fistful of dollars to pay the driver, so while rummaging in his backpack for British pounds, he was able to hear Austin read the lead story.

"The INRA confirmed today that one of its members, Catherine Reid, was killed on Sunday, when the bomb she was carrying exploded prematurely." The news report continued but Peter remained stunned and motionless as he stared at television crews outside his family home.

THE END

Acknowledgements

Thank you to my reader base who have provided so much positive support and made UNDER CURRENT CONDITIONS a BOSTON GLOBE BESTSELLER.

Again, I am indebted to Mary and Chris for their invaluable editing assistance. The most difficult challenge when writing a novel is not putting words on paper, but rather taking them off!

Thank you, Tom Williams, Esq. You are a wonderful friend, mentor and attorney. You provided the spark of inspiration for this story and loaned me your copy of COCAINE: AN UNAUTHORIZED BIOGRAPHY, by Dominic Streatfeild. This awesome book was an invaluable resource.

I measure my personal wealth by the quality and quantity of friends which, in my estimate, makes my net worth greater than anyone on the Forbes List. Thank you, William J. Burns, Esq., CPA for your continued counsel and support. Thank you, John Carroll, for being the best friend anyone could ask for.

Thank you, Dave Bailey for designing another awesome book cover. To me, your name is synonymous with the word, "talent".

A huge THANK YOU to Michael Dern, MD for diagnosing my cancer. Thank you, Andrew Wagner, MD, and the wonderful medical staff at Beth Israel Deaconess Medical Center in Boston for looking after me so well. Thirty years ago, when I decided to make Boston my home, I had no idea just how important that decision was!

Thank you to the men and women of the armed forces of the United States of America for sacrificing so much so we can enjoy the privileged lives that we do.

Thank you to all First Responders who serve us 24/7-365.

Also by Kyle Darcy ...

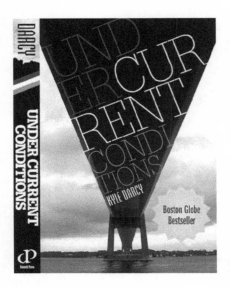

UNDER CURRENT CONDITIONS

Instinct − A subconscious evaluation of people or situations without rational evidence to support the response or feeling.

UNDER CURRENT CONDITIONS chronicles the consequences of trusting the wrong person - a business acquaintance, a friend, or even a spouse. Beginning in Boston, Massachusetts in 1999, the story is based on actual events which culmanate in 2009 with a precedent setting international murder trial.

UNDER CURRENT CONDITIONS
is a
BOSTON GLOBE BESTSELLER

CPSIA information can be obtained
at www.ICGtesting.com
Printed in the USA
LVHW092057010620
657146LV00006BA/22/J